PEACE, LOVE & YOU KNOW WHAT

BY JOAN LIVINGSTON

Casa Rosa Books

This is a work of fiction. Names, characters, places, and incidents are a product of the author's imagination. Any resemblance to actual persons, events, or locales is entirely coincidental.

Cover and book design by Michelle M. Gutierrez

ISBN-13: 978-0692731185 (Casa Rosa)
ISBN-10: 0692731180

For Hank

PART ONE
LAST WEEKEND

DON'T THINK TWICE

Tim shut the book. Nobody should have to know this much geology to graduate. He would have to fake his way through the final exam unless Mack showed up with a copy, his mission tonight, but it was after two and the stupid hippie hadn't returned. He probably ran into a girl and deserted his roommates back at 221 Winter Street, which was no big surprise, because the guy thought with his dick.

Tim leaned back in his chair so two legs were off the floor. His head rested against an oily spot on the kitchen's wallpaper. He was just another shaggy hippie at Westbridge State College, with brown hair to his shoulders and a full beard. He wore a dirty white T-shirt and bellbottom jeans, the standard issue these days.

The geology final was multiple-choice so the odds were decent he'd pass. It's all he needed. He was a history major. This stuff was of no use to him.

Across the table, Manny bent over his book. The bare bulb glared from the ceiling, giving his black hair and beard a soft halo. The shade broke when Manny did a stunt with a baseball, but everybody was stoned, so they thought it was a scream when the glass popped and shattered.

Tim patted his pocket. He had two Winstons left. He fished one from the pack as Manny scowled and held his long hair back with a fist.

"What were we thinking taking geology? I can't remember a damn thing," Tim said.

Manny raised his red all-nighter eyes.

"We got any Coke left? No? We're outta coffee, too. Shit, we should've bought speed from that guy."

Manny's face was back over the page. Above them in the attic, a type-writer tapped. Joey had been holed up all day and night working on a take-home exam. The tapping stopped, and the steady click of a boot heel started. Joey's leg moved without him. What did the guy expect? He lived on coffee and cigarettes. When he got cut, he probably bled brown. The three of them let Joey live for free in the attic after he kept crashing on the mattresses in the living room. At least they no longer had to look at his scrawny body twisted in some dirty sheets at noon.

Everybody loved Joey. He was smarter than any of them. When somebody bitched about the war and goddamn Nixon, he recited "Anthem for a Doomed Youth" by heart before going off about the English poet Wilfred Owen getting killed during World War I. Tim only remembered the first line: "*What passing-bells for those who die as cattle?*" Above them, Joey's big brain was thinking up something else profound. His foot moved. By now Joey could have run one-legged up the street and back.

The typing restarted. The foot stopped. Joey was getting it all down.

Tim held a butt between his fingers.

"Manny, how about taking a break?"

"Swell idea." Manny pushed his book aside. "Got another one of those?"

Tim tossed him the pack.

"Here."

"How do you think Mack made out?"

Tim blew the smoke above his head.

"We'll find out soon enough. I just heard his car pull up."

Manny rubbed his beard.

"Hot damn, it's about time he showed."

Mack marched upstairs, through the hall, and into the kitchen. He had the outlaw look going, with a full beard and red hair to his shoulders although he kept it clean and tied low so he could fit it beneath a cowboy hat. His fringed suede jacket, a gift from an old girlfriend, hung open over his white T-shirt. He grinned as he raised a stack of papers.

"Look what I scored." He tossed the papers on the table. "It's not the final we're taking tomorrow. It's last year's, but I heard from a reliable source the prof doesn't change them much. Check it out. I think we're gonna be okay."

Tim and Manny leaned forward and read.

"Holy shit, you even got the answers. Jesus, Mack, where'd you cop these?" Tim asked.

Mack chuckled.

"Didn't steal 'em. Didn't have to." He lowered his voice. "You know the lab assistant?"

Tim nodded.

"Her? The girl with the mustache who never says a thing?"

"I didn't even have to mention money. She had something else in mind."

Manny rolled his eyes.

"Oh, God, I can imagine."

"Hey, I did it for the team. Besides, it wasn't half bad. Her little mustache kinda tickles." Joey's boot pounded a beat above them. Mack glanced at the ceiling and shook his head. "Crazy freak." Mack tossed his hat on the table as he dropped onto a chair. "I dunno about you boys, but when this is over, I wanna party. None of this hanging out in the living room shit, hoping some girls show up. I don't wanna be emptying change jars to buy bottles of Ripple or GIQs of no-name beer, or have somebody fishing a baggie of dried pot he hid under his mattress." He stared one-eyed at Manny. "I mean a real party. I mean a bash bigger than any we've had."

Tim and Manny stubbed their cigarettes into an ashtray filled with roaches and butts.

"Bigger than the Halloween party last year?" Manny asked.

For the Halloween party, a gang of them swooped in dressed as Mexican bandits, carrying knives, whips, and even a gun loaded with blanks, which scared one guy silly when it was fired point-blank at his chest. He kept stammering, "You don't feel the bullet that kills you," until somebody handed him a beer and said, "Yeah, yeah, I read that in Hemingway, too."

"Bigger," Mack said.

"How about St. Paddy's Day?" It was Manny again.

On St. Patrick's Day, they had beer for breakfast and walked half-drunk to campus, lasting one class before returning to 221 Winter Street to finish the job.

"Absolutely bigger." Mack smirked. "In a week, most everybody'll be

5

gone. Summer jobs. Hitting the road. But we'll be stuck working in a stinking furniture factory."

Tim saw the summer ahead, sitting in his shorts in the overcooked apartment, or going to Angie's to watch the Red Sox on the set above the bar, or the VFW for ten-cent draft night, which was okay if you didn't mind the stony stares from the townie patriots. Once in a while, somebody in exile would find their way back to Westbridge. It happened last year when guys with fresh haircuts and trimmed beards knocked on the door of 221 Winter Street for a fix of tribal fun.

Mack leaned back in his chair.

"Listen to this. I'm even gonna blow my tax refund on this bash rather than pay my old man back for the brake job on my Fairlane. For once we'll have enough pot and booze. If we run out, we'll take up a collection and make runs to the package store. I'll invite the Roach Motel gang. Those freaks always have decent grass, and some of the professors, you know, the Dirty Old Bastards Club. Those guys are kind of a pain cause they always make moves on the best girls, but they're usually good for a coupla bottles of the hard stuff." He chuckled. "We might even have food. I'll talk to the girls across the hall."

Mack slapped the table.

"We're gonna need something with enough good vibes to last us a month or two. Something wild. Something really wild." He kicked an empty into the pile near his chair. "Picture this: a joint filled with freaks, high and happy and without a fuckin' care in the world. There's no war going on, and nobody has to worry about getting drafted." Mack's voice got louder. "I'll move my stereo into the living room, so we have dance music. We'll get people on their feet. The Stones. Motown. Old Sly. Maybe we'll make a trip to the pond to skinny-dip at midnight. Picture this. Hairy guys. Naked girls. Hanging loose. Gettin' it on. They can crash here or at one of the other pads in town." He took a breath. "We'll start Friday after the dorms close and end Sunday before graduation starts. We'll get anybody who's awake to go." He wagged a finger. "We'll scare the shit outta old Dean Shirley Hendricks."

Mack chuckled.

"It does mean we gotta clean up this dump." He hooked his thumb toward the bathroom door. "No girl's gonna want to use that toilet."

"Who are you inviting?" Manny asked.

"Everyone and anyone who's a freak or a friend of a freak."

"What about the guys on the first floor?" Manny asked.

"The math majors? Those straights? We have to invite them. We're gonna make too much noise not to. Who knows? Maybe they'll loosen up."

"Make sure Lenora hears about it," Tim said.

Mack's lips curled beneath his red mustache.

"A party without Lenora? Our queen? No way. Tim, maybe you should do the asking." His grin got bigger. "She should be over that last guy by now. Doesn't it take about six weeks? What was his name? Tadd?"

"No, it was Brad," Tim said.

"Brad. What kind of a name is Brad? Sometimes I wonder about Lenora's choice in guys. Glad he's outta the picture." Mack's brow pinched. "I believe it's time to finally make your move, Tim. She'll be gone next week."

Tim sighed. Lenora's last relationship was a close one. Things were getting heavy with the guy, a friend of Joey's hiding out from some trouble in California. But Lenora's romances lasted three months tops, the guys drawn by her open heart, soaking in her love as if it were sunlight, until it drove them away. Tim held her while she cried enough times to know the story. Her ex-boyfriends said they were living in the here and now. They reminded her about the war in Vietnam. Her response? War was all the more reason to be in love. They didn't see it her way. She took the breakups hard, sobbing in her room, playing dreary folk songs like Dylan's "Don't Think Twice, It's All Right" and snarling at the lines. She stopped eating, got real skinny, drank, and smoked too much pot, even embarrassing herself a little in public. She wrote sad or hateful poetry until she came to her senses or lost interest.

Manny shook a finger.

"I have two questions about Lenora. First, how in the hell did she manage to graduate on time? I mean she's always partying with us. And second, how did she save up enough bread washing dishes in the dining hall to go to Europe?"

Tim shrugged.

"Easy. Lenora can focus."

"Focus."

"She may hang around us bums, but she always gets her papers in on time," Tim said. "She's smart, too. Take the time she took philosophy. She

7

said it went way over her head. You know what I mean, crap like if we didn't have a god, would we need to invent one. She tells the professor she used to hypnotize her sister and make her go back into past lives."

"Shit, no," Manny said.

"Shit, yes. The prof went so nuts he struck a deal with her. All she had to do was give a lecture to each of his classes, and he'd give her an A. No papers, no exams."

"Lenora's something else," Manny said. "What are we gonna do without her?"

Tim didn't answer. He didn't want to think of Lenora leaving Westbridge.

"I don't have a fuckin' clue," he said finally.

Mack's arms were folded behind his neck. He hummed, waiting for the conversation to return to him.

"Manny, what do you think?" Mack asked.

"I'm in. What about you, Tim?"

"A three-day orgy? Why not?" Tim turned toward Mack. "Uh, any word about the other problem we talked about?"

Mack squinted.

"You graduating on Sunday? I'm still working on it. I need to call in a few favors. Don't look so worried, Timmy boy. Your widowed mother will see you get a diploma. She'll bawl her eyes out and call your name in that sweet, little voice of hers." He gestured toward the exam on the table. "Have I ever let you down? Look how I made out tonight."

Manny's head bobbed.

"Mack, you're the man."

Tim glanced at the exam. They wouldn't sleep tonight until they went over the answers a few times, but right now, Mack's idea for a three-day orgy was more interesting. Tim stood and grabbed the broom leaning against the fridge. He jabbed the ceiling.

"Joey, get your ass down here. You'll wanna hear this."

The typing stopped. They watched the ceiling as Joey's boots walked above them. Grinning, Mack went to the sink and drank from the faucet, holding his ponytail so it didn't fall into the dirty dishes.

THE HARD TRUTH

Heads down, Tim and Manny staggered through the campus of West-bridge State College. They were semi-sure they'd get a decent grade on their geology final, thanks to Mack. But this being their third all-nighter in a row, and with another ahead, they were out of it.

"I think you're right. It was quartzite. I put that down, too," Tim said.

"How about five? Pre-Cambrian shield?"

"Think so."

Manny gave him a scared smile.

"Shit, maybe we did okay."

The two bumped shoulders, drunk with fatigue, swapping answers, as they jaywalked the quadrangle's grassy square toward the administration building. They ducked through the auditorium door, propped open because the weather was warm, and hit a left to the newspaper office. The office, if it could be called one, used to be the ticket booth for the auditorium. It was all the college spared for *The Hard Truth*.

Mack, the editor-in-chief, was already there, moving and stacking bundles of newspapers printed specially for graduation. He was the second person to finish the geology final, and he had a smug smile when he handed the bluebook to the professor, telling him, "Thanks, I got a lot outta your class," which made the man nod and grunt. Then Mack gave Tim and Manny two thumbs up before he split.

Mack tossed copies of the newspaper to Tim and Manny. The headline across the top of the front page said: "Hello cruel world!" It was Tim's idea. He was one of the paper's reporters, actually assistant editor, but as usual, Mack took his idea and ran with it. The paper was chock full of anti-war, anti-Nixon, and anti-establishment stories.

Lenora wrote her farewell column, called "Who the heck is that?" Her last was about the janitor who's been cleaning up after students for over twenty years, watching as one class leaves and another takes its place. Tim murmured. He recognized the guy. He had a profound limp because of a clubfoot, and Lenora wrote he took off his shoe so she could see it. She got him right as she did the other people she wrote about, like the retarded guy who rode his bike around campus. Then there was the cook behind the counter of Jimmy's Coffee Shop. His name wasn't Jimmy, it was Ralph, and he named the joint for his older brother, who got killed in Korea.

Manny opened his copy to the centerfold where the names of the Class of 1972 were printed. His fingertip pressed the paper.

"Tim, your name's here. See? Timothy Patrick Devlin. It's above Lenora's name. It says you're graduating Sunday."

Tim peered over Manny's shoulder.

"My mother will like that a lot."

"Huh? I thought you needed two more courses to graduate," Manny said.

Tim grunted as he fell onto a chair beside the wooden table they lifted from a classroom. Manny sat beside him.

"You're right. I don't have enough credits, but I can't tell my mother that. You met her. I'm supposed to be outta here and getting a job. She works the nightshift at the bread plant back home. You think she'd understand the five-year plan?"

Air came out of Manny's mouth in one big "ha."

"Tim, right now I can't think of a damn thing."

"That makes two of us."

Tim's elbow was on the table as he pushed his jaw into his hand. He shut his eyes and felt himself slip away until a girl's laughter jerked him awake. He blinked. Lenora came through the door, wearing one of her costumes, a black skirt hanging to her sandals and a gauzy top with strands of beads. Hair so brown it could be black fell halfway down her back. She swirled around with her hands in the air and stomped her sandals.

"Alleluia, I'm done. Can you believe it? No more papers. No more finals. I finished my last shift at the dining hall." She spun again. "Guys, I'm a free woman."

Mack came toward her with his arms out.

"Jesus, Lenora, I'm gonna miss you."

Mack hugged Lenora tightly and tried to nail her with a kiss. He thought it was cool to stick his tongue in the mouth of any girl he met. But Lenora told Manny and Tim he wasn't very good at it. Too much spit. And his breath smelled like cooked meat.

She held her hand against Mack's chest.

"Knock it off, Mack. I don't want a kiss from you."

Mack moved against her hand. His face came closer.

"Aw, Lenora, you don't mean it."

"Yes, I do. I'm not your girlfriend, and I don't want to be. I don't mind you giving me a hug, but keep your tongue to yourself. Or next time I'll bite it off."

Mack stepped back.

"Whoa, I guess she told me off good."

Manny glanced up from the open newspaper.

"You mean well, don't you Mack?"

"Shut up, Manny. I don't need a fuckin' grammar lesson, especially from a history major."

"Hey, don't insult me. You're the one who's supposed to be the English major."

Mack shuffled to his desk, muttering, but Tim was positive he'd get over it. Lenora was too important to all of them. The girl had been with them during good trips and bad trips, protests and parties. Once, she talked a cop out of giving Mack a ticket after he got caught driving through a stop sign. The way she worked the pig was pure magic. By time they drove off, the man had lost his blank cop face and started smiling.

Tim couldn't forget how she held his hand as they watched the draft lottery on TV, and then cried when he pulled an eight, which meant he was heading to Vietnam for sure. Lenora found a friendly doctor to write a note that Tim had a chronic skin rash, so he wouldn't have to go. She went with Tim to the induction physical, and when he came outside, she hugged him and said, "They're not taking you from me."

Why did she have to leave?

Lenora sat on the table.

"How'd you guys do on your geology final?"

Tim glanced at Manny.

"We made out okay. I mean the answers came to me almost like magic." Tim paused. "Hey, Lenora, what are you doing Friday, Saturday, and Sunday?"

Her legs swung beneath her long skirt.

"Except for graduating? I'll be packing. Why? What'd you have in mind?

Tim eyed Mack, who had his back to him.

"See, we're having a little party at the house, and we wanted you to come."

"Three days? A little party? You're putting me on."

"No, I'm not. Right, Manny?"

"It's true, Lenora. So, are you coming?"

"Of course, I will. It's my last weekend in Westbridge."

EVER-LOVING QUEEN

enora, Tim, and Manny walked toward Jimmy's Coffee Shop, only a block from campus on Main Street. She linked her arms in theirs so she was in the middle, which was the way she liked it. These were her guys. She met Tim at freshmen orientation, hitting it off from the start. Mack, Manny, and Joey came the next year. She was their ever-loving queen. That's what Mack called her. She didn't mind at all.

"Let me guess. The party was Mack's idea."

Tim grinned.

"Give the little lady a prize."

She looked from one hairy face to the other. They walked in step, as they often did, taking a coffee break, or heading to 221 Winter Street to hang out or to the coffeehouse or any number of places in Westbridge. They marched together in protests, once when the college fired a leftist professor in the philosophy department, but mostly because of the war. The boys she loved were doing brave or stupid things to keep themselves out of Vietnam. And then those four kids got killed at Kent State when they brought in the National Guard. Everyone knew it could happen at Westbridge, so they shut the campus for the semester.

Like her, like most of the kids at Westbridge State, Tim and Manny were the first of their families to go to college. Tim was from a big Irish family who lived in South Boston. Manny was a full-blooded Portagee. She was, too. He grew up in a dirty city on the ocean, where the Portuguese either fished, like Manny's father Manny, or worked in the mills, like his mother, Maria. Lenora grew up in a town across the bay from Manny's city, but they never met until they came to Westbridge. Lenora and Manny's grandparents came from the same village in the Azores Islands, so they liked saying they both went way back. Maybe they were long-lost cousins. Lenora and Manny cultivated the bond, cracking inside jokes.

Manny would say, "Lenora, I met a Portagee the other day."

And Lenora would ask, "One eyebrow or two?"

The three friends stopped in front of Jimmy's and looked across the street toward the commons, which formed a grassy oval in the center of downtown. The statue of Lord Randall Westbridge stood full-sized with his hands outstretched as if he were accepting blessings from above. His face had a fatherly expression, stern but loving, as he gazed at the kneeling men who planted geraniums around his pedestal. The college sent the crew to spruce up the town for commencement.

"How long do you think those flowers are gonna last before somebody rips them off?" Lenora asked.

Tim and Manny shrugged.

"Maybe for graduation if they're lucky," Tim said.

It was around ten, so Jimmy's was filled with working class townies on a break and bleary-eyed students hunched over textbooks. The air smelled of grill grease and cigarettes. They moved behind the flannel flank of townies toward the cook, Jimmy's brother. A copy of Lenora's column, the paper spotted by grease, was taped near the register.

The cook's gold tooth showed when he grinned.

"Hello, honey, nice to see you."

Lenora smiled as she gestured toward Tim and Manny.

"You look real busy, but my friends and I'd like to order."

"Sure, honey, what'll it be?"

"Go ahead, Tim. Only coffee for me." She pointed toward a corner table. "Hey, there's Joey."

Tim gave their orders. The cook poured their coffees and turned toward the grill, scraping charred bits to the side with his spatula before breaking eggs onto the hot surface. They grabbed their mugs and made their way to

Joey who sat beside the jukebox. Joey pushed his black glasses up his nose. His long, blond hair was a mess.

Lenora sat across from Joey. Tim took the chair beside hers. Manny frowned at the pieces of napkin and spilled sugar on Joey's side of the table.

"How come I always have to sit next to Joey? Let me sit next to Lenora for a change."

"No way," Tim said.

"Jesus, Joey, what a mess." Manny used a napkin to wipe the table. "How much coffee did you drink anyway?"

"I don't remember," Joey said.

"Shit, look at you. You're such a wreck."

Joey raised his mug.

"If I change with all the winds that blow/ It is only because they made me so."

"What'd you say?" Manny asked.

"Longfellow wrote it," Joey said.

"Longfellow. It's Longfellow," Manny mumbled. "He can remember poetry and who wrote it, but not how much coffee he drank."

Lenora lifted her mug as Manny talked up the three-day party, about who was coming, what they were planning. Beside him, Joey's hands twisted a matchbook into a useless lump. His leg jumped beneath the table.

Manny paused.

"Do you mind, Joey?" he said. "I feel like there's something living under there."

Joey glanced at his leg as if it weren't a part of him.

"I can't help it. I'm a little nervous today."

"A little nervous? Lenora, can't you make him stop?"

"Sorry, Manny. I don't possess that kind of superpower."

The cook barked that their orders were ready. Manny reached between two townies at the counter for their plates. The men glared. One of the townies got up to stick coins into the juke, and afterward Merle Haggard started singing he was an Okie from Muskogee. Lenora knew what was going down. The townies were waiting for Tim, Manny, and Joey to do or say something to confirm their idea that college boys were weaklings and not as smart as they thought.

Tim nodded at Joey.

15

"You eat?"

"I had something." Then Joey said quietly, "But I'll take one of those pieces of toast if you don't want it."

"Help yourself," Tim said.

Lenora watched Tim pour pepper over his egg.

"You sure love pepper," she said.

"Wanna try?"

Lenora didn't answer, because someone knocked at the window. Lenora's roommate, Geneva, squeezed her face against the glass and stepped back, laughing.

Joey hooted.

"You should see your face, Lenora. What's the matter?"

"I'm not talking to her."

"What for?" Joey said. "What'd Geneva do this time?"

"She let a junkie stay at our place."

Joey leaned forward.

"She did what?"

"You see that guy who's been walking around campus with a guitar case and hair to his butt? Him. If you wanna know, there's nothing in the case, except dope."

"Wow."

Tim and Manny listened as they chewed.

"Geneva met the guy somewhere, felt sorry for him, and, get this, she has the nerve to take off, sticking me with the creep," Lenora said. "I guessed something was wrong when he kept nodding off. Then I found his works in the bathroom sink."

Joey pulled on his mustache.

"Hot damn, what'd you do?"

"I hunted Geneva down and told her either he goes or I call the cops. He was gone when I got home."

Lenora set her mug hard on the table. Geneva was outside the window talking with Nina, who was taking her place at the apartment. Good luck to Nina. The stuff Lenora put up with living with Geneva. It was Geneva who told their last landlord they were nurses. He kicked them out after he found out it was a lie, and they had to move into the ratty apartment they rented in the Brown House. Then there was the time Geneva had an affair with one of the married professors from the Dirty Old Bastards Club, and since her bedroom only has a sheet for a door, Lenora could hear them going at it. She did other crap, like being late with the rent check and wearing Lenora's clothes without asking. Taking in the junkie was the absolute worst, however.

"It's always something with Geneva," Lenora said. "I sure as hell won't miss her."

Tim put down his fork.

"But you'll miss me. Won't you?"

"Sure, I'll miss you, Tim."

His blue eyes didn't blink.

"What will you do when you come back from Europe?" he asked.

"No idea. All I can tell you is I won't be living in Westbridge. You've gotta know when it's time to move on." Lenora's head tipped to one side. "Tim, don't give me that sad look. Be happy for me. We'll still be friends."

"It won't be the same without you around."

She patted his hairy cheek.

"We can do something different. Okay?"

Tim opened his mouth but didn't say more. Geneva and Nina stood beside their table. They wore matching tie-dyed shirts and no bras. They reeked of patchouli.

The townies swiveled on their stools.

Both girls smiled brightly.

"You know Lenora. But I don't think you've met these guys." She pointed as she said each one's name. "They live with Mack. You remember, the guy who's having the party."

Tim, Manny, and Joey glanced at each other.

"It's our party, too," Manny said.

"Oh, yeah, I forgot. Lenora, you going?" Geneva asked.

Lenora folded her arms and stared at her roommate.

"I thought I told you not to wear my earrings, Geneva." Her voice was flat and tight. "Of course, I'll be there. It's my last weekend."

A spoon rattled across the table and onto the floor.

"That's right," Joey said. "She's outta here."

ABOVE IT ALL

Tim crawled through the living room window onto the porch roof where Mack, Manny, and Joey waited for the beers he carried. He passed around the cold, open bottles and stretched out on one of the sleeping bags they spread over the shingles. Above him, a full, fat moon was stuck between the limbs of the large maple in the front yard. Tim closed his eyes and listened to the neighborhood. Somewhere south on the street, a woman called her kids to come inside. He imagined them running sweaty in the dark like he and his brothers once did. The woman's voice was high as if she were singing her children home. She wasn't angry or loud.

He remembered his own mother, sitting on the front stoop of their triple-decker, watching the kids in the neighborhood play hide-and-seek among the parked cars. She smelled like the sugary dough of the day-old bread and donuts she brought home.

Tim took a sip of beer. This was the first time he and his roommates got stoned since finals began. They pledged to lay off the stuff until the last exam, in one of those all-for-one, one-for-all moments. Joey taped a calendar to the refrigerator and marked each day as it passed. Today was the end, so Mack broke out his stash. Tomorrow was the first day of the party. Mack said he wanted to make sure it was the primo pot the dealer promised although there wasn't anything he could do since the guy had already split for the West Coast. The dealer claimed it was Panama Red, which was probably a load of bull, but the pot was heavy. Tim sighed, lost in the soft folds of his high. Beside him, Joey's boot tapped the shingles. They made him stay in the middle, so he wouldn't fall off the roof.

Mack had his mind on the party.

"We made a dump run today. We need to do another tomorrow before the party starts. But the place is starting to look presentable. Joey, you did a nice job in the kitchen. Glad to see you finally put your nervous energy to good use." Mack stopped for a gulp of beer. "People will drift in early. The important thing is to pace ourselves. I don't wanna use up all the best pot on the first night. We'll have to mix in some of the weak shit Manny bought."

"It's not my fault. The pot I smoked was great. It just wasn't the pot the guy sold me."

"You fell for that old trick." Mack sniffed. "Anyway, we'll make the first beer run after we hit the dump. Joey here is treating us all to breakfast Saturday morning, and the girls across the hall are making dinner that night."

Manny sat up.

"Food? We're gonna have food?"

"Uh-huh. Saturday afternoon we're having a ballgame. It'll be us against the Roach Motel tribe. We need to settle a score after that basketball game this winter. Roach Brother Bob said they'd take us on."

Manny groaned.

"Man, those guys play dirty."

"This game, we'll play it their way, nice and dirty. Forget about it for now, will you? The big question is who's gonna clean the bathroom?" Mack belched. "I don't hear any volunteers. I tell you what. We'll draw straws later."

The rest murmured their approval. No one talked. They just floated on the porch's roof.

Manny broke the silence.

"Boy, I hope I get laid tomorrow. It's been a while."

Manny was bummed when his girl dumped him a few months ago, especially after she found another guy right away. His buddies tried to help, taking him out drinking and listening to his sob stories, until Mack told him to snap out of it. Manny was wasting his prime sexual years.

"Anyone in mind?" Mack asked.

"I dig the new girls who write for *The Hard Truth*," Manny said.

Mack snorted.

"Those girls? The freshmen? They're not opening their legs for a hairy Portagee like you. They're looking for some rock star, hippie god. Besides, they're cock teasers."

Manny moaned.

"Oh, no, cock teasers."

Mack cleared his throat.

"Manny, those sweet young things don't mind showing off their titties and shaking their tight, little asses in your face, but try touching 'em."

"Shot down, eh, Mack?" Manny said.

"Funny one, Manny. I don't need to work that hard to get laid. I'm only trying to help you out, so stop being such a wise ass and listen up."

"Brother, here we go again," Tim muttered as he elbowed Joey.

"Tell me about it," Joey said.

"Hey, you two, shut up," Mack said. "It's my turn."

Mack began his take on the screwable girls on campus. They had heard the speech many times. If there were a course at Westbridge State College called Screw 101, Mack would be the man to teach it. He was the self-proclaimed authority, claiming to have done it with more girls than anyone in the school's history. He got a dose of the clap once and crabs twice. He also sweated through a couple of late periods. For Mack, happiness was a girl on the pill.

Mack never tired of saying the girls outnumbered the guys three-to-one when he came to Westbridge as a freshman. Deciding those were favorable odds, he broke up with his steady girl from his hometown and moved from his parents' house into 221 Winter Street. The guys who lived there were the freak pioneers of Westbridge who had abandoned the two lousy frats on campus when they realized smoking pot and dropping acid were more fun than chug-a-lugging beer from a fish bowl. They didn't want to stand outside a dorm with a bunch of horny guys, begging girls to toss their underwear out a window. The war was on, getting harder and hotter, goddamned Lyndon Johnson was in charge then, and they were all hanging onto their college deferments as long as they could.

"Manny, my advice is if you want to get laid, you're better off with someone easier to get," Mack said. "Someone like Lenora's roommate, Geneva."

"Geneva? You screw Geneva?"

"Sure. She's pretty hot. Ask Professor Burke."

"Burke and Geneva, I forgot."

There was the flick of a lighter, and then Mack spoke.

"How could you? It was only last year. She was in his philosophy class. You know how Ned Burke gets with the girls in his class. He has them over one at a time in his office so he can size 'em up. He's smart about the girls he chooses. Not too pretty. He looks for the kind who wanna date their father, but a smart father who writes poetry, listens to jazz, and dresses cool. He sees them on the sly, so it's exciting until old Inez Burke finds out. Burke tells the girl there's no way he can leave his wife. Sometimes Inez sees the girl herself."

"Is that what happened with Geneva?" Manny asked.

"Nah, dummy, Ned had a heart attack. Jesus, Manny, pay attention, will you? Remember when he was dancing at the Halloween party with her? He started grabbing his chest. Then he dropped to the floor. Lucky somebody knew mouth-to-mouth. It kept the guy alive, but I think his bad ticker's slowed him down some." Mack chuckled. "I asked him to come anyway."

"How about Mrs. Burke?"

"Inez? She'll be there. Somebody's gotta keep an eye on Ned. Shit, I hope I'm not like him when I get old."

A car slowed below them. They recognized the engine. Nancy, who lived across the hall, was home. She got out of the car.

"I see you hippie degenerates up there," she yelled through the maple tree. "You don't fool me. I know what you're doing. Shame on all of you."

"Yeah, why don't you come join us?" Mack called.

"Maybe later."

The front door slammed and deep inside the house Nancy's feet pummeled the stairs. Everybody quieted. Nancy shared the one-bedroom apartment across the hall with Lorraine. Those libbers didn't take crap from any guy, especially them. It meant they couldn't use their phone or raid their refrigerator for fear of castration. Both women wore Army fatigues as if they were living in a war zone, but then again, they were always on the frontline of any protest on campus, stirring up the crowd with chants and passing around signs. After the Kent State shootings, Nancy and Lorraine led a crowd of protesters downtown. The town cops showed up. Many of the kids and a couple of the liberal profs, members of the Dirty Old Bastards Club, broke ranks, but Nancy and Lorraine went to jail, clenching their cuffed hands in a power salute as the cops hauled them off in a cruiser. Afterward, the Winter Street gang took up a collection to pay their bail.

"How about Nancy?" Manny asked.

"She's actually got a decent bod under all that Army Navy surplus shit she wears," Mack said. "But she doesn't shave her pits or legs. Big bush, too. That's a turnoff for me. You might dig that, Manny, being a hairy guy yourself."

Only Mack laughed.

"Okay, asshole, what about Lorraine?" Manny asked.

"Nope, don't waste your time on her. She's not interested in men at all, if you catch my meaning. At least Nancy swings the other way sometimes."

Tim squashed a mosquito on his chin, surprising himself when he felt skin instead of hair. He took a lot of ribbing from the others when he shaved this afternoon, but he expected it. Of course, he cut himself and his skin was tender from the blade since he hadn't been without a beard for over three years. When he walked into the kitchen, Joey stomped the floor and howled like a lunatic. He yelled for the others. Tim said he was going to shave, but they all thought he was messing with their heads.

Shaving his beard was part of the plan. On Sunday, he was showing up at graduation in the cap and gown Joey snagged for him from the administration building. Once again, Mack worked his stud magic, this time with a secretary in the registrar's office who got Tim's name on the official list. Tim was to get in line in front of Lenora, Devlin was before Dias, and then step across the stage when they call his name and take whatever they hand him.

He rubbed a rough patch on his jaw. He still had hair to his shoulders but the clean face would please his mother and maybe confuse Dean Hendricks, so she wouldn't recognize him until it was too late. Besides, no one would dare make a scene in front of all those parents. Tim drained the beer. Manny and Mack were still at it. Manny gave him a girl's name, and Mack summed her up with a phrase or two. Big tits. Fat thighs. Gives good head. Screams her head off. Nice ass. Tim knew most of them. He had been with a couple. Mack's comments were cheap shots.

"What about Lenora?" Manny asked.

Mack murmured.

"Lenora. Wish I could say I did. Any of you?"

There was a chorus of no's.

"I kissed her once," Joey said.

"You did what?" Manny asked.

"Big deal. I've kissed her, too. Lots of times," Mack said.

"This was different."

"Sure, Joey."

"Mack, let him finish," Manny said.

Moonlight bounced off Joey's glasses.

"We were in the newspaper office, sitting on one of the desks. We were shooting the shit like we always do. She looked at me with those big, brown eyes of hers, and I kissed her. She kissed me back. It was really nice. I actually thought something was gonna happen."

"You never told me you kissed Lenora," Tim said.

"Shut up, Tim. I want to hear what happened next," Mack said.

"I told you. Nothing. She said she needed to go to the bathroom, but she didn't come back. I waited and waited. I asked Geneva to go check on her, but she was gone. Weird, huh? We never talked about it. She acts like it never happened. I don't understand what's up with that."

Mack tossed his empty bottle backward through the open window.

"Jesus, Joey, you fuckin' blew it," he said.

Tim watched clouds sail across the moon. Beside him, Joey said, *"She walks in beauty, like the night/ Of cloudless climes and starry skies,"* and then, "Lord Byron."

A FORGIVING MOOD

Lenora looked up from the box she was packing when she heard rats fighting behind the wall beside her bed. She pounded on the black-painted wall.

"Knock it off you, little fuckers."

The rats scurried to another part of the building. But they'd be back. They had a nest in the corner of her room, according to an ex-boyfriend who had knelt with his ear to the wall. He called her over to listen, but she couldn't do it. She didn't want to think about rats living in this old apartment building.

No one had ever seen the woman who owns the Brown House. They just spoke to her over the phone, listening to her pack-a-day wheeze, and if a tenant didn't mail the check on time to her post office box, or it bounced, she sent her son, a middle-aged man with fat, soft hands and thin, slicked-back hair, to get the money. When there was a vacancy, neither had to show an apartment or advertise since there were so few rentals within walking distance of campus. Word spread fast and the place was gone within a day or two. The apartments at the Brown House were passed down through generations of students, who put up with the bad plumbing, cracked linoleum, and botched renovations to escape the dorms. They left behind stained mattresses and shabby furniture when they moved out.

The first party Lenora went to as a freshman was in one of the ground-floor apartments. She and Geneva, whose room was next to hers at Faulkner Dorm, came here after being ignored by the frat guys at the get-acquainted mixer. Lenora wore a plaid wool jumper her mother sewed. Her dark hair was short and set with curls so she looked like the good Catholic girl she was then. She and Geneva arrived at the party about a half-hour after the cops had cleared out the place, and by time they knocked on the door, only a couple of guys were drinking in the kitchen. They offered them beer and hits off a joint. The beer was sour, and Lenora didn't get high from the joint. One of the guys teased Lenora about her dimples, and he gave her and Geneva a ride back to the dorm so they could make their curfew.

Lenora folded the box's flaps and set it aside. It wasn't her idea to paint the room black, including the ceiling and floor. It came that way. The landlady told her over the phone she wasn't paying to repaint the room some normal color.

"Nothing wrong with black," the woman told her. "It don't show dirt."

Actually, black didn't show anything. When Lenora walked into her room at night, she felt as if she were stepping into a hole.

She heard the downstairs door slam and feet on the steps. Geneva came inside the bedroom. She handed Lenora her carrings.

"Sorry about that. It's just that you have such nice things. I can't help myself."

Lenora was silent as she put the earrings on the bureau.

"You're still mad at me about the junkie. I can tell. I didn't know, and when you told me, I got rid of him."

Lenora stooped for a sweater on the floor.

"What do you want? A medal?"

"A medal?" Geneva's head cocked to the side. "No, I wanted to ask you if Nina can crash here this weekend. She can sleep on the couch. Is that okay?"

Lenora eyed her roommate. Suddenly, she was in a forgiving mood. She could afford to be. Next week, she'll be in Europe while Geneva sweats it out on the top floor of a rat-infested apartment house and works in the office of a construction company.

"Why not?"

"Cool. She's downstairs. I'll go tell her."

Lenora shook her head.

"What if I said no?"

Geneva waved her hand.

"I knew you wouldn't."

GOT IT EASY

enora stirred a wooden spoon through the batter and lifted the empty box of Betty Crocker brownie mix to see if she missed anything.

"Oh, yeah, the most important ingredient. Hand me the baggie, Geneva."

Geneva reached for the bag of pot on the drain board of the kitchen sink. She tossed it beside the bowl.

"Here, you go. How much you putting in?"

"The recipe on the box calls for a handful," Lenora joked.

Lenora dumped crushed leaves into the batter before she gave it a stir and poured it into a pan. She glanced up as Nina came from the bathroom. Her brown hair was done up in a towel. Lenora slid the pan into the oven and checked the time. She left the mess on the table because she was going to make a second batch. The small oven had a single rack, so she could only bake one pan at a time. Lenora sat down, taking the pins from her hair and knotting it tighter. She swiped the sweat off her upper lip.

"Hot enough for you, Geneva?" Lenora asked.

"Tell me about it. It's gonna suck to be here this summer."

Geneva had another year or so to go. She should be getting her diploma, too, on Sunday but she got behind. She was staying put for the summer rather than go home.

Nina sat at the table.

"Don't say that, Geneva," she said. "We'll have fun. It looks like lots of people are sticking around. Like those guys from Winter Street."

Geneva ran a finger along the edge of the bowl and licked the batter.

"Uh, don't expect too much from those boys. You'll see. They'll show up here begging for free meals like they always do. I'll have to tell 'em the cook moved out." She tipped her head at Lenora. "Mind if we roll a joint?"

"Go ahead."

Lenora tossed Geneva a package of Zig-Zags.

"Lenora, I was telling Nina about the old days. Remember freshman orientation and that talk Dean Hendricks gave us girls? She told us to cross our legs and never wear black patent leather shoes, cause sex-crazed boys could see up your skirt. Who in the hell wears patent leather shoes anymore?"

Lenora snorted.

"That woman's a witch," she said. "She tried to get me fired from my dishwashing job. She had the nerve to tell my boss I was an immoral person. Do you believe that? I was too immoral to scrape garbage off plates. My boss told her to get lost. I was his best worker. He even gave me a raise to totally tick her off."

Geneva concentrated on rolling the joint.

"How about freshman initiation at Faulkner Dorm?" she said.

"Those girls were sick," Lenora said.

"Nina, you should've seen what they made us do," Geneva said. "We had to wear our clothes backwards and eat with our hands in the dining hall. They dragged us out of our beds in the middle of the night and told us to sing stupid songs. Remember when they made that girl strip to her underwear and jump rope?"

Nina batted her eyes.

"You're shitting me."

"It was the last year the college let 'em do that." Geneva licked the paper to seal the joint. "It was the last year for a lot of things. Like having no boys in your dorm room. Freshmen had to study from eight to ten. Curfew on the weekends was eleven, and if a girl was late, she got written up. We fixed 'em though. Didn't we, Lenora?"

"Uh-huh. We signed out like we were going home for the weekend. Then we came and went as we pleased."

Geneva raised the joint in triumph.

"We left the basement door near the laundry room unlocked." Geneva giggled. "Jesus, all that sneaking around we had to do. Nina, see how easy you got it?"

Geneva lit the joint. Rats scratched and squealed in the wall behind her. Lenora leaned over to pound the plaster.

"Cut it out," she growled.

Nina frowned as she took the joint.

"What in the hell's that?" she asked.

"Rats. Don't worry. We haven't seen 'em yet, but they bug the hell outta me," Lenora said.

Geneva made a snuffling laugh.

"They're all over this building," she said. "Did you know the Brown House used to be a whorehouse?"

Nina handed the joint to Lenora.

"Really?" Nina said.

Geneva raised her hand.

"God's honest truth. Men would come up from the railroad station to get their kicks. Now some old hag owns it and makes a ton renting to college kids. Wait 'til you meet her son."

"Is her last name Brown?" Nina asked.

It was Geneva's turn to smoke, so Lenora answered.

"Nah. It's some Polish name. Everybody calls the house that cause of the shit brown siding. Geneva's right. Her son's a real trip." She opened the oven door to peek at the brownies. "He's a middle-aged blob with wet hands. You don't wanna touch 'em. You don't want him staring at you with his little pig eyes, but he does."

"Tell Nina what he said about the rats."

Lenora took the joint from Nina.

"He said they were squirrels. I've got a good mind to call the Board of Health." She took a hit, and then smiled as she let out the smoke. "But it's a cheap place to live and it's not half bad. Eh, Geneva?"

"Yup, home sweet home."

The rats made a racket in the walls again. Geneva knocked on the wall this time.

"You wanna go together to that party at 221 Winter tomorrow?" she asked.

"I like those guys," Nina said. "Especially Mack."

Geneva licked the batter again.

"Mack? You'd better watch out for that one. Mack thinks he's God's gift to women. Somebody ought to tell him it's not how long his dick is that counts but how long he can make it last."

Nina blinked.

"Really?"

"Yeah, his idea of a special night ain't so special if you ask me," Geneva said. "Manny. Joey. Tim. The others. They're just a bunch of hairy, horny losers."

"They're not losers. I'd rather do it with them than one of the Dirty Old Bastards." Lenora grimaced. "Whoops. Sorry, Geneva."

Ned Burke was a taboo topic. They didn't talk about him when Geneva slept with him, and Lenora tried to make a point of not being around when he was over during their brief affair. She did take pity on Geneva after Ned had his heart attack. Lenora went with her to the hospital, telling the nurses they were Ned Burke's daughters. She stayed in the hallway, keeping a watch for his wife, but Geneva didn't stay long in the hospital room. She took one peek at her beloved Ned, hooked up to machines and without his teeth, and she hauled ass out of there. She was shook. She said he was so old.

"That's okay. I had it coming." Geneva sighed. "Think he'll be there?"

"Ned Burke? At the party? Professor Groovy wouldn't miss a good time like that."

Nina giggled.

"You're bad," she said.

Geneva frowned.

"Lenora's just trying to be funny."

"Aw, Geneva, remember those T-group sessions? Professor Groovy pairing us up and telling us to touch the other person. It was supposed to free our inhibitions." Lenora stuck out her tongue. "One time I got Joey, and when I touched his hair cause he finally washed it, Groovy laughed like a jackass. He expected me to grope his crotch instead. Poor Joey got so scared he grabbed one of my necklaces, and beads went flying everywhere." Lenora's head fell forward as she laughed. "Remember what Ned did to you? Feeling you up like that in front of everybody?"

"Inez Burke started flipping out in the kitchen when he squeezed my boobs," Geneva said. "What'd she say? 'Jesus Christ, Ned, you're scaring that poor girl to death.'"

"You should've seen the look on your face," Lenora said.

"Well, it wouldn't hurt for you to loosen up once in a while and have some fun. You don't have to fall in love all the time."

"What are you talking about?"

"Lenora, you get so hung up on guys," Geneva said. "Live a little, will you? If this was my last weekend in this joint, I'd go out with a bang. Look at it this way. You're not coming back. Do what you want for once. Tell me, Lenora. What do you got to lose?"

"Oh, yeah? Thanks for the advice, Miss Lonely Hearts."

"Always glad to be of help.

Lenora checked the oven. The brownies were getting a nice crust.

"Hand me that pan, Geneva. I've got more work to do." She lifted the baggie. "Looks like we've got enough for another joint. Up for rolling one?"

BEER RUN

Mack braked at the red light and glanced in the rear-view mirror at Manny, who stared straight ahead at something the rest of them in the car couldn't see. The stupid hippie dropped a tab of acid, Purple Owsley he bought from a guy who didn't want to bring it home.

The light changed and the car darted forward.

"Tim, how's he doing back there?" Mack asked.

Tim, who was jammed between Manny and two cases of beer that couldn't fit in the trunk, bent forward.

"You okay, bro?"

Manny grinned.

"Yeah," he said, stretching out the word.

"He's fine," Tim said. "Mack, the real question is how's Joey doing. I don't think it was such a cool idea leaving him in charge back there. Suppose the cops show up? Joey'll start twitching all over the place, and he'll get busted for sure."

"Somebody had to stick around. Don't worry. The night's young. No casualties so far, well, except for Manny." Mack's head swiveled toward Big Ray who rode shotgun in Mack's two-door Ford Fairlane. "You done rolling that joint?"

"Keep your shirt on, Mack."

Big Ray rolled a skinny joint with his fat fingers and hummed with The Beatles as they sang "Here, There and Everywhere" on the Fairlane's eight-track player. The grass was dry and twiggy, so it kept falling onto Ray's big gut. He picked up the pieces and tried again. He wore overalls built for a farmer as large as him, but no shirt, so even in the back seat Tim got a strong whiff of fat man's BO, which was sweat and something else.

When Big Ray was at Westbridge State, he was the editor of the campus paper for two years. Just about anytime anyone stopped at the newspaper office, Ray was hunched over a portable typewriter as he wrote one of his no-holds-barred editorials, punishing its keyboard with two fingers so fat their skin looked ready to split. "That bastard Richard Nixon is going to get us all killed" began one. He called Dean Shirley Hendricks "an uptight broad" and President David Longo, "a member of the he-man capon club." Ray was the one who changed the name of the school paper from the *Westbridge Gazette* to *The Hard Truth*, which pissed off the school's board of trustees so much they threatened to cut off funding. But in what was now a permanent part of Westbridge lore, Ray stormed into the board's meeting and told the stuffed shirts what this world needed was the hard truth, so they backed down.

Big Ray lived in a dumpy apartment in a dumpy city near Westbridge, where he worked nights in a dumpy pizza joint. He didn't have a car, so he hitched. Or he got one of the Winter Street freaks to give him a ride, bribing them with beer and some of that sorry-ass homegrown pot he got off the pizza drivers. Ray must be blowing half his paycheck on the beer stowed in the trunk and the back seat. That's why he came along for the ride. The man was psyched to be in the thick of it again. Instead of swearing about the heat in front of a pizza oven, he was squashed in the front seat of Mack's Ford Fairlane, getting high with his best buddies.

Ray lit the joint.

Mack's eyes flicked toward the rear-view mirror.

"Doesn't look like Manny needs any of this. Manny, what're you looking at?"

"Boats."

"Boats. You would, you Portagee."

Mack was next, holding in the smoke, while he took a left to avoid the main drag. Downtown Westbridge was an absolute joke. Except for the pizza and sub place on the corner, the place was dead, so there was nothing worth seeing. Besides, it was a lousy idea driving through the center of Westbridge in a smoke-filled Ford with five cases of beer and Manny tripping his head off. The townie cops, a predictable brand of fuzz, always parked a cruiser there Friday nights. Even so, Mack was the model, stoned driver, keeping the speed limit, but not too slow, using signals, and stopping the car where it was supposed to stop. He held the joint over his shoulder for Tim.

"Take it," Mack said hoarsely, choking back the smoke.

It was weak weed Ray bought off a pizza driver, but nobody was about to pass up a freebie. Tim held the smoke in and let it go with one long, hard blow.

"Thanks, Ray," Tim told him.

Ray made a happy hum.

The three of them passed the joint while Manny watched moving pictures on the back of Mack's seat. They now rode through one of Westbridge's nicer neighborhoods. New Cape Cods were mixed in with the old Victorians. Some of the college's professors lived on this street. Mack slowed the car as they passed a development of ranch houses built last summer on what used to be a great field of corn with a vegetable stand on the corner. The farmhouse and barns were gone.

Ray swept his hand across the Fairlane's windshield.

"There, my dear friends, stands the American dream. That's why the best of our generation is fighting in Vietnam, so white-bread, middle-class slaves can live in shit-box houses like that." He slammed a fist on the dashboard. "Let 'em have ranch houses with two-car garages. That goddamn Nixon."

"Right on, brother. You tell 'em," Mack said.

"It's about time the American people woke up and see they're being duped." Gobs of spit flew beneath Ray's thick mustache. "Our boys are getting killed in those jungles, and for what? So, these assholes can live in a house that looks just like the one their neighbors have. This country is fucked up."

Everything, man, was cool. Big Ray was back in form, ranting about the system like he used to do in Westbridge. They were bringing five cases of beer back to Winter Street and The Beatles were singing "Good Day Sunshine" on the eight-track. Mack turned up the volume as Ray slapped the beat on the dashboard. They grinned from the buzz. Totally cool.

Then Tim saw Lenora. She was stuck inside the shadows along the tree-lined sidewalk, so at first he wasn't certain. But he recognized her gait. Those long legs moved fast beneath her skirt, the one with the slit up the side, so you caught some skin when she moved. A bag hung from one shoulder.

"Mack, stop the car. There's Lenora. See her? She's near those trees. Over there."

Tim leaned forward. He pointed over Big Ray's shoulder toward the next street corner.

"Hot damn, it is Lenora," Big Ray said. "What in the hell's she doing in this neighborhood?"

Mack beeped the horn, but Lenora had already seen the car. She stepped into the street and raised her thumb as if she were hitching. Big Ray rolled down his window, and Lenora leaned laughing into the smoky car. Her spicy scent drifted inside.

"Nice to see you guys."

She glanced up when a red pickup with a bad muffler gunned past. One guy yelled "hey, hippie assholes," and another threw a beer can out the window that nearly hit Mack's car. Lenora frowned. Three guys were in the cab. Tim recognized them from dime draft night at the VFW as townie patriots who liked to talk tough.

"Get in, Lenora. I'll give you a ride," Mack said.

Lenora poked her head inside the Fairlane. Her loose, dark hair fell onto Big Ray's chest.

"What are you gonna do? Strap me to the hood?"

"Nah, nah, there's room in there with Manny and Tim. Hurry up. We gotta get back to the party. We left Joey in charge." Mack shoved Ray's arm. "Ray, let her in. Those townies could be trouble."

Lenora stepped aside as Big Ray gripped the roof to ease his body from the car's front seat.

"The townies stopped the truck and asked if I wanted a ride, as if I would," Lenora told them. "They circled around, so I cut through a yard. I thought I lost them going this way. I was supposed to get a ride with Geneva, but she took off without me."

Lenora pulled the seat forward. She was trying to see how she was going to fit in the back. Tim grinned and slapped his thigh. Her mouth fell open. He expected that. They were freshmen the last time she saw him clean-shaven.

"Come on, Lenora, I won't bite," he told her.

She covered her mouth as she laughed.

"You shaved."

"Yeah, I shaved. Get in."

Tim grabbed her wrist, yanking her forward, so she fell giggling onto his lap. Big Ray settled into the front seat and slammed the door. Lenora swung her legs over Manny. His lips melted into a goofy grin.

"Lenora, it's you."

"Yeah, it's me, silly."

Mack put the car in gear, jerking Lenora back so she fell against Tim's chest. His hands slipped beneath her bag and around her waist.

"Manny's tripping," he said in her ear.

She nodded at Manny. His hand rested on her thigh where the skirt came away.

"You okay?" she asked.

Manny fingered a strand of her beads.

"These are pretty, Lenora."

"Here, you can have it."

She slipped the necklace over Manny's head. She adjusted the string of red and turquoise beads on the tufts of black hair sticking over the top edge of his T-shirt. Manny murmured as he patted the beads.

"Manny, those are nice colors for you." Lenora's head swung toward Tim. The corners of her mouth curled nicely. "So, why'd you shave?"

"My mother's coming Sunday. I wanna surprise her."

"Sunday? You're graduating? How's that possible?"

"Well, almost, but my mother doesn't know that. Joey found me a cap and gown. I'll just walk across the stage and take whatever they give me. It's not a real diploma anyway. They mail it to you later."

"Won't she find out? They're not gonna announce your name."

"Yeah, they will. Right, Mack?"

Mack's blue eyes shot back in the rear-view mirror.

"Yup, the fix is in."

Tim lowered his voice. "Mack made friends with a secretary in the registrar's office."

"Oh, brother."

36

Big Ray called over his shoulder.

"Lenora, you got food in that bag? I smell something good."

She laughed.

"Uh-huh. Brownies. They're not bad. I had one before I left while I was waiting for that damn Geneva to show up."

"You put pot in them?" Big Ray asked.

"Course, I did. I'll make sure you get one when I pass them around."

Lenora touched Tim's cheek.

"I like you like this, Tim. You look like a new man. What do you think, Manny?"

Next to them in the dark, Manny's voice mooed, "Smooth."

GOOD VIBES

The music, something Motown, was cranked on the second floor. People shouted and laughed. Feet pounded the floor. The air was filled with sweet, funky smoke. The freaks and their queen could feel the good vibes as they unloaded the cases from the trunk of the car. Manny stood staring up into the large maple in the front yard. His mouth hung open as he said, "ooh."

It was 221 Winter Street code that when somebody took acid, they weren't left alone. No one was going to do something crazy like jump off the roof or out a window like that actor's daughter, although people did have bad trips. It happened before, but it turned out the trippers, like the guy just back from Nam, were a little shaky before they swallowed the tab. Manny wasn't shaky. But no one wanted him tripping his brains out and wandering the neighborhood. He could get lost or scared. Or someone could call the cops.

Lenora grabbed Manny's arm.

"You're coming with me."

Mack and Tim went first, carrying cases of beer up the stairway and dodging the girls who sat on the steps. Big Ray was next. His feet plodded the treads. He breathed heavily through his mouth as he tried to keep up.

"Let us through, people," Mack called out. "More beer here. Gotta get it in the fridge."

Nancy and Lorraine's door was open when Lenora and Manny reached the landing. She poked her head inside. The party spilled into their place although it appeared to be a libbers-only crowd. Their idea of party clothes was tank tops and fatigues. There were lots of heavy boobs and unshaved legs among the sisters.

Nancy shouted "Hey!" and waved her over.

Lenora raised Manny's hand as if they were cuffed together.

"Can't. I'm babysitting Manny. He's tripping," she said.

Lenora used a finger to push Manny forward. Tim said he dropped acid around six, so he probably wouldn't be coming down until after midnight or later, if the stuff were really Owsley. Manny stopped, and when Lenora leaned forward, she saw the kitchen was packed.

"Wait a sec, Manny."

She shifted the bag on her shoulder and gripped the back of Manny's jeans to guide him through the crowd. Pot smoke swirled in the light cast by the blue bulbs screwed into the ceiling. Tim loaded beer cans into the fridge while Mack high-fived his greaser high school buddies who showed up for every party. They smoked a little pot and wanted to get in on some of the free love, but they couldn't get their heads around the peace stuff. This time, one of the greasers brought a dog, a mongrel cowering in a corner.

The kitchen was so full people sat on the counters and stove. A girl with her pregnant belly out to there got a seat at the table. The father, the guy who did air guitar on the steps of the administration building, stood beside her. Lenora went to the wedding, held at the home of the bride's bewildered parents in a Boston suburb. The happy couple lived on the first floor of the Brown House and both hoped to finish school next year.

She heard her name across the room. Geneva stood near the window. Nina, her new roommate, was with her.

Lenora flipped her off.

"Thanks for the fuckin' ride, Geneva." She adjusted her grip on Manny's jeans. "Keep going. I've got you."

She pushed Manny through the hall, where the line was six deep to use the bathroom, and toward the living room, where it was wall-to-wall freaks. She tugged Manny's belt so he stopped in the doorway. She hadn't seen this many longhairs inside a building since they took over the gym to protest the philosophy professor getting fired. The guys had hung sheets over the living room windows and put red bulbs in the lamps. A small square in the center of the room was cleared for the dancers, who moved their sweaty bodies and jerked their arms to Sam and Dave's "Soul Man" as if they were living in the ghetto, but, of course, they were attending a small state college in Massachusetts.

People gathered in bunches on the mattresses and ratty furniture shoved against the walls. Lenora knew everybody. It was like a tribal meeting of the Westbridge clans. The Roach Motel crowd was on her left, sitting beneath the black and white poster of Clint Eastwood wearing a serape in the movie, *A Fistful of Dollars*. The Sampson brothers, Bruce and Bob, who lived next door to each other at the Roach Motel, another college dump, passed a bong to their followers. They sat together on a striped mattress, so it looked as if they were adrift on a life raft.

Roach Brother Bruce, who lasted one semester at Westbridge, claimed he was a warlock, but he was actually a burned-out speed freak with a heavy Rasputin brow. He was harmless unless he got paranoid from doing too many drugs and started carrying a gun. His younger brother, Bob graduated three years ago. Roach Brother Bob went to Boston for a year to make it in advertising until he decided it was a drag working for the man no matter how much he got paid. So, he was back in Westbridge living in the string of cinderblock apartments at the Roach Motel and doing whatever for money. He was Lenora's first boyfriend on campus. She was a virgin then, and she cried for three weeks when he gave up on her fast. She found a better opportunity with a guy she met back home. They tripped on mescaline and she bled on his sleeping bag.

To their left, Howard Keith, who taught art at Westbridge, picked at the shredded fabric on the arm of an upholstered chair. Professor Keith was a frequent guest at these parties. He was not a member of the Old Dirty Bastards Club but of the more exclusive Queer Professors Club. Professor Keith never hit on any of the guys though. He came strictly for the entertainment. Last Halloween, he arranged the screening of the 1930s movie, *Freaks*, at the Westbridge Coffeehouse, held Friday nights in the basement of the Unitarian Church. The movie was a sellout.

The liberal Unitarian minister, a man with owlish eyebrows, sat beside Professor Keith. The good pastor could always be called upon to say a few profound words about peace at any protest. His reputation did take a serious nosedive, however, at the Kent State protest, because he hit the road when the cops showed up. Disappointed protesters debated whether the minister could possibly be a nark or a sellout, but all appeared forgiven during these three days of peace, love, and you know what at 221 Winter Street.

"Coming through, Lenora."

Big Ray had a pipe clenched in his mouth that spewed sewer smoke. He carried a can of beer in each hand. Lenora slid Manny to the side as Big Ray's big belly plowed forward like the bow of a ship. The dancers yelped and parted to give Ray the way to the couch where Rico, Westbridge's Prince of Darkness, sat with his coven. Ray told one of the young girls hanging onto Rico to shove off so he could sit. It wasn't that Ray liked Rico. Not many people did. But if Big Ray sat on one of the mattresses, he wouldn't be able to get up easily.

Lenora held onto Manny.

"You all right, Manny? See any Portagees in here?"

His shoulders shook with laughter.

"One eyebrow or two?"

"One."

She laughed with him.

"Nope. Not even two."

Joey hung out with some of the regulars. She flashed a peace sign at the guy who ran away with a Christian acting troupe. He came back a Jesus freak although that only lasted a few months, which was a relief because they all got tired fast of his salvation bullshit. One couple made out next to a hippie dad who was in his sixth year at Westbridge. His two blond-haired girls, both under five, ran shrieking around the room.

Lenora recognized the freshmen girls from the newspaper office. They were decked out in short, tie-dyed halter-top dresses and white knee-high boots as if they were go-go dancers. One of the girls painted a peace sign on her cheek that was melting in the heat. Lenora frowned and shook her head. She heard them say Rod McEwen was their idea of a great American poet. No fooling. These girls could take her place at Westbridge after she left. Well, that wasn't happening yet. Not this weekend anyway. She was still the queen, and she could do whatever she wanted.

"There's Joey. That looks like a good place to sit."

She steered Manny toward Joey, who watched their approach. He pushed his misshapen, black-rimmed glasses back up his nose.

"How's it hanging, bro?" Joey said.

Manny made a horsy laugh.

"It's hanging just fine."

"Joey, can we park here?" Lenora asked.

"Girls, give 'em some room."

Lenora made a satisfied smile as she squeezed between Manny and Joey. She threw her bag onto the bare mattress. Somebody put Dylan's *Blonde on Blonde* on the stereo, confusing the dancers for a moment, until the guys from the Roach Motel started chanting the chorus to "Rainy Day Women 12 and 35." They spread their arms toward the ceiling and joined them.

"Great party, Joey," Lenora said in his ear. "This is huge. Who'd you invite?"

"The whole world, I think. Mack went a little crazy."

"Hey, I brought something."

The others watched as Lenora pulled the package of brownies from her bag. She was unwrapping the aluminum foil when she heard her name. It was Tim. He knelt on the mattress in front of her and handed her a beer.

"I was looking for you, Lenora," he said.

She stuck a brownie in his mouth.

"Well, here I am, Tim."

SHAKE THAT THING

Tim and Lenora sat against the wall as they took in the show. The grownups had finally left the kids alone: the art professor, the minister, and the hippie dad, who carried his sleeping daughters, one on each shoulder. Whoever was left was drunk or stoned or both.

Mack half-dragged Geneva into the living room. She squealed her head off as they slipped through the dancers, jerking to the Rolling Stones' "Satisfaction." One of the Roach Motel girls took off her top and twirled it above her head, so her titties bounced wildly as she danced. Not to be outdone, Mack did some Cossack dance moves, even trying to kick from a squat, goofy stuff, but he made it work, so the other dancers stopped to give him room. Geneva fluttered around him, giggling as people clapped to the music and cheered. Mack fell on his ass after a few high kicks, but he was back on his feet, spinning and daring the others to try. His high school buddies standing in the doorway pointed their beers at Mack and laughed with their heads thrown back.

"Mack's such a showoff," Tim whispered to Lenora.

"What else is new?"

Manny tripped on the other side of her. He hadn't left except to take a leak. Lenora waited outside the bathroom door for him.

"Manny, you still alive? Blink twice if you are," Tim said.

Manny lifted his hand.

"Close enough."

Joey sat several feet away, talking it up with another heavy thinker, a guy who returned to Westbridge on the GI Bill after being stationed in Europe. He was into that expat thing, wearing a beret and smoking a pipe. The two were deep into William Carlos William's *Kora in Hell Improvisations*. Joey rushed to the attic to get his copy, dog-eared and filled with his notes. The two passed a joint and read the best passages aloud while the expat's foxy German wife chain-smoked unfiltered Gauloises.

"Read that line again. I think I heard something new there," Joey told the expat.

One of the freshman girls was passed out next to Ray on the couch, long deserted by Rico who split before midnight. He and his coven were driving cross-country to California the next morning. Lenora told Tim the other freshman girl was puking into the bathtub.

Someone passed Lenora a joint, and after taking a hit, she gave it to Tim.

"Tastes like the primo pot Mack bought," he told her.

"Yeah? Pass it back to me," she joked.

Tim held the joint aloft, making Lenora reach for it. She grabbed his side, tickling him so hard he fell back, and then she was lying on top of him, laughing with him. He stuck the joint between her lips. She held the smoke in her mouth and blew it into his.

"Take a hit."

Tim did as he was told. He would have done anything Lenora said. She took the joint and brought it to her lips.

"You're such a crazy girl."

Smoke streamed through her mouth as she laughed. She held the roach.

"Uh-oh, all gone."

Somebody changed the record. Sly and the Family Stone played "I Want to Take You Higher." Lenora rolled off Tim, and he said, "Hey, come back," but she sat against the wall to get out of the way of the stampeding dancers. The volume was up so loud, the funky guitar riffs buzzed through the speakers. Sly wailed like a tomcat. It was a miracle the cops hadn't showed up, but Mack spread the word everybody had to stay inside even though the apartment was a million degrees. After the girls complained the line was too long for the bathroom, the guys were allowed to take a piss in the backyard, but they had to be quick and quiet about it. Trees separated 221 Winter Street from the houses on either side. Old people who went to bed early lived in both, and they must be deaf because they never complained. Mack's theory was that the old coots watched with binoculars.

Tim sat next to Lenora. On her other side, Manny grinned like he tasted something good. She crawled forward to get her bag a clumsy dancer had kicked. Her blouse slid forward so her back was bare. She wasn't wearing a bra, of course. Lenora was the first girl on campus to stop doing it on purpose. Tim remembered the day she walked into the dining hall without one. They were second-semester freshmen then. He noticed the nice sway of loose breasts beneath her top. When she caught him staring, she said, "They needed a little air." His dick got hard, just like it was now.

Then there was the time he saw her asleep in the bed of a former Winter Street roommate. The door was open, and he couldn't help staring. The top sheet was thrown off, so he saw everything about her.

"I bet you'd like a piece of that," the guy said.

Tim didn't answer. He held his breath and wished.

Now, he admired the curve of Lenora's waist. If he were Joey, he'd have the right words to describe her, but he wasn't, so he didn't. All he thought was that soon she'd be gone.

He ran a finger lightly along the sharp ridge of her spine. She glanced back, surprised.

"Sorry. I couldn't resist."

She didn't stop smiling as she patted his bare cheek and sat back beside him. He closed his eyes. He had his arm around her, and she fit there so easily, he sighed.

Lenora jiggled her head to the beat, getting into the music. Roach Brother Bruce, who danced by himself, reached for her.

"Come on, Lenora, shake that thing."

She turned toward Tim.

"I'll be back."

He could have kissed her. Instead he said, "I'll be right here."

Lenora got to her feet, stopping a second to steady herself. Her hands were in the air, and she made those broad hips go back and forth in a bump and grind. She wiggled her finger, but Tim shook his head. He wasn't much of a dancer, but neither was Roach Brother Bruce, because suddenly he was gone, sucked into the crowd. Lenora shrugged. It didn't matter. People were dancing anywhere they could. One of the Roach Motel girls jumped on the couch, waking the freshman girl, who staggered away. The girl put so much into her dancing she jostled Big Ray, which normally would have ticked him off, but her squirming butt was in his face, so he was one happy guy tonight. Even the couple hot and heavy in the corner stopped to dance.

Lenora's blouse rose high enough that Tim got a look at her breasts when she lifted her arms. Her skirt split wide and showed thigh as she shimmied. Tim, high and horny as hell, knew he better get up there with her. He kicked off his sandals. She extended her hand to help him up.

"I'm lousy at this."

"It's easy," she told him. "See?"

Her hips were going. No way he could move like that. She was playing him, and Tim didn't mind one single bit.

A BIG, BAD LOVE

Tim and Lenora danced to a slow song. They were the only ones on the floor. It was after three, which was the last time they went to the kitchen for beer but found nothing in the fridge. Guys too hopped up to sleep or those who didn't get lucky were in there listening to Ray bitch about the war. The rest were either passed out or asleep or getting it on in a darkened corner of the apartment.

Neither spoke as they moved in circles. Aretha Franklin's voice came through the stereo's speakers. She sang about love. A big, bad love. Lenora knew all about it. It was the kind of love that got her into trouble and broke her heart. She liked how she felt with Tim, but she wasn't looking for that right now. This was her last weekend. She was leaving for Europe, and after that, who knew what she'd be doing.

She blew on Tim's neck.

"This is nice," she told him.

His "yeah" was soft.

Tim's face came closer. They kissed and they kept on kissing as he backed her toward his room. He shut the door. They pulled at each other's clothes, laughing, as they fell onto his bed.

NAKED

Lenora opened her eyes. Manny stood a few feet away in the moonlight pooled on the floor beside Tim's bed.

"What's the matter?" she whispered.

"Can I sleep with you?"

"What's wrong with *your* bed?"

"Willy and Mary are using it."

Lenora glanced at Tim. He snored lightly.

"You still tripping?"

"No, I've been down for a while. Please, Lenora."

"All right, sleep on top of the sheet."

She watched, amused, as Manny dropped his pants.

"Geez, Manny, what the hell are you doing?"

"Getting ready for bed."

"But you're naked."

He lifted the sheet.

"So are you. So's Tim."

She snatched the sheet. She glanced back at Tim. His eyes were closed.

"Course, we're naked. What do you think we've been doing?"

Manny grinned.

"I know. I could hear you two in the other room. Everybody could. You make a lot of noise, Lenora."

Manny's dick stiffened. She began laughing. This was too crazy for words.

She held the sheet for Manny.

"Get in. But you're gonna have to be very, very quiet."

Stifling a giggle, she crawled over Manny. She rose above him, straddling his legs as she poked his hairy chest.

"Don't move a muscle."

Manny watched through half-closed lids as she ran her hands all over him. Her dark hair fell forward. She played with his dick. The boy was gone. Totally gone. Manny started to speak, but she covered his mouth.

"Shh. Don't wake Tim," she whispered.

Manny nodded and stifled a moan as she pushed him inside.

"Ooh, this feels good," she moaned.

Lenora rocked slowly until Manny gripped her hips to make her go faster. He grunted. He was nearly ready to lose it. She checked on Tim. He was awake. Shock was on his face, or maybe it was lust.

"Get ready, Tim," Lenora cooed, as she patted his hairless cheek. "Your turn's next."

EARLY RISERS

enora opened her eyes. She lay between Tim and Manny. Air came from her mouth in an oh-my-God kind of sigh as she remembered what they did. All night she wanted to be with Tim, but the thing with Manny, and then Tim again? She wasn't that drunk or stoned. She sighed again. She couldn't explain it.

The top sheet was bunched around the three of them. To her left, Manny snored lightly. He rolled so his back was to her. Tim's arm was draped over her waist. His chin, now covered with soft, short whiskers, was tucked into her hair. She smiled about Tim shaving for his mother and trying not to disappoint her about graduation. Lenora saw the woman once. She was a first-generation American whose parents came over on the boat from Ireland about the same time Lenora's grandparents crossed the Atlantic from the Azores and Madeira islands. She called her son, "Timmy," and said she was proud of her youngest boy, the first of her large brood to go to college. He wouldn't have to drive a truck or work on car engines like his brothers. He wouldn't work in a factory like his father, who died in an accident when Tim was only seven. Her Timmy was going to be a teacher or have a desk job somewhere.

Lenora met Tim's mother at Jimmy's, where he took her and one of

50

his sisters, who was pregnant with her third baby. They came from South Boston to bring Tim his winter clothes. He lived in the dorm then. Tim's mother insisted Lenora join them for lunch. Later, Tim told her that his mother said, "I like your pretty girlfriend."

"You tell your mother I'm not your girlfriend?"

He gave her a shy smile. No, he didn't.

Lenora squinted at the alarm clock on Tim's dresser. It was after ten. She needed to get to the bank before noon to close her account. She was leaving with her parents right after graduation Sunday.

She gently moved Tim's arm and rolled him away. He murmured and made smacking noises with his lips.

"Tim, I'll be back later."

She kissed his cheek.

"Yeah, yeah," he whispered back.

She threw off the sheet and rubbed the dried semen on her thighs as she scooted to the end of the mattress. She glanced at Tim and Manny. They were still asleep. She lifted the sheet and let it fall over them before she searched the floor for her clothes. She dressed.

Lenora shut the door quietly and stepped into the hall. She ducked inside the living room, where people were still sacked out, to find her bag. She walked past the closed bathroom door into the kitchen where Joey scrambled eggs at the stove. Coffee the color of dirty river water popped in the glass bubble of the aluminum pot. Hung-over early risers sat at the table or paced with paper plates. No one spoke.

Joey was making morning-after eggs, his specialty. He mixed whatever was left in the liquor bottles with the eggs, so the stuff in the skillet was as green as bird shit. He threw in a little bit of herbs from a jar, maybe it was basil or oregano, so he thought it was gourmet cooking. No one had the heart or nerve to tell him otherwise. Certainly, Lenora didn't.

Lenora's foot tapped the cracked linoleum near the stove.

"You're up early," she said.

"I never went to sleep. Maybe I did for an hour or two before dawn." His head swung toward the kitchen table. "I went early to Foodtown to get the groceries for breakfast. See?"

"Wow. Eggs and toast. Coffee. I'm impressed."

Joey gave the eggs a stir.

"Want some? Grab a plate."

51

"No, thanks. I gotta get to the bank before it closes. I'll be back later. Tell Tim that for me, will you?" She checked the bathroom door. The knob turned. "It's about time."

Mack came from the bathroom.

"All yours." Mack made a snorting laugh. "Ha, I know where you were last night." He laughed again. "I saw you leave Tim's room. Didn't think I knew, huh?"

She rushed past him.

"I sure as hell don't care if you did," she said as she shut the bathroom door behind her.

THREESOME

Mack kicked the leg of the bedstead, but Tim and Manny didn't wake up. The top sheet was twisted around Manny's torso. Tim slept on his side, naked, with his hands between his thighs. Mack kicked harder. Both blinked up at him.

"I hope this ain't what it looks like." Mack smirked. "Shit, I wish I had a camera. I'd blackmail you both if you ever got rich and famous some day."

The sheet fell to Manny's crotch as he bolted upright. He checked the narrow space separating Tim from him. Tim, too, eyed the spot. Glass beads, black and red, from Lenora's necklace, were spilled over the wrinkled sheet.

Mack sniggered.

"Looking for somebody?" he asked.

"Yeah, Lenora."

Tim gave Manny a hard shove.

"Shut up, Manny."

Mack's mustache rose when he grinned.

"Lenora, eh? She's long gone. I caught her sneaking out, but she wasn't interested in talking to me. She told Joey she had places to go, people to see." He tipped his head. "Don't worry, you perverts, she said she'd be back later."

Tim eyes were small and hard, but they didn't stop Mack.

"Threesome, eh? I gotta hand it to you. And with Lenora, too."

"Give it a rest, Mack," Tim muttered.

Mack sat on the corner of the mattress near Manny.

"I was sure Tim was gonna score. Lenora was wet for him all night. I have to say, Tim, it was a smart idea shaving. Looks like she got off on it. I'll have to remember that one." Mack scratched the red hair on his jaw. "What I can't figure out is how in the hell Manny got in on the action. Tim, you must've been taking a leak when this hairy ape jumped in your place."

Tim's jaw was tight.

"Mack, sometimes you can be such a fuckin' asshole."

Mack shook a finger.

"Man, oh, man, somebody's a little touchy today. Manny, what's the story?"

Manny laughed. Mack waited, but he didn't say a thing. Neither did Tim. He was out of bed, grabbing his jeans off the floor and throwing them over a shoulder. He scratched his naked butt as he left the room.

Mack nodded at Manny.

"How about it?"

Manny untwisted the sheet.

"What time is it, Mack?"

"Around noon. We've got some food going in the kitchen. Joey's taken over."

Mack watched Manny lift the sheet nailed to the ceiling to go to his side of the room. He came back with a fresh shirt. Mack wasn't going to get anything more from Tim. His best shot was with Manny. This was too rich: Lenora getting it on with those two sorry guys. He should be so lucky. He only got to screw Geneva's new roommate, Nina, who was still zonked out in his bed. She was heavier than he liked and she had a funny-shaped mouth like it was made for yelling, but he wasn't complaining. She was planning to stick around Westbridge all summer. That took care of one problem, although he'd have to be smart. He wasn't looking for anything serious with her.

But Lenora was something else. Lenora was their queen.

Manny pulled up his jeans.

"What's there to eat?"

"Breakfast is on Joey. We even have coffee."

Manny zipped his fly.

"Coffee? I could use some of that."

They walked to the kitchen where Joey was still at command at the stove. He lifted a spatula.

"Guys, you're just in time. Get yourself a plate. There're some spoons in the sink."

Mack stared at the green eggs. Joey pulled toasted slices of bread from the oven to stack on a platter. The top crusts were missing.

Mack tipped his head.

"Uh, Joey, what's with the crust?"

Joey turned his back to those in line.

"They were a little moldy. I cut that part off." He lifted a slice. "See? Good as new."

"Those egg cartons look dirty," Mack said. "Wait a minute. Where'd you say you got this stuff?"

"Foodtown. Where else?"

"Uh, Foodtown doesn't sell moldy bread and eggs in dirty cartons. Where'd you really get them?"

Joey lowered his voice.

"Okay, but don't tell anybody. I found the eggs and bread in the trash at Foodtown. Don't worry. They're still okay."

"You gotta be shitting me," Mack said.

"I did buy the coffee and jelly. The paper plates, too. That okay with you?" He lowered the flame beneath the frying pan. "You don't have to eat any of it if you don't want to. There'll just be more for the rest of us. Right, guys?"

A line of freaks near the stove nodded.

Mack shrugged.

"You're right. I'll take a pass. Gotta get more beer anyway." He waved. "See you all later at the ballgame. Don't forget we're going swimming at the pond. No suit? No problem." He jabbed a thumb at Manny. "Manny, grab your sandals. We've got some business to take care of. Breakfast is on me."

MIND-BLOWING PROPORTIONS

Tim went left on Winter Street for a quick walk around the block to clear his head. It rained earlier this morning, and the sun lifted the moisture into the air and cooked it there. Today was going to be a scorcher. A swim later would feel great.

He was only a few houses away from 221 Winter when he saw Mack back his Ford from the driveway and head in the opposite direction. Manny was in the front seat. Neither noticed him. He knew what was going on between those two. Mack was pumping Manny about what happened last night with Lenora. It wouldn't take much. Manny wasn't the kind of guy who could keep something like that to himself. He pictured the happy idiot jabbering away. Tim didn't blame him. He felt like a happy idiot himself. What Lenora did with the two of them was an experience of mind-blowing proportions.

Tim couldn't believe it when he saw Lenora on top of Manny. The guy was going out of his gourd. Then Lenora was looking at him, telling him to get ready, as if she had to say it. He shook his head. She lay beside him, and the two of them went at it on his side of the bed. He didn't know what Manny was doing while that happened. He didn't care. Tim would have said or done anything so she wouldn't leave. After they both came, her voice mewing some sweet song, she stayed wrapped in his arms until they both fell asleep. He smiled to himself. Manny didn't get her again.

He picked up a few stray empties as he ran up the stairs of 221 Winter Street. He smelled food as he came through the door. Joey hovered over the stove.

"Yo, brother, grab a plate. Never mind. I've got you one and a clean spoon, too," he told Tim.

Tim watched as Joey dropped a spoonful of green egg onto a paper plate and reached into the oven for two pieces of toast. Big Ray, who had one of his overall straps unbuckled, sat across the table, shoveling food into his mouth and wiping his mouth with the back of his hammy hand.

Joey set a plate in front of Tim.

"Here, you go. Chow down."

Tim took a whiff.

"What *is* this?"

"Mostly eggs. A little Wild Turkey and a secret ingredient."

Tim poked the eggs with his fork.

"What's the secret?"

Joey didn't answer. He was back at the stove, whistling and cooking up another pan of eggs for whoever was next. Flies swarmed over the beer bottles and cans piled in boxes against the wall. Trash spilled from the can. The linoleum was black and sticky.

Tim stared at the green eggs.

"It ain't half bad if you put enough salt and pepper on it," Big Ray said. "I think there's some Tabasco sauce around here somewhere. Just watch out for the chip on the top of the bottle."

Tim slid the plate toward Ray.

"Here, help yourself. I'm not hungry."

"You sure?"

He grabbed Ray's empty plate.

"Please. You'll make the cook very happy."

Joey brought over a mug of coffee.

"Wow, you wolfed that down. Want some more?" He nodded toward the stove. "There's plenty."

"I'm full. Thanks, buddy." Tim patted his stomach. "Did you see Lenora leave?"

"Oh, yeah, I forgot. She gave me a message for you. She said to tell you she'd be back later."

Tim whistled as he strolled to his room. He didn't bother looking at the mess in the living room. Mack would come back and make everybody clean up before they hiked to the pond. He was good at getting people to do things like that.

The couple who slept in Manny's bed was leaving his room.

"Hey, you two, there's food in the kitchen."

"That's what we heard. You going to the pond?" the guy asked.

"Yeah, later."

Tim stood near his bed. Black and red beads were scattered over the sheet. He held a few beads in his palm, liking the way they caught the light. Maybe Lenora would ask for them back, maybe not. He remembered a small jar in his dresser that could hold them.

He thought he heard her leave this morning. He thought she kissed him.

This wasn't Lenora, the girl who fell in love like no one else. The more he thought, the more confused he got. What had gotten into that girl?

He checked the alarm clock on his dresser. He had enough time to go downtown for something decent to eat. He would try to find Lenora.

PLAY BALL

The score was tied, three-up, in the third inning of the freaks' softball game, with the Winter Street team scoring on a blown catch by the Roach Motel's rightfielder who was tripping on acid and had no business being out there. He wasn't even close to the ball when he thought he caught it. Most everyone had already stripped and hit the pond at least once. The water was still dick-shrinking cold because it was only May, but it woke up anyone still hung over from the night before. They would all swim again after the game before heading to Winter Street. Lorraine, Nancy, and the rest of the libbers were treating everybody to a dinner of U.S. Government Surplus Food. They promised macaroni and cheese, baked beans, and mystery meat salad sandwiches.

The Winter Street and Roach Motel freaks were psyched about another contest of supremacy. Sometimes when things got too uptight between the two tribes, they challenged each other to a game of touch football or basketball to set the record straight. Or they made stupid dares like the time the Roach Motelers bet the Winter Streeters they couldn't run a pirate flag above the administration building, which of course they did. The prank even made the Boston paper because Dean Hendricks made such a stink about it. She even offered a reward, but no one ratted out Joey who climbed onto the roof from the dean's office after asking a friendly custodian to unlock the door.

One night, the tribes had a footrace at the college's track, but it was after everybody had been drinking hard and bragged they were much better athletes in high school than any of them actually were. By time they reached the finish line, they were bent over, grabbing their sides and huffing. Guys puked on their shoes. Softball was definitely more their speed.

Fans sat in the grass and beneath the trees around the softball field set up in the large clearing near the pond. Westbridge State College owned the pond and the acreage around it. The talk was eventually it'd be used for dorms if the school ever got that big. For now, the college let it be, except for sending a grounds crew to mow once in a while. That hadn't happened this year though, so the grass was calf-high except where a hundred feet had trampled it down. No one was supposed to swim or hang out here. No-trespassing signs were posted everywhere, but the freaks ignored them. Besides, no one had ever seen a Westbridge cop get out of a cruiser and walk the half-mile road to the pond. They were safe.

They set up the diamond on the flattest part of the field so third base had to be a tree. The teams agreed a runner just had to tag the bark and any ball hit off the tree was fair. It was an automatic double if the ball hit the no-trespassing sign. The rest of the bases and the gear were swiped from the supply closet at the athletic department.

Of course, it was supposed to be a friendly game of softball, but no one would guess that by the way Mack and Roach Brother Bob, the team captains, were carrying on. Things got hot and heavy over an extra hard slide Bob made at home. The two freaks were red-faced and beard-to-beard as they argued. Big Ray, who was umping, stood back to let them duke it out. Everybody else grooved on the show. They all howled when some guy threw an empty beer can toward home plate and yelled, "Rumble."

Joey, who was playing first, saw the whole thing. Nancy, the Winter Street catcher, was blocking home plate, waiting for the relay from Tim at short when Roach Brother Bob plowed into her like a linebacker. Ray jumped back as if he suddenly stepped barefoot on something hot, moving faster than anyone had ever seen him. Nancy was flat on her back with Roach Brother Bob sprawled on top of her. She raised her hand to show she had the ball. Winter Street fans cheered.

Ray hooked his thumb and shouted, "You're out!" He yanked off his mask and checked Nancy. "You okay?"

She pushed at Roach Brother Bob.

"Yeah, but tell that motherfucker to get off me," she said.

Roach Brother Bob and Mack wouldn't let it go. Spit flew from their mouths as they yelled at each other. Joey stood next to Manny between first and second, finishing a joint while they assessed the battle at home plate. Joey shook his head as Manny took the last toke.

"Boys will be boys," Joey said.

Manny scratched the back of his head. He glanced toward Tim, who sat leaning against third base.

"You see Lenora around?" Manny asked Joey.

"Not here. This morning I did. She was heading out the door. She looked a little ragged."

Manny grinned.

"Guess where she was coming from."

Joey raised his hand.

"I heard all about it. I think everybody has. Why in the hell did you tell Mack?"

"You know how he gets. Fucker should sign up for the FBI, the way he worked me over. Took me out to breakfast, let me buy whatever I wanted. On him, and Mack's such a cheap bastard. He acted like we were best buddies." He shrugged. "Lenora's a big girl. I think she can handle it."

"Is that so?"

Joey strolled toward Tim, sitting in the shade of third base.

"Don't you wanna hear more?" Manny called after him.

Joey waved his glove.

"Nah, I'd get too jealous."

Joey crouched. Tim grunted a greeting. Joey wasn't expecting to hear anything about Lenora from Tim. He was a person he trusted to keep any information to himself. Joey could say anything to Tim like the time he told him he got picked up hitchhiking by a pervert who had a thing about feet. After a few miles, the guy started talking about Joey's boots and saying things like, "I bet there're some men who'd pay money to touch a fine pair of boots like those." His voice sounded sick when he said it. But Joey had been waiting for a ride for a couple of hours, and he wasn't about to tell the driver to let him off in the dark in the middle of nowhere. Tim didn't even wince when Joey told him the guy paid him twenty bucks. He knew Joey was always broke.

Neither spoke. Like the rest of the crowd they watched the show near home plate and waited for things to blow over.

"Look, asshole, that's the way the game's played in the big leagues," Bruce, the older Roach brother, yelled.

"As I recall, asshole, this ain't the big leagues," Mack said back. "What are you complaining about? He was out at home anyway. Your catcher made the play."

"But it was a cheap shot. She could've gotten hurt."

Mack pointed toward Nancy, who scowled as she rubbed her elbow. A Red Sox cap was planted backwards on her head. A couple of her libber friends, who played in the outfield for Winter Street, stood in solidarity beside her.

Roach Brother Bob opened his mouth, but Big Ray wedged himself between the two.

"Whoa, take it easy, boys." He turned toward Nancy. "Nance, you okay?" He continued after she gave him a stony nod. "Let's break this up and play some ball."

Mack's eyes were nearly closed.

"Tell that prick to take it easy. I don't want anybody getting hurt," he said.

Big Ray's fat hand was on Roach Brother Bob's shoulder.

"No more hard plays. That all right with you Bob?"

"Yeah, yeah, sorry, Nancy."

Nancy gave him a half grin.

Ray raised two fingers to signal the outs.

"Everybody back on the field. Play ball!" he barked.

Joey stood. That's when he saw Lenora circle the edge of the crowd. She wore a top with thin straps like a man's undershirt, but a satin butterfly with sequins was sewn on the front. Her long purple skirt swayed as she walked. Her hair hung in one thick braid.

"A thing of beauty is a joy forever:/ Its loveliness increases; it will never/ Pass into nothingness; but still will keep," Joey said softly.

"What'd you say?" Tim asked.

"It's a poem by Keats."

"Jesus, Joey, don't you ever give that brain of yours a rest?"

Joey chuckled.

"There goes Lenora," he said.

He nodded toward the crowd. Lenora stopped to talk with one of the libbers. Her head was tipped back.

"She's here?"

Joey didn't have to say more. Tim was on his feet. He looked as if he was going to chase after her, but Mack growled for everyone to get into position. Roach Brother Bruce was at the plate and Mack was getting ready to pitch the ball high and inside to the hairy mother.

SKINNY DIPPING

enora sat with the happy hippies chilling at the pond and celebrating the Winter Street team's come-from-behind win. She watched Tim, Joey, and Manny horse around in the water, dunking each other and making wild jumps off a large boulder. They were naked like the rest of the swimmers except for Big Ray, who was too embarrassed to be seen that way, so he rolled up the legs of his overalls and went into the water up to his knees. Lenora hadn't been in yet.

Tim stood on the boulder, whistling sharply. He waved his arms and shouted her name.

Lenora shook her head and shouted back, "Too cold. The water's too cold."

She watched as Tim made a flat dive into the water, swimming toward shore until it got too shallow, and then he was running and grinning like he had something in mind. Pond water dripped from his naked body. She cowered and yelped as it splashed on her.

Tim got ahold of her wrists.

"Come on, Lenora, time for you to get in the water. You look too hot sitting here."

She held back and dug her feet into the grass. She kept saying no. Her laughter was breathy and high.

"Okay, okay. Let me take my clothes off first. "

Tim released one wrist.

"Sure, Lenora, but I'm holding on. I know what'll happen. You'll run off as soon as I let go." He pointed toward her skirt. "Hurry up, or I'll get Manny and Joey to help me."

She looked toward the pond where their hairy, smiling faces floated above the water.

Joey hollered through two hands, "Come on, Lenora. The water feels great."

"Don't lie to me. It's effin' cold." She kicked off her sandals and tugged at Tim's hand. "What's the matter? You don't trust me?"

"Uh-huh. You'll split as soon as I turn my back. You won't even say bye."

Her skirt slid down her hips into a dark purple bunch at her feet.

"I did say bye this morning, but you wouldn't wake up."

"Sure, sure, I went looking for you all over town. I even went to your apartment, but you'd vanished into thin air."

"You must've just missed me. I had a million things to do today."

"One of them didn't include leaving a note, did it?"

She tucked her free hand on the band of her red satin panties. Tim gave it an appreciative glance.

"You're enjoying this, aren't you?" she said as she yanked the panties to her feet. "There's no way I can take this top off with you holding my hand. You're gonna have to let go."

Tim chuckled.

"Only for a second."

He grabbed her hand when she was done.

"Wait, my beads."

He watched as she pulled each one over her head. She made a teasing smirk.

"I'm ready."

"Okay."

She ran with him into the water, screaming because it was so cold.

"Dive, dive," he yelled, and when they came up for air, Tim dragged Lenora toward the boulder where Manny and Joey waited. She laughed the entire time.

A WESTSTOCK MOMENT

Mack kept telling anyone who listened it was a Woodstock moment. Now he told Joey who sat cross-legged on the grass. A mob of naked girls and guys were in the water. They had plenty of pot. They even had music. Some of the folksy freaks, the coffeehouse regulars, got out their guitars and harmonicas to play a decent version of "I-Feel-Like-I'm-Fixin'-to-Die Rag" while one of the Roach brothers, Bob, the younger, a little bummed because the Winter Street team won, hammered away at the bongos. They weren't Country Joe MacDonald and the Fish, but they weren't half bad. People were paying attention to the singing, because they wanted to join in on the parts they knew.

Mack didn't make it to Woodstock. His father's car got as far as the New York border before the engine blew. So, he became the guy who almost went to Woodstock, although the story changed over time. Mack's car kept getting closer and closer to Max Yasgur's farm. Next, everyone expected Mack to make it. Eventually he'd be backstage with the performers, smoking weed with Jimi and grooving with Sly. A few of the other Westbridge freaks went to Woodstock, including Manny, who didn't remember too much, because he was on acid most of the time. But he said there was a lot of people and it rained. He thought he got laid.

Mack, who had been in the water twice, sat on the grass with his shirt off, catching some rays. Joey passed him a lit joint. Mack brought it to his lips as he checked out Nina, Geneva's new roommate, who slept topless in the shade.

"Yup, it's a Woodstock moment all right."

"I'd say it was more like a Weststock moment."

Mack blew out the smoke.

"Good one." Mack gave Joey the joint. "Check out the knockers on that one. See the girl next to Ray. Who is she?"

"She's one of the townie girls who hangs out at the Roach Motel."

"No wonder they lost. They got too distracted."

"Nah, it's cause Lorraine had that hit." Joey's hand made a sweet arc in the air. "Right over the outfield. She was a good pickup."

"I don't think either of us will be picking up Lorraine, if you get what I mean."

Mack kept talking with Joey about the game, but his eyes were on the pond, watching Lenora, Manny, and Tim splash each other. Lenora's braid flew wildly, and she giggled as she fended off their attacks. Her breasts rose above the water when Tim grabbed her around her waist. She yelled for Manny as if she were in trouble.

Shit, how long was this threesome going to last? Manny told him all about it. Lenora was the one who said to get in bed with Tim and her. She was the one who got on top of him. Then she did it again with Tim. Mack got horny thinking about it.

Mack raised his eyebrows. He remembered when one of the Roach Motel girls announced at a party last year she'd take on any guy who wanted to give her a try. Guys were going in and out of the bedroom all night. Mack took a turn, but he ended getting a blowjob instead. That was his idea. She said she was on the pill, but he wasn't taking any chances on another dose of the clap.

Lenora wouldn't do anything like that. Maybe he didn't know her as well as he thought. Maybe he had overlooked an opportunity.

Joey slapped Mack's arm. He held the smoking joint. Mack took a hit as he watched Lenora pick her way over the stones. She held her hand over her crotch, but he still saw her dark bush. She said something back at Tim and Manny, waving at them before she bent for her pile of things and ran to the woods. Mack craned his neck. The end of her braid bounced against her back. He handed the joint to Joey.

"Finish it."

Mack stood. Joey raised an eyebrow.

"Leaving?

"Yeah, catch you later, bro."

Mack strolled toward the woods. By time he reached Lenora, she was on her knees searching through her pile. She glanced up when she heard him coming.

"Hey, Mack, what's happening?"

"Nothing. Looks like you were having fun down there."

"Yeah, those guys are nuts."

She hesitated like she was thinking something over, but then she stood up with her back to him, pulling on her panties, shiny and red. She bent for her top. Lenora had it bunched around her neck when she faced Mack.

"You gonna stand there and watch me dress?"

"I've got a better idea."

He stepped forward so he was close behind her. He had his hands on her breasts, playing with them and liking the way their nipples got hard. He made a sound deep and low in his throat.

Lenora's voice hissed.

"What in the hell are you doing? Get your fucking hands off me."

He slipped his hand down the front of her panties. He began kissing her neck.

"Come on, Lenora, lighten up. Let's have some fun."

Lenora twisted and chopped at him with her elbows.

"Cut it out, Mack."

"That's it. Put up a little fight, Lenora. I can play this game. Just you and me in the woods." He growled. "I see a nice spot over there."

"Let go of me."

Mack had Lenora in his arms, half-carrying her, but it was a struggle because she was slapping and kicking. She called him all kinds of names. Then Lenora gave him a hard shot with her fist that sent him backwards over a tree root to the ground. She yanked down her top and went for her skirt. Her movements were sharp and tight.

"You're such a fuckin' asshole."

Mack sat on the ground. He had a good mind to grab her ankles, but she'd holler her head off.

"It's okay to do it with two losers, but not me."

"That's what this all about? I slept with Tim and Manny, and not you?"

She slipped her feet into her sandals.

"What about those guys?"

"Get lost. I don't have to explain myself to you or anybody else."

She snatched her bag and left.

Mack stayed where he was. Shot down by Lenora? Impossible. He shook his head as he saw her purple skirt between the trees. What a bitch.

He lay on the grass and stared up through the leaves, so heavy he couldn't see the sky. He listened to the voices echo up from the pond. The crowd was thinning. Freaks were heading back to 221 Winter Street. He wondered if Lenora would show up. Of course, she would. She wasn't just a bitch. She was a cold-hearted bitch. He had been right about her after all.

Mack started back to the pond. At the end of the woods, he stopped and worked the zipper of his fly. Near the shore, Manny stared at him. Mack grinned and gave the chump a big thumbs-up.

THE BEST PART

Joey's leg jumped beneath the kitchen table as he twisted a book of matches. He still hadn't slept, and it didn't appear he was going to any time soon. His eyes flitted around the room. Sunburned freaks went in and out, filling up on food and drink.

Tim sat across the table, trying to finish his macaroni and cheese, but the paper plate jiggled over the tabletop.

"Jesus, Joey, what you doing? You humping somebody down there?"

Joey looked down at his leg and laughed. He willed the leg to stop, and it did long enough for him to apologize before it started up again. He tossed the matchbook onto the table and shrugged.

"I'm just a nervous kind of guy, I guess."

"No shit. No wonder you're so skinny. Did you eat?"

"Yeah, but I'm thinking of going for seconds. I really liked the sandwiches. I thought the piccalilli added something to the mystery meat." Joey slapped his belly. "Cookies and watermelon. We're eating like kings tonight."

Tim glanced up from his plate.

"I don't think kings eat mystery meat."

"Don't knock it. It's one of the best meals I've had in a long time." He pointed to the line in the hallway to Nancy and Lorraine's place. "That's probably true for most of them, don't you think?"

"If you like the food so much, I bet Lenora will get you more."

Joey raised a finger.

"Great idea."

Joey grabbed his paper plate and fork, and then got in line behind Nina, Geneva's new roommate who Mack almost left behind at the pond. The girl woke up with red marks on her back from where the sun came through the trees. She looked as if she was going to cry when she didn't see Mack. She grabbed for her clothes. Then the jerk came out of the woods, greeting Nina like he missed her something awful with a big, sloppy kiss, so obvious he had something to hide, at least to Joey, and afterward he talked to Manny in code. Tim was still in the water with one of the Roach Motelers, the last to leave the pond.

Nina turned around in line.

"Having fun?" she asked.

Joey's fingers shredded the edges of the paper plate.

"Yeah. How about you?"

"Uh-huh." She checked the stairway. "Where'd you say Mack went?"

"Packie run. He and Manny went to the one in East Westbridge. He says if he keeps buying so much booze at one place, the owner will tip off the cops." Joey nodded, skipping the part about two girls who went along for the ride. "I think he's just being a little paranoid."

Joey stood near the table of food. Lenora laughed. She pointed a spoon at him.

"You need a new plate."

Joey laughed too. He held half a plate. The rest was in pieces on the floor in the hall. Lenora handed him a new one.

"Macaroni and cheese?"

"Huh-huh. Could you give me some of the crust? It's the best part."

Joey grinned as Lenora dug at the edges of the pan. She kept at it even after Nancy came beside her and started telling Joey she saw him in line already. Nancy's cheek was scraped badly from when she got hit in that collision with Roach Brother Bob at home plate.

"Didn't you hear what Lorraine said? No seconds until everybody's been fed."

Joey's feet danced.

Lenora lowered her voice.

"It's my plate. Joey's holding it for me."

"You like crust?" Nancy asked.

"It's the best part."

Nancy pressed her lips and jabbed her head toward the left. She wasn't buying any of it, but she wasn't about to call Lenora a liar. Lenora winked at Joey as he held the plate with two hands. She handed him a sandwich.

"I'll take care of it for you," he told her.

Joey carried the plate of food into the kitchen. Professor Ned Burke, holding two bottles of red wine, one under each arm, and dressed in beatnik black, stood near the sink. Mrs. Burke, whose first name was Inez, was beside him. Joey set the plate on the kitchen table. The arrival of the Burkes was more interesting than eating.

A couple of the other Dirty Professors were already in the living room, smoking weed and trying to impress girls with their worldliness and bottles of scotch. Everyone in the kitchen greeted the Burkes as if they were royalty. They all hoped they could be like them when they were old. They wished their parents were.

The Burkes' time was in the fifties when they hung out with other hipster people. Ned liked jazz and met Henry Miller when he lived in Paris. He settled into the life of an academic after he was hired to teach philosophy at Westbridge State College. Then when he found himself again in the late sixties, he dropped acid, claiming it brought him nearer to God than church. Inez Burke, who came from old money, put up with all of that and his screwing around with wide-eyed coeds.

"Ah, here's a friendly face," Ned told Inez. "You remember Joey, of course. He's a fellow poet."

Inez nodded. She wore pointed eyeglasses and a pageboy like her husband.

"It's nice that you both could make it," Joey said.

Ned clasped the back of Joey's arm and hand in his special poet's shake. He and Joey had a special bond. Sometimes Ned stopped by *The Hard Truth* office or Jimmy's Coffee Shop to chat. Ned bought Joey coffee and told him about the cool life in Paris and New York. They talked about poetry. Once the Burkes invited him to dinner. Inez served steak. Joey had never seen real silverware before, and he had to remind himself it'd be bad karma if he filched any of it.

Inez leaned forward as Ned raised a bottle of red wine Her breath smelled like cigarettes.

"Joey, honey, see if you can find us a corkscrew and a couple of clean glasses." She lifted her eyeglasses. "Is that a ham sandwich?"

Joey rifled through the drawer next to the sink.

"Ham sandwich? Almost." He raised a rusted corkscrew. "Will this do?"

FIFTEENTH PRESIDENT

Mack peered into the rear-view mirror and swore when he saw the flashing blue light of a cruiser in the distance. He and Manny were coming back from the packie in East Westbridge after they dropped those girls at the bus station. The trunk was filled with cases of beer. Mack was giving Manny some of the juicy details about what happened in the woods between him and Lenora. In Mack's version they got it on, a little hurried, but that couldn't be helped. Lenora wanted it so badly. Manny kept saying, "I don't believe it" although he ended up believing everything Mack told him.

The cruiser was close to the Fairlane's back bumper. Mack pulled to the side of the road. Now, he had something else to think about.

"Shit, are you carrying?"

Manny patted the pack of Winstons in the pocket of his T-shirt.

"I've got a couple of joints in here."

Manny's head swiveled toward the back of the car.

"No, no, don't do that. Don't make any fast moves." He stopped the car on the shoulder and killed the engine. "In fact, don't do anything."

Mack watched in the side-view mirror as the cop got out of his cruiser. Mack didn't recognize the pig. He must be a rookie because he wore aviator shades over his smooth pink face although it was getting dark. The cop stopped, checked what Mack and Manny were doing in the front seat before he gave the car the once-over. Mack's eyes shifted toward Manny. Thank God they hadn't been smoking dope. The beer they drank at the pond wore off long ago.

"Be cool," Mack said under his breath.

The cop stood beside the driver's side of the car, peering through the windows into the empty back seat. He didn't have enough hair to shave. Mack smiled as if he were happy to see the cop when he leaned toward the open window.

"Evening, officer. Is there a problem?"

The cop sniffed.

"Did you know, sir, your car has a taillight out?"

"Sorry, officer, I didn't. Bulb must have just gone out. I'll be sure to take care of it right away."

Mack kept his voice smooth and light. The cop slipped his shades into the breast pocket of his uniform. His eyes were tiny blue dots.

"License and registration, please."

"Yes, sir."

Mack stretched past Manny to open the glove box. The cop watched, but only a dumb ass stashes pot in a place like that. He found the registration and rolled his hip so he could get his wallet out of his back pocket. He handed the papers to the cop, who studied him and Manny as if he were taking an exam. He bowed to see Manny, who sat stone-faced straight ahead.

"You there. What's your name?"

A bead of sweat dropped in a shiny track from Manny's forehead to his beard.

"Manuel Ferreira. Everybody calls me Manny."

"Where are you two boys from?"

"We go to school at Westbridge," Mack answered.

"Westbridge, eh?" The cop studied Mack's license. "What's your major, Mr. MacKenzie?"

"English," Mack said.

"English." He hummed. "What about you, Mr. Ferreira?"

"I'm a history major."

The cop's tight expression didn't change.

"History major?" He cleared his throat. "Mr. Ferreira, who was the fifteenth president of the United States?"

Manny blinked twice.

"James Buchanan."

"Buchanan?"

"Yeah, he served before the Civil War."

The cop nodded as he handed the papers back to Mack.

"I'll let you off with a warning this time, Mr. MacKenzie. But get that light fixed. It's a safety hazard."

"I will, officer."

Mack chuckled as the cop returned to his cruiser.

"James Buchanan. That's a smooth one." Mack shook his head as he put the car in gear. The cop was still sitting in his cruiser. "How in the hell did you remember that?"

Manny rubbed his beard.

"Easy. When I was a kid, the local dairy had pictures of all the presidents printed under the bottle caps. Remember those little bottles we got in the cafeteria? If you collected all of them you got a big prize. A bike or something like that. It was fixed, of course. I kept missing two presidents. James Buchanan was one of them."

"Did you ever get him?"

"Not until now."

Mack slapped the steering wheel and laughed with Manny. He shoved an eight-track into the player. What they needed now was a little Cream, that smack head Ginger Baker beating on the drums like a maniac and Clapton killing them with his guitar. A half-mile up the road the Fairlane's headlights flashed on the "Entering Westbridge" sign. Mack was nearly home free. He checked the rear-view mirror to see if the cop tailed them.

"Manny, how about firing up one of those joints? I remembered something else I wanted to tell you about Lenora."

JASMINE

enora was done serving food at the libbers' pad, and after a few hugs from hairy women, she went to the kitchen next door for a beer. She stuck her head into the fridge, feeling for the coldest bottle. Behind her, Mack bragged about his run-in with a cop. Guys slapped Manny on the back and said, "James Buchanan, fifteenth president of the United States." Listening to them, Lenora would have thought the two of them were in the SDS and got away with burning down a warehouse filled with draft records instead of carrying a couple of joints and having a rear taillight out.

She used the church key to open the bottle before chucking the cap into a trashcan where it clinked through the pile of empties. Tim was at the kitchen table with Joey. They shared a bottle of Jim Beam and both looked a little wasted. Tim gave her a shit-eating grin as he raised the bottle and called her name. She giggled when he slapped his thigh.

"Come on, Lenora, join us." Tim's words slurred. "Don't make me come over there and get you again."

Mack turned around. The red hair around his mouth twitched.

"Back for more?" Mack said in a mocking voice.

"In your dreams, asshole."

77

She didn't even wait for a response although she heard the hoots as she dodged the crowd in the kitchen and hallway. She glanced back, but Tim stayed where he was.

The Roach Motelers were holed up in the same corner in the living room as last night, heavy in discussion with a couple of the Dirty Professors. The folkies moved their show inside, but who knew how long they'd play before someone cranked the stereo and drowned them out for some hard-core dance music. That guitar strumming was okay for protests and coffeehouses, when you wanted to put war and lost love into song. Folk music can be too much of a downer although some of the drama club freaks were into it, grooving in the middle of the room in a stoner ballet. They came in ruffled shirts and hats with plumes they copped from the drama department's costume closet. One of the guys wore a black cape that swirled so widely it whipped the bandana off the bongo-player's head.

Inez Burke sat alone in the middle of the ratty couch. Her hand swept toward the worn, torn cushion when Lenora asked if she could join her. The flame from her lighter flickered in her eyeglasses. She blew the smoke in one noisy stream. Her attention was on her husband, Ned, who sat with Professor Thomas Mitchell aka Professor Itch, another member of the Dirty Old Bastards Club, on a mattress in the far corner of the room. Some sweet young thing with a beaded headband and straight hair to her ass hung onto Itch, a tenured member of the English department. Itch's wife divorced him last year, cleaning him out, so he could only afford to live in one of the cinderblock apartments at the Roach Motel, which ticked off the administration but upped his social life immensely.

Lenora drank from the bottle.

Inez cleared her throat.

"Lenora, did you hear *The New Yorker* is going to publish one of Ned's poems? He was so pleased, as you can imagine. It was the first he wrote after his heart attack." Her words slipped against each other. "Ned read it at the coffeehouse this spring. I believe you were there. He called it 'Jasmine.'"

"I remember the poem. I liked it."

Inez smiled.

"Ned wrote that for my birthday."

"He wrote 'Jasmine' for you?"

Inez took a drag from her cigarette. Her tight lips curled as she forced out the smoke.

"The flower of his middle age." Of course, that's me. Do you think Ned could have written it for anyone else? For one of these *girls?"*

Inez waved around the room. Of course, Lenora thought Ned wrote it for one of these girls. Everybody at the coffeehouse did, and they all wondered which one it could be. If the stories were true, he probably slept with half the girls at this party and tried to with the other half. Across the room, Ned sat on a mattress and joked with Geneva. Her breasts jiggled beneath her see-through top as she laughed at some witty comment he made. It was a bold move for Geneva. Certainly, Inez knew about the fling.

"Of course, not," she told Inez.

Ned rose and strolled across the room. He moaned softly as he lowered himself onto the sagging cushion beside his wife. He leaned past Inez for the wine bottle at her feet. It was three-quarters gone.

"Where's your glass, my dear?" he asked.

Inez exhaled smoke.

"They didn't have anything clean enough, so I've been drinking from the bottle." She flicked ash onto a plate of half-eaten food on the end table. "Help yourself."

Ned chuckled and took a swig.

"Lenora, I hear you're leaving for Europe next week. Where do you start?"

"Paris. I fly into Orly."

Ned sat back. He beamed at Inez as he set the wine bottle on the floor.

"Paris. It's been a while. We're hoping to make it next year. I'm taking the spring semester off to write and do a little traveling. I wanted to this fall, but the college couldn't spare me. We have such a small department."

Inez's cigarette hissed when she stuck it into a pile of baked beans.

"Tell me, Lenora. How bad is the bathroom?"

"It's been getting a real workout, but for these guys, it's all right. Just don't look in the bathtub."

"That's fine. I don't plan on taking a bath."

Inez wobbled a bit as she made her way through the crowd. The hem of her black maxi skirt swayed.

"Is your wife okay, Professor Burke?"

"Inez was a sport to come tonight." He glanced at the wine bottle next

79

to his foot. "She's fine, I hope."

Ned wanted to talk about Paris. He told Lenora about a café he liked and a cheap, but clean pension on the Left Bank. She must go to a certain bookstore there. The bookstore owner was an old friend. He might be able to give her a place to stay. She definitely should mention his name.

"I warn you. He does like pretty girls." Ned sniggered when Lenora rolled her eyes. "But as I recall, Lenora, you play hard to get."

"As I recall, Professor Burke, I wasn't playing."

"Touché, my dear. I thought for certain we would have gotten to know each other much better during that little one-on-one I scheduled in my office."

Lenora set the empty on the floor.

"I thought we did."

Ned chuckled. His thighs hung open in a wide, manly pose. His arm rested on the back of the couch.

"Ah, I was interested in something more intimate, and you clearly wanted to talk about philosophy. Unbelievable."

Ned showed straight teeth when he laughed.

"That's right, Professor Burke."

"Ned, call me Ned. Please. Everybody else does." He settled into the corner of the couch. "I used to see you early in the morning washing dishes in the dining hall. That couldn't have been pleasant. I heard how Dean Hendricks tried to get you fired from that job. Between you and me, Shirley's a frigid, old bitch." His head shook. "They pay peanuts for those kitchen jobs. How ever did you manage to save enough for your trip?"

"I didn't spend any money, except for rent and food. Then the English department gave me that award, and I'll get some graduation money from my folks. My tickets are paid for, so I figure I'll have around six hundred when I get there."

Ned hummed.

"Europe can be so expensive." He bent toward her and whispered. "Why don't we go somewhere private?"

"Professor Burke."

"No, no, dear, it's nothing like that."

Lenora checked the other side of the living room.

"What about your wife?"

"Don't worry about Inez. She'll understand." He stood. "Trust me on this one."

A few heads turned as Ned followed Lenora through the crowd. She took a right into the hall and another into Tim and Manny's room. Ned shut the door. Lenora stood, hugging her middle, as Ned chose the corner of Tim's mattress. He scrutinized the disheveled room.

"What did you want to tell me, Professor Burke?"

Ned made little puffing noises through his nose.

"Lenora, you're always in such a rush. Have a seat. Please." He raised his hands. "I promise I won't molest you although, frankly, these days I'm flattered by your concern."

Lenora sat on the mess of tangled sheets. Ned's eyes were lively as he reached into his back pocket. He opened his wallet and removed a small stack of bills. He did a quick count.

"There's over two hundred there. It's not enough, but it'll help with your trip."

He thrust the money toward her.

"I'm sorry. I can't take it."

"Of course, you can," Ned crooned. "I'm not asking you to do anything, if that's what you're worried about."

Lenora's lips parted. The bills shook slightly in Ned's hands.

"My dear, it'd make me very happy. Inez will be pleased, too. Some of the best times we had together were in that beautiful city."

She folded the bills in half.

"Thank you, Ned."

"Please remember me when you raise a glass in Paris. A little toast to my health would be nice."

"I will, Ned. I promise."

She smiled as she leaned forward. Her thin arms wrapped around Ned's neck. He made a rumbling laugh.

"Ah, so, this is what it took to get you to hug me."

Lenora was about to reply when the bedroom door swung open and slammed against the wall. She jerked back, but it was too late. Inez stumbled through the opening.

"Ned, what in the hell are you doing with that girl?" she yelled.

Lenora jumped up from the bed and backed toward the window. Inez charged forward, screeching, but Ned grabbed her waist and wrestled her onto Tim's bed. Inez's legs kicked beneath her maxi skirt. Her arms swung wildly.

Ned took his eyes off his wife for only a moment.

"I strongly recommend you leave now," he told Lenora. "I don't know how much longer I can hold my wife."

"I'm real sorry," Lenora said, and then she booked.

MAYBE

nez Burke hollered as Ned led her down the stairway. Joey helped the
professor half-drag his drunken wife, who kept squirming and flinging
her free arm. Joey, who held onto the other, dodged her flying fist. Ned
had his arm around his wife's waist while he spoke to her in low, sooth-
ing tones as if he were settling a spooked horse, but they had no calming
effect on Inez.

"Ned, you gave your word. You said you were done. And, Christ, it had
to be *her*."

She missed the step, but Joey had his grip, so she didn't fall.

"Inez, it's not what you think. Nothing happened in there with her.
Absolutely nothing."

"That's what you say all the time. I should've divorced you years ago.
The shit I've had to put up with. All those stupid girls."

"Please, Inez, you're making a scene."

Her head arched back so she looked upstairs. Joey did the same. People
were knotted at the top.

"What in bloody hell are you all staring at?" she snapped.

No one answered.

Tim squeezed through the crowd, holding Inez's purse aloft.

"I found it near the couch," he announced.

Tim was down the stairs behind Inez. Ned grunted as he adjusted his hold around his wife.

"Let's take the steps a little more slowly." Ned's voice was a sleep-inducing monotone. "Inez, you had a little too much to drink tonight. I'm certain you'll see things differently tomorrow when we're able to talk calmly about this."

"There you go again, you patronizing son of a bitch."

Inez gave Ned a savage poke in the gut that flattened him against the wall. Ned's feet slipped on the stair tread and he groped for the railing to keep from falling. A laugh stuttered in his throat.

"Nice shot, Inez. You almost got me that time." He took the purse from Tim, jamming it beneath his arm. He grabbed his wife's wrist. Joey had the other. "Let's see, dear, if we can muster a little dignity."

Tim stayed back as Ned and Joey helped Inez down the steps and through the front door. Joey was thankful the Burkes parked their white Cadillac in the driveway. Ned pinned Inez against the side of the Caddy as he fished the keys from his pants pocket. She had stopped resisting. Her head was down.

"Do whatever you can, Joey, to keep her on her feet."

Joey gently held Inez against the car. She lifted her chin. Her glasses dammed back tears.

"I feel so humiliated," she said.

"Hang in there, Mrs. Burke. It's gonna be okay. You'll see."

Ned unlocked the door and tossed the purse in the back seat. He went for his wife, holding the back of her head while he eased her into the front seat. He plucked at the hem of her skirt, so it fell in place. He removed her glasses and let them dangle on their silver chain. Her face set into a melancholy gaze.

Ned glanced at Joey.

"Thanks. I've got her now." He shut the door and scooted around the front of the car. "Give my apologies to Lenora." He said over the hood. "Nothing happened this time." He paused. "Honest."

Joey moved back as the large, white car left in one smooth whoosh. He followed the Caddy's taillights through the dark tunnel of trees until they were gone, and then he walked across the street. He sat on the curb. From behind his ear he pulled a cigarette he bummed off Manny. He dug for matches in his jeans pocket to light the end. He took a drag, hoping the smoke kept the bugs away.

He liked stepping away like this and letting things settle in his brain. Sometimes in the middle of the night, when he was done reading, he sneaked down from the attic and walked the streets, even in winter. He liked listening to what the night air carried. Right now, except for the cats yowling in a nearby yard, the only noise came from 221 Winter Street. Every window was lit and filled with moving people. It was an absolute miracle nobody called the cops.

His right knee began its bounce. He watched it move without him. He couldn't help it. Those who knew him knew that, too. He figured he had a lot to be nervous about even when he was a kid. He worried about things like whether his parents would move away without telling him, or he'd go blind without warning. That's why he liked reading poetry. Their words were pools of water that swirled softly in his head. They calmed and interested him.

Joey sucked on the butt. He had to find a job if he wanted to stay in Westbridge for the summer. He went to the furniture factory where the other guys got work, but the foreman took one look at his nervous shake and said he couldn't run machinery. Maybe he'd be okay if they sanded by hand, but there wasn't enough of that to hire him. He had one lead on a job as the weekend dishwasher and janitor at Angie's Bar, which had to be one of the lowest jobs in Westbridge, but at least he'd get a free meal and two beers a night.

If that didn't happen, he would have to go back home and work again at his cousin's car lot, cleaning cars and running titles to the registry of motor vehicles. It wasn't hard work, except when he went with his cousin to repossess cars. His cousin was smart. He kept a spare key, and if someone stopped paying the loan, they went to the deadbeat's neighborhood to steal it back. Joey let his cousin drive the repo, especially after some maniac took a shot at them. At least there were gaps in the work, and he could hide in the back seat of one of the cars, reading poetry and thinking. His cousin, of course, didn't want to hear about any of *that stuff*, as he called it. It's too bad Joey couldn't find a job where he read poetry and told people what it meant. He could, but he had to finish school, and then he would have more school.

Joey's leg bounced hard.

Mack was right. It was a great weekend although for Joey the party began the minute he handed in his take-home exam on Ralph Ellison's *Invisible Man*, and Dr. Roberts, a woman who terrorized her students with her intelligence, peered over her reading glasses and said, "Mr. Franklin, how would you grade this paper?" His leg shook. "I think it's my best work," he told her. She surprised him with a smile so slight it didn't even look like a smile, but her eyes had a pleasant cast, so it must have been.

Lenora used to live in the same building as Dr. Roberts until she and Geneva got evicted for lying about being nurses. The professor was the one who ratted them out to the landlord, but Lenora didn't hold it against her. She said Dr. Roberts didn't want students gawking at her love life with another woman, a professor from Westbridge's history department. What did Lenora say? "We all need some things to keep to ourselves." He took another drag of the cigarette. That Lenora. Really, what were they going to do without her?

Tim came through the front door and across the street toward Joey. He stood in the middle of the road with hands outstretched.

"What in the hell was that all about?"

Even in the semi-darkness Joey could see Tim was one mixed-up guy. He waited until Tim took a seat on the curb beside him.

"The way I understand it, Inez found Ned and Lenora together in your room. Ned said nothing happened, and I think I believe him, but old Inez didn't see it that way. I ran when I heard her screaming bloody murder. It sure sobered me up fast."

"Lenora was with Ned in my room?"

Joey's leg jumped.

"They were hugging on your bed. That's what Mrs. Burke kept saying. But she was pretty loaded. She could barely walk, but, man, she could throw a punch. She almost made Ned fall downstairs." He whistled. "I don't know what happened in there between Lenora and Ned. All I saw was Lenora getting the hell out, and Ned was on top of Inez, holding her down, so she couldn't get away. I think maybe Mrs. Burke finally had enough."

Tim shook his head.

"Manny stopped me up there just now. He wanted to tell me something about Lenora and Mack at the pond this afternoon, but I blew him off. I don't wanna hear anything about that."

Joey gave Tim a playful shove.

"Hoo-hoo, boy, better hold onto your heart. Lenora's splitting for Europe. She's gone, man. So what if she wants a little fun before she goes. There's nothing wrong with that. Guys do it all the time."

Tim blew out air.

"I gotta ask you something." He paused. "Do you think I'd ever have a chance with Lenora? Be honest, now."

"Tim, I'm not the person you should be asking this question. She's upstairs."

"Yeah, yeah, I wanna hear what you think."

Joey squashed a mosquito against the side of his neck. He knew what Tim wanted him to say: of course, she could fall in love with him. It was all over Tim's face whenever he saw Lenora, his lopsided grin, the soft eyes. He was plain nuts about her. Did he have a chance? Shoot, what in the hell did he know about women or Lenora in particular? She kissed him once and took off. He still didn't understand what happened there.

Tim waited. The butt trembled in Joey's hand.

"You can take this for what it's worth. When I see you two together, you seem to have something going I don't see when either of you are with other people. She's always smiling and laughing when you talk with her. If you're not around, she wants to know where you are." The butt sparked when he flung it into the street. "Hmmm. I'm guessing maybe."

"Maybe? That's the best you can say?"

"How long have you known Lenora? Four years? And you're asking me this question on her last night here? Geez, Tim, look at the guys she falls for. They're those take-charge kinda guys. They've got something going and they're not shy about moving in on her." Joey sniffed. "So, maybe."

"Maybe. That's what I think sometimes. I sure did last night." Tim grimaced. "But the thing with Manny. You heard about that?"

"Everybody has, cause Manny's got a big mouth and Mack's got a bigger one." Joey shrugged. "To tell you the truth, it's nice to see Lenora being free and easy. She gets so damn serious." His foot tapped the pavement. "I say enjoy her while we have her. She's not going be around much longer."

"Yeah, yeah."

"Then to the lip of this poor earthen urn/ I learn'd the secret of my life to learn/ And lip to lip it murmur'd; 'While you live/ Drink! For once dead, you never shall return.'" Joey slapped his forehead. "Damn mosquitoes. That's

Omar Khayyam."

"I get it." Tim made a deep humming noise. "When I left Lenora, she was sitting next to Big Ray. Think he's next?"

"Ray? No fucking way."

Tim hooted.

"I don't think so either."

"Let's go back inside. The bugs are killing me," Joey said.

"Yeah, I wanna see how she's doing."

"Who?"

Tim elbowed Joey's side.

"What do you mean who? Lenora, of course."

Joey's mouth opened in a toothy smile.

"Just testing you."

They were in the middle of the street when Tim stopped and grabbed Joey's arm. A car with its headlights off came their way. The driver flashed them high and low. Tim yelled, "what the hell," and both ran to the sidewalk when the car pulled into the space left by Ned Burke's white Caddy. It was Mack's Ford Fairlane and laughter came from the car's open windows.

Mack was the first one out.

"You should've seen your fuckin' faces," he said.

Geneva, Nina, and the two math majors from downstairs followed him from the car.

"What's with the lights?" Tim asked.

Mack folded his arms.

"We were on a little secret mission in the center of town. Right, girls?"

Geneva and Nina came around the car. They were giddy, and the math majors who lived on the first floor, in awe of their energy, stayed out of the way.

"You should see what we did." Nina giggled. "You tell 'em, Mack. It was your idea."

They clustered beside Mack's car.

"We were in the center of town fixing up Lord Westbridge. Now the old lord isn't such a stiff. He's one of us. A real freak." His head jerked as he laughed. "Geneva found the wig. Then we got one of Big Ray's old tie-dyed T-shirts in a closet. We didn't think Ray would mind. It had a big rip on the side. I even gave up one of my headbands." He gestured toward

Geneva and Nina. "The girls made a sign for him to carry. It says 'Make love not war.'"

Geneva pawed the air as she laughed. The math majors, grooving on their first act of civil disobedience, stepped closer as they laughed with her.

"Mack, tell him about the cop. That's the best part," Geneva said.

"Oh, yeah. Like I thought, there was a cruiser up there. I parked behind Jimmy's and scouted it out. Get this. It turns out the cop was sleeping." He snorted. "Well, he was until Geneva and Nina started squealing like little girls when we got done and woke him up. You should've seen us run when he got out of his cruiser. The lazy bastard didn't even walk five feet. He shined his flashlight and went back inside. Can you fuckin' believe that?"

Nina jabbed her thumb at the math majors.

"We almost lost one of these guys when we were hiding from the cop," she said.

"It was a trip man." Mack leaned his backside against his car's fender. "Tell me, did anything happen while we were gone?"

Tim and Joey glanced at each other.

"The Burkes did have to leave a little early. Other than that, things have been pretty cool," Joey said.

Mack grinned at the second-floor windows.

"Pretty cool, huh? We better get upstairs and heat things up. I still have some of the primo pot left," he said.

ONE HAPPY TRIBE

The party was in a sweaty frenzy as Stevie Winwood began wailing, "Gimme Some Lovin'" over the stereo. Most had been dancing since Mack and the others returned, it had to be almost two hours, and now everybody was up and singing. They danced in the living room and those who couldn't fit, danced in the hall and kitchen. They were high and grooving like they were one happy tribe. Mack danced bare-chested in the middle of the room with his arms wrapped around Geneva and Nina's waists. Even Big Ray was on his feet.

Lenora danced with Tim. Her arms were around his neck and their bodies bumped. Barefoot and breathy, Lenora was into it. Her dark hair flew around her. She forgot about the bad scene with Inez and forgave everyone for kidding her about it. She kept switching between Tim and Manny, although staying mostly with Tim, and once with Joey, but he was impossible to dance with because he had absolutely no rhythm.

Somebody cranked the music louder. Lenora leaned toward Tim.

"I hate to say this, but I gotta go," she said in his ear.

"What for? Stay here with me. The party's not over yet."

"It's almost four."

"I wish you wouldn't go."

His hands were on her hips. She pressed against him.

"Why don't you kiss me goodnight, Tim?"

They slowed to barely a dance, and they kissed right there, a long one. Lenora opened her eyes. She smiled as she touched Tim's cheek.

"I'll see you in a few hours. We'll walk together. Devlin comes before Dias. Remember?"

The corners of Tim's mouth twitched.

"Yeah, see you then."

She slipped from Tim to Joey, who shuffled in place and punched toward the ceiling. She ruffled his hair and mouthed, "I'll see you."

She spun away, slapping hands with everybody, hugging some, saying all their names: Big Ray, Mack, Geneva and Nina, Roach Brothers Bruce and Bob, the libbers Lorraine and Nancy, Professor Itch and the other Dirty Old Bastards.

She stopped to dance again with Manny. He sang, too.

Lenora found her sandals and bag in the corner. Tim watched her leave, and he waved when she waved. Then she was through the crowd, down the hall, into the kitchen to say her byes, and out the door.

She paused at the top of the stairs to slip on her sandals. Behind her, the apartment buzzed in a heavy riff. Lenora murmured. She was with Geneva the first time she came to 221 Winter Street. Tim told her about a party. She got high smoking pot and listened to The Beatles' *Sgt. Pepper*. They kept playing the last part of "A Day in a Life" where the orchestra drags on a sound for twenty-four chords, at least that's what Tim told her, and it drove them all nuts each time they listened to it.

She checked behind her one last time and said, "See ya, everybody."

Lenora walked down the stairs, and she was almost out the door when she heard her name. Joey had both hands on the railings as he took the steps three at a time. He made a thudding leap onto the bottom landing.

"Lenora, wait up. Where are you going?"

"Home. I've gotta get some sleep. My parents will kill me if I don't show up for my graduation."

Joey slid his black glasses up the bridge of his nose.

"You can't walk alone through town this time of night. It's not safe. Let me give you a ride home."

"A ride? Thanks."

"Wait here."

Joey ran toward the backyard. Lenora gazed up at the lit windows, feeling as if she left something behind. She watched the front door, but it didn't open.

She twirled and laughed when she heard a bell. Joey pedaled a bicycle over the grass.

"A bike? I thought you were borrowing somebody's car." She walked around the bike. "Tell me, hot shot, where am I suppose to sit?"

He patted the handlebars.

"Right here, Lenora."

"On the handlebars? Shit, I haven't done that since I was a kid." She looked him in the eye. "How stoned are you anyways?"

"Not so stoned I can't ride a bike."

"Good enough." She hitched the strap of her bag onto her shoulder. "Shit, I must be crazy doing this."

Joey held the bike as Lenora hoisted herself on the handlebars, tucking her skirt between her thighs as she balanced herself on the narrow bar. She squealed his name when the bike wobbled badly, but he pulled it straight, standing as he pedaled and used the full length of his legs to put some speed and balance into their ride. Her laughter rose so high, she could have been singing or screaming or both.

"Hold on tight, Lenora."

"Don't worry. I am. Just don't drop me."

They traveled up Winter Street, past the darkened houses. Lenora cried out when the bike took a hard left, nearly falling, but Joey kept it upright. They cruised through the squat, brick buildings of campus and across the grassy quadrangle where a white, canvas tent was set up for graduation. Joey panted as he pedaled uphill toward downtown, past Jimmy's and the cobbler's shop where they all bought their Jesus sandals. Both howled when they saw Lord Westbridge decked out as if he was one of them. Mack bragged about it at the party, so they circled the commons twice to get a better look. Then they sailed past the hardware store, the Five and Dime, and Angie's Bar, long past its last call.

Joey's face pitched forward.

"Hang on, Lenora. We're coming to the end."

Joey steered the bike in an arc across the street, aiming for the driveway of the Brown House and letting its steep slant slow the bike until it finally stopped. Lenora leaned back, laughing and falling against Joey as his foot hit the ground.

"Here we are, safe and sound," he announced.

Lenora eased off the bike, thanking Joey as she brushed out her skirt.

"Wow, Joey, that was a lot of fun."

Joey held onto the bike. He grinned.

"Yeah, but I think I went deaf from all your screaming."

"I was screaming?"

"The whole time."

Joey squinted as Lenora lifted his glasses and used the bottom of her top to wipe fog off the lenses. She touched his hair, pushing it back behind his ear, and played with the ends of his beard. His brain was working, but the boy didn't have a clue what she was doing. She handed him back his glasses.

"Thanks for the ride," she told him.

"You said that all ready."

"Yes, I did." She pointed toward the bike. "Why don't you leave it in the hall? Nobody's gonna take it."

His mouth opened, but nothing came out. Lenora's skirt twirled around her ankles as she walked toward the Brown House. She peered over her shoulder.

"You coming or what?"

"Lenora, what's going on?"

"Aw, Joey, haven't you every wondered what it'd be like? Here's your chance."

Joey pushed the bike over the grass as he ran to catch her.

POOR JOEY

ina and Geneva came flying through the front door of the Brown House and down the grassy slope in front of the building. Tim saw them from the back of Mack's Fairlane where he, Mack, and Manny listened to Steppenwolf on the eight-track player. Nobody talked. They were all hung over even after coffee and chow at the greasy spoon diner in East Westbridge. Tim's head hurt from the booze and lack of sleep, but he'd live. He remembered what Joey told him yesterday as that nervous nut jumped around the kitchen like somebody had hot-wired him. "I can sleep the rest of my life." That's what Joey said.

They all crashed this morning for a couple of hours, and when Tim woke, he found Nina, Geneva's new roommate, asleep in his bed. He had gotten so high, he couldn't remember if anything happened between them. Worse, for a few minutes when the girl's arm was slung over him, he thought she was Lenora and they were alone. He was bummed because she wasn't. He blew it not following Lenora after she left. What was the big deal about staying at the party? He got more wasted and ended up having a girl he barely knew in his bed.

"What in the hell are those girls so excited about?" Mack asked from the front seat.

Manny rubbed his temples.

"Not a clue, but, geez, they're loud," he said.

Tim watched the girls, laughing and grabbing at each other as if they were running a foot race. Something definitely was up, but he wasn't that interested. He had other things to think about like how he was going to get away pretending to graduate. Thank God, Lenora will be next to him. Maybe, she was already there, waiting.

"Listen to that Nina. Jesus, what a mouth on that girl," Mack said.

Tim raised himself so he could check his face in Mack's rear-view mirror. He looked a little foolish with a black mortarboard planted on top of his head. His gown was unzipped over the shirt and pants he borrowed from one of the math majors downstairs. He wore one of their striped ties. His brown hair stuck out in crazy angles beneath the mortarboard. Maybe he should have gotten a haircut after all. He turned his jaw and lifted his chin. His face had a fresh set of cuts, because he insisted on shaving again this morning. He was in no condition to use anything sharp, but showing up with stubble would be worse than having a full beard.

Geneva beat Nina to the car.

"Shit, you're not going to believe what we just seen." Geneva made a squealing laugh as she poked her head through the car's open window. "Remember how Joey was MIA, and we searched all over the place for him? How we almost called the cops in case he got picked up?"

Mack adjusted the player's volume.

"Yeah?" he told her.

Geneva jerked her thumb toward the top of the Brown House.

"He's up there with Lenora. Nina and I walked in on them."

Mack snorted and spun his head toward the back seat. Tim avoided his glare. Lenora and Joey. How in the hell did that happen?

Manny stuck his head out the car.

"Joey? Joey's up there?" Manny ducked back inside. He, too, stared at Tim. "You gotta be shitting me. Joey and Lenora doing it? What in the hell's going on with that girl?"

Nina and Geneva made a conspiratorial laugh.

"I'd say plenty." Geneva raised her eyebrows. "Her door was open and the covers were off. They were curled up together. Naked. I didn't know Joey had one of those uncut dicks. I never saw one of them before." She winked at Nina. "Ever wonder what's that like?"

Nina yanked open the front door and pulled the seat forward so she could get in the back.

"Dunno," she said. "Haven't tried one."

Nina stood halfway in the car, waiting for Tim to move over for her. Lenora and Joey. It was unbelievable.

Manny slapped Tim's arm.

"Jesus, Tim, wake up. She wants to get inside."

Nina had already given up. Her mini-skirt was hiked high up her thighs as she climbed over Tim to sit in the space between him and Manny.

"And here we were all worried about poor Joey," Geneva said as she slid into the front seat.

"Poor Joey, all right." Mack studied the steady flow of traffic toward campus. "Shut the door, Geneva. We gotta get going. Did you wake 'em up?"

Geneva snorted.

"Nah, but they probably heard us leave. We were laughing so hard. Right, Nina?"

Nina didn't answer. She tried to get Tim's attention, but he just sat there doing nothing.

PROFESSOR ITCH

Lenora swore when she saw the clock beside her bed. She thought she heard voices, probably Geneva with somebody else, but now the apartment was quiet. She shook Joey's shoulder. He opened one eye and moaned.

"Joey, I have to get going or I'm gonna be late for graduation."

He mumbled and rolled toward the wall.

Lenora ran to the bathroom to wash at the sink, and when she got back, Joey still hadn't moved. He told her he didn't sleep the night before. He maybe got a couple hours the night before that if he was lucky. She pulled the sheet over his shoulders. She smiled as she thought about them riding the bike through town and the blown-away expression he had on his face when she told him to come upstairs.

Joey was so eager to please in bed, almost surprising her, but of all the guys at Westbridge, she expected that of him. They would be sitting at Jimmy's or some other place, and Joey acted like his mind was somewhere else, as if he were in another universe or something. Then he would say something absolutely brilliant, like a piece of somebody's poetry or an observation, and she realized he was paying attention after all. He had been finding the words to express how he felt. He did that last night. Just when

97

Lenora thought Joey was finally falling asleep, she heard his voice. She remembered what he said, because they took a course in Irish Lit together. It was something by the poet William Butler Yeats.

She pulled a mini-dress over her head, the one with a pink and purple paisley print. She hurriedly pulled a brush through her hair, tearing at the small knots before she tossed it into an open box. Joey didn't respond to her voice, so she grabbed her cap and gown off the dresser and made her way downstairs, through the first floor hallway, and then out the front door.

Lenora hurried toward the town center. She picked up her pace when she heard the bell of the Westbridge Congregational Church sound the half-hour and she realized her alarm clock was a few minutes off. She might be late after all. A line of cars traveled without a break past her. This was Westbridge's second-busiest traffic day of the year. The first was moving-in day when carloads of nervous or relieved parents dropped their children and their belongings at the dorms.

She stood at the curb waiting to cross at the stoplight. She could use a cup of coffee and something to eat from Jimmy's, but she didn't have time. She was glad she told her parents to meet her after the ceremony. They would have flipped out if they had found her and Joey in bed.

She draped the black gown over her shoulder and stuck the cap into her bag. She needed to make a run for campus although her leather sandals weren't good for it. Then she heard the friendly beep of a car horn. A few cars back, one of the Roach brothers, Bruce, was at the wheel of his piece of junk station wagon, brown with cracked wooden paneling on the sides and rusted-out fenders. He pulled the car toward the curb. Professor Thomas Mitchell, aka Professor Itch, a Dirty Professor from the English department and Bruce's neighbor, dressed in full academic plumage sat in the front seat. His thin gray ponytail drooped below his tam. His gown hung loosely over an orange and black dashiki.

"Do you need a ride, Lenora? We're going to commencement," Itch said through the open window.

"Gee, thanks."

Itch reached behind his seat to unlock the back door.

"Get in, get in."

"Where's your MG, Professor Mitchell?"

Itch made a choking laugh as Lenora hurriedly shoved empty beer bottles and newspaper toward the other side of the back seat. The air was heavy with fresh pot smoke. Roach Brother Bruce stuck his left hand out the window before he drove the station wagon back into the line of traffic, leaving black dust where Lenora once stood.

"The MG had a little accident last night. Totaled, I'm afraid." Itch made the laugh again. "But I learned a valuable lesson. Never let a drunk drive your car no matter how pretty and young she is." Itch was half-turned in his seat. His lip was fat and split. The skin was bright purple around one bloodshot eye and high on his forehead. "We almost made it home. You know the oak tree next to the driveway? She didn't quite get the car around it."

"Are you all right?"

"Oh, yes, my head only glanced the windshield." The sleeve of his robe fell to the crook of his arm as he waggled a finger. "She took the curve a little too fast. She's back at my place sleeping it off, poor thing."

For the past four years, Lenora witnessed Itch's transformation from a dignified, tenured professor of British Lit with a devoted faculty wife and three smart kids to a letch who lived in a cinderblock apartment. There, he lured co-eds to read his novel-in-progress, which never progressed past the first two rough chapters. It was a pickup line that didn't work on Lenora, who took two courses with the man. Itch was a good lecturer, she'd give him that. Shakespeare was his thing. He could recite *Macbeth* by heart, doing all the voices. His Lady Macbeth was dead on, a remarkable performance that was a must-see for anyone literary who went to Westbridge State College. Nobody skipped class when Itch performed *Macbeth*.

Itch joined the Dirty Old Bastards Club during Lenora's sophomore year. He let his hair grow and shed his suits for black turtlenecks, like his buddy Ned Burke, or a shirt woven by peasants in some Third World nation. He started showing up at T-group sessions and student parties, first with his wife, then without her after she decided they were too weird. She kicked him out after one of his girlfriends had an abortion in New York, a bit of a scandal he almost kept from the administration. It was a relief to the grownups on campus when Itch and his wife divorced.

The traffic was stop and go around the commons. Lord Westbridge stood unmolested on his pedestal, and Lenora smiled, wondering when somebody in charge saw his hippie getup and rushed to take it down. She sat forward as a cop directing traffic let a line of families cross the street.

Itch spoke over his shoulder.

"Don't worry, Lenora. They can't start without me." Itch cleared his throat. "I'm giving the commencement address."

Lenora giggled.

"You're the speaker? I thought you were on the outs with Dean Hendricks."

"I believe I still am. The speaker was supposed to be the head of the history department, but he was diagnosed with mumps on Friday, poor soul, and in what had to be a extremely vulnerable moment, Dean Hendricks remembered what a bang-up job I did seven years ago when I spoke at the reunion." He raised a finger. "She set some ground rules. No profanity or any references to drugs. She didn't want a lot of peacenik stuff either. She said she wanted me to give the kids a nice sendoff and not embarrass the college. I told her not to worry." He winked his good eye. "Besides, I can't afford to lose this job. I have child support."

"What are you gonna talk about?"

He raised a roll of white paper.

"It's all in here. I wrote it this morning." He nodded. "Bruce heard some of it."

"It's heavy, man." Roach Brother Bruce peered in the rear-view mirror before he steered the station wagon sharply toward the right. "Hang on. I've got an idea."

They entered the alley next to the Five and Dime and through a parking lot leading to a side street. The station wagon lumbered through the best part of town, past Itch's old Victorian his ex-wife now owned, then the president's house where Lenora once attended a Christmas tea when she was the class secretary her sophomore year, and finally, behind the administration building. Kids wearing caps and gowns clogged the roadway. Roach Brother Bruce stopped the car.

"Looks like this is as far as I can take you both."

The hinge on Itch's door cranked as he thanked Roach Brother Bruce for the ride. Lenora bent forward to peck his cheek above the line of his beard.

"I'll see you sometime," she told him.

Roach Brother Bruce raised two fingers in a V.

"Have a beautiful life, Lenora."

"That's what I'm planning on," she told him.

Lenora walked with Professor Itch through the crowd. He chatted about his speech. He was so inspired this morning it took him only an hour to put it together. She grasped the back of Itch's arm when he stumbled in his sandals. The man seemed in no rush to get wherever he had to be. He was more interested in talking with her and greeting students.

"Do you know where you're going, Professor Mitchell?"

He made a tittering laugh.

"Lenora, that's a question I often ask myself."

"No, no, I didn't mean it that way." She stood on her toes. "There's the rest of the faculty. See Professor Burke? Oh, never mind. Come with me."

Lenora hooked her arm in his and guided the man toward the right direction.

RABBLEROUSING FRIENDS

im waited among the Ds for Lenora. Mack dumped the car back at the
apartment and woke up anybody who was still left. Then they fired up
a couple of joints before they made the short walk to campus, singing
and carrying on as families stared and pointed from inside their cars.
Tim watched for Lenora's arrival ever since they regrouped behind the administration building with the other graduates. One of Dean Hendricks'
do-gooders gave the group the evil eye, because the hairy freaks wore what
they all had on last night, even Big Ray who tried to find a shirt his size
in the closets at 221 Winter, but gave up and wore just his overalls, so
he looked more like a hog farmer than a recent grad of Westbridge State
College.

The dean's do-gooder girl, wearing white heels and lipstick, nodded
when Tim gave his name. It was on the list, thanks again to Mack, who
wore such a smug smile Tim was convinced he'd get busted.

Tim spotted Lenora finally on the edge of the crowd, as usual looking
like she knew what she was doing and where she was going. Her gown
was draped over one shoulder. He didn't see Joey or anybody else with her.

Manny saw Lenora, too. So did Mack, who said it out loud.

"I don't see our buddy Joey anywhere. She must've ditched that guy, too."

Mack snickered.

Tim moved away from Mack and Dean Hendricks, who barked orders on the sidelines. He didn't hear much after she said she expected them to act like adults now that they were graduating from this fine state institution of higher learning. They should all be proud to show the world their Westbridge State College rings. Tim looked at his bare hands. He didn't dare show his face to the woman although honestly he didn't think Dean Hendricks would recognize him. He checked himself enough times in the mirror during the past couple of days to know. But as far as the dean was concerned he was a marked man.

Two years ago, Dean Hendricks called him into her office after he wrote an unflattering profile of her in *The Hard Truth*. He got plenty of juicy stuff from students, alum, and a few ousted professors. He even found an old college classmate, who said she was destined to make everybody's life miserable. The woman never married so Westbridge State College was her life, as one professor who tried to cut the woman a break, said. To be fair, Tim asked to interview the dean, but she turned him down when he wouldn't allow her to read the piece first.

He could see Dean Hendricks sitting behind her desk, where with one half-spin of her chair she could spy on what was going on in front of the administration building, from couples making out to that crazy freak doing air guitar on the steps. The nail of one manicured finger tapped the front page of *The Hard Truth* as if she were sending him code. She took off her reading glasses and bored her brown eyes through his skull.

"It seems to me, Mr. Devlin, you went to a lot of trouble for this article although I am imagining its purpose was to embarrass me."

The leather cushion crackled as Tim shifted in the seat. He knew he was in trouble when a dean calls him mister while treating him like a kid.

"It's a shame when people don't have anything nice to say about you." She pressed her lips so tightly they nearly disappeared. "Then again, maybe they did, and you decided not to include it. Was that it, Mr. Devlin?"

Tim started to speak, but she raised her hand as if she were about to dismiss him.

"Not that long ago, students were expelled for less. Much less." She cleared her throat. "Fortunately for you and others here, times have changed. I'm going to say this: I don't like what you wrote about me, not at all. You may think you're smart, but now that you've decided to draw attention to yourself, I plan to honor that decision. Believe me when I say I will keep my eyes on you. You and your rabblerousing friends, your day will come."

Tim hoped Dean Hendricks now thought he was one of those commuter students who lived at home and kept a low profile during the four years he attended Westbridge. Maybe he had been busy studying to be a high school teacher. He wasn't a troublemaker at all. Those bothersome guys from 221 Winter Street were hanging around him, because they loved making such pests of themselves.

Still, he had a bad case of nerves thinking how it would embarrass his mother if he got discovered. Dean Hendricks would call one of her goons to escort him off stage. His poor mother would start crying, his sisters, too. He would get expelled for sure. Why did he think he could get away with something like this? He should have told his mother he slacked off and couldn't graduate on time. He would have taken some heat from his mother, but she would have gotten over it eventually. The woman did love him.

Christ, if he were Joey, his leg would be moving like he was dancing by himself.

Lenora stopped in front of him.

"There you are, Tim." Her dark brown eyes traveled from one guy to the other. "I see the gang's all here."

Mack smirked.

"Almost."

"That's right," she said. "Joey's not here."

"Gosh, I wonder where old Joey could be," Mack said. "You see him around, Lenora?"

Lenora's lips trembled so slightly no one could tell if it was her intention to smile, frown, or spit in Mack's face. Mack waited for what it might be. He didn't lose his stupid smirk. Tim bet on a frown and a smart remark, but Big Ray broke the standoff.

"Let's head out, Mack. I wanna get a seat."

"Yeah, yeah, as I recall Geneva said she'd save you one." Mack patted Tim's shoulder. "We'll catch you later, bro. You, too, Lenora. Maybe we'll find Joey after all. I'll let you know if we do."

Lenora didn't answer. She thrust her arms into the sleeves of her robe and worked the zipper. She tried to fit the mortarboard over her hair.

"I feel like such a mess. Help me with it, Tim, will you?"

Tim adjusted the cap and smoothed the strands of hair from her face. She reached into her bag for a couple of black hairpins.

"I thought you weren't going to make it in time," he told her.

"That makes two of us. I had to hitch a ride with Itch and one of the Roach brothers." She lifted the strands of her love beads, so they hung over the front of her robe. Her eyes batted softly. "You wanna tell me something, Tim?"

He pushed the pins into her thick black hair. He smelled the soap she washed with this morning.

"Yeah, I'm scared to death. This is a really stupid thing I'm gonna do."

She nodded.

"Don't you worry none. I'll be next to you the whole time."

He reached for her hand. Its skin was smooth and cool. Then he and Lenora moved with the line. He heard the crowd cheer loudly when the first graduates reached the tent.

A SENSE OF HOPE

J oey sped his bicycle through downtown, working the pedals hard, until
he coasted downhill toward campus. He discovered Lenora was gone
when he woke up minutes ago. He threw on the clothes he found on
the floor and fled. He thought he remembered Lenora try to wake him.

He pedaled the bike to the driveway behind the administration building and slowed when he reached the quadrangle. He recognized Professor
Mitchell's voice as it boomed from a speaker, but Joey couldn't tell what
the man was saying. He circled the tent until he found Manny, Mack, and
the others standing outside. He dropped the bike in the grass and stood
behind Manny, raising himself on the toes of his torn Converses, so he
could see. Inside the tent, families and graduates fanned themselves with
programs.

"What's Itch talking about? What the hell happened to his face?" Joey
asked.

Manny ignored him.

Itch paused. He nodded as his good eye swept the rows of graduates.
His hands burst open as if he were singing gospel.

"I feel a great sense of hope when I look at the fresh, young faces before
me. I think I speak for my colleagues when I say I have enjoyed the chal-

lenge of teaching students who are so unfettered they are unafraid of new ideas, and in that way you have taught us a great deal. I am convinced you have the potential to change the world in a positive way." He pounded the podium softly as he leaned into the microphone. "Now get out there and show us what you can do."

The crowd erupted into applause. The graduates were on their feet, clapping and cheering. Geneva and Nina stood on chairs, screaming their heads off.

Mack made a two-finger whistle.

"Far out," he said.

"Old Itch outdid himself. Even Dean Hendricks is congratulating him." Manny pointed toward the stage. "You should've heard him, Joey. He talked about the war and everything. He threw in a little *Macbeth*. Even did the voices. He quoted Dylan and John Lennon. Too bad you missed it, Joey."

At the podium, Professor Mitchell beamed as his colleagues gathered to congratulate him. Professor Ned Burke put his arm around his pal to lead him back to their seats on stage. The Winter Street tribe, still caught in a great rush of triumph for their loyal friend, didn't let up. Itch had spoken his mind and he had spoken for theirs. The man wasn't a sellout.

"Yeah, too bad," Joey said.

Joey nearly lost his footing when Mack slapped his back. He pushed his black-framed glasses up his nose.

"That's okay. We all know where you've been, Joey, you old dog." He stuck his thumb toward the front of the tent. "We're all so relieved to see Lenora was able to make it on time." He lowered his voice. "So how was she?"

Joey shook his head.

"Jesus, Mack, I think being an asshole must come naturally to you."

DEVLIN BEFORE DIAS

t was almost Tim and Lenora's turn to walk the stage. They followed their row to the front of the platform and up its steps as Dean Hendricks read aloud the names of each grad. Beside her, President David Longo shook hands and handed blue folders from the stacks on a table, all the while saying a few pleasantries, nothing personal, because truthfully, he didn't know any of the students.

Lenora searched for her parents among the well-dressed crowd. She saw them seated toward the front near the center aisle. Her father, who fixed smashed cars for a living, wore his Sunday suit in honor of his oldest daughter's college graduation, a first for the family. She saw her mother beside him and her two sisters. She gave them all a small wave. Then she scanned the crowd until she found Inez Burke sitting with the other faculty wives and a few of the college's bigwigs. Inez wore dark sunglasses and didn't crack a smile.

One girl was ahead of Tim. Lenora remembered her from freshman year when they were in the same dorm. The bottom edge of her shiny, blond hair slid sideways across the back of her robe when she walked forward. Lenora pressed her hand against the small of Tim's back. The poor guy was ready to lose it if the slightest thing went wrong. Throughout Itch's speech, his fingers squeezed her hand tightly.

"Try to enjoy the speech," she kept telling him.

"I can't. What if I get caught?"

She wanted to say it was an absolutely dumb idea pretending to graduate. Of course, she didn't.

"Stop worrying. I won't let it happen," she answered back.

Dean Hendricks announced the blonde's name and gave her a puckered smile while President Longo went through the motions. Then the dean's head was down as she searched for her place on the sheet of paper. She said "what?" as the flesh between her brows formed a sharp crease above her glasses so deep it appeared the contours of her face would never rebound. President Longo smiled vacantly at Tim, then Dean Hendricks when she didn't say the next name. Instead, she gestured for her assistant who stood several feet away on the stage. Both women eyed Tim, the paper, Tim again, and then the paper.

President Longo said, "What's the matter?"

Tim muttered, "Oh, shit," as a woman Lenora recognized as his mother walked up a side aisle toward the edge of the stage and aimed a Brownie camera toward her loving son. Her cheeks were round from smiling. Her eyes were the same blue as Tim's. She snapped a picture of her son waiting on the edge of the platform for whatever was going to happen. Lenora stood beside Tim and gripped his shaking hand.

"I'm a dead man," he whispered.

All Lenora said was, "Shh."

President Longo moved beside Dean Hendricks. Their heads were together while they talked. The crowd in the tent buzzed. Everyone wondered what was holding up commencement. So did Ned Burke, who gave Lenora a wondering look.

Lenora mouthed the words, "Help Tim."

Ned's gaze shifted toward the scene at the podium, where Dean Hendricks held her hand over the microphone while she argued with President Longo, and then it was back at Lenora. The man was swift enough to figure it out. He weighed what he could do. Lenora figured if there was ever a time for Professor Groovy to take a chance for his friends, it was now. Her lips formed, "please." Ned Burke slapped his thighs as he stood to join the trio.

Lenora leaned forward.

"Stay cool, Tim. Everything's gonna be fine," she whispered.

The black tassel from Tim's mortarboard jiggled while Ned studied the sheet of paper President Longo gave him.

Ned's finger jabbed the print.

"His name is on the official list from the registrar's office. I see it right here. It can't be a mistake."

President Longo's head fell forward in a neat little chop.

"What are we waiting for?" he said. "Let's get on with the ceremony."

Dean Hendricks snatched the paper from Ned.

"Very well," she huffed.

The dean glowered at Tim as she waited for President Longo to get settled beside the table stacked with folders. Lenora didn't dare risk a smile when Ned gave her a wink. She got in place behind Tim.

Dean Hendricks' voice wobbled over the microphone, "Timothy Patrick Devlin." Tim sighed as his name carried through the speakers to the rear of the tent, where the Winter Street tribe howled and banged on the folding chairs. Manny raised a chair above his head as if it were a trophy.

Dean Hendricks winced.

President Longo held out his hand when Tim stepped toward him.

"Congratulations, young man. Here you go."

Tim took the folder and stepped to the edge of the stage as his mother took another picture.

Dean Hendricks bent toward the microphone.

"Lenora Correia Dias."

Another cheer exploded from the back of the tent when Lenora started forward. She took her folder from President Longo, and then turned to wave to her parents and sisters when they rose from their seats. Way in the back, Joey and Manny pumped the air with both arms. Big Ray, Geneva, even Mack, and the others made as much noise as they could. Tim grinned and clutched his blue folder. Lenora nodded as she strode across the stage toward him. This was it.

PART TWO
CHANGES

A GONER

J oey twisted the chin hairs of his beard as he read the typewritten lines on the paper. The poem was called "Pussy Willow," a bitter rambling thing about, what else, unrequited love, and another student submission for the *Westbridge Review*. Joey knew the guy who wrote the poem. He was one of the math majors who lived on the first floor of 221 Winter Street, and who, as Mack rightly predicted, had a life-changing experience at last year's graduation orgy when he got laid and stoned for the first time. So did his roommate, and the two of them immediately stopped shaving, cutting their hair, and taking so many showers. They swapped Oxford shirts with fruit loops on the back for tie-dyed T-shirts. They and the bong they built from lab equipment became a fixture at Winter Street and Roach Motel parties this year although they were not part of the inner circle. Mack said studying all those numbers made them too linear, whatever that meant.

Joey read the poem again, the third in the stack on the wooden table in front of him. He thought he recognized the girl. She had dirty blond hair down to her shoulders and never showed her teeth when she laughed, which was often. Frankly, the math poet didn't have a chance.

He fired up a cigarette and stared at nothing. He stopped playing with his beard now that he had something else in his hand. He poked the butt in the air, spilling ash onto the paper. No one was supposed to smoke in the *Westbridge Review* office, which was tucked in the landing of the second-floor mezzanine of the administration building's auditorium. The table and chairs were arranged next to the windows near the metal filing cabinet Joey lifted from the science building and the couch Manny found at the curb on trash day. The couch smelled like cat piss when it got hot. But it was March and the mezzanine was unheated so that wasn't a problem today, because it was cold enough Joey had to wear his winter jacket.

Joey, who was the *Westbridge Review's* editor this year, a position he inherited from Lenora, didn't mind the space at all. It was about as covert an office as you could get. The janitors never cleaned although once in a while one showed up to ogle the girls, bum cigarettes, or tell dirty jokes. Even Dean Hendricks forgot they were there, which was fortunate. No one bothered them, so they could hang out for hours shooting the shit about writing or whatever moved them. Sometimes they sat in the balcony to watch the drama club horse around on the stage below. Couples made out there, and in one case, someone, Lenora actually, had a breakup. It was a classic moment. The guy didn't think she cared so much. He sure didn't know Lenora. She bolted from the balcony, yelling, "You want some space? Go ahead. Take all the fucking space you want and stay out of mine." Her voice echoed through the auditorium. The cast on stage rehearsing a scene from "Brigadoon" stopped mid-song to cheer her on in their kilts. The guy split fast. No one could understand what she saw in the pretend hippie anyway. Just because you grow your hair and wear embroidered denim shirts doesn't mean you're automatically in the brotherhood.

That Lenora. She sent them a few postcards from Europe, squeezing as much as she could on the backside in the tiniest print. Then they heard nothing from her, not even when she was supposed to be back home in September. Totally MIA. She forgot his birthday, and Lenora never did that. They didn't hear from her at Christmas. Tim called her parents' house in the fall, twice but had no luck. Her mother or whoever the woman was that answered said she wasn't there. He couldn't leave a number for her to call back, because the guys at 221 Winter Street never bothered to have the phone hooked up. When Joey asked around, nobody heard from Lenora, not even her old roommate, Geneva. Tim talked about borrowing

Mack's car to go see her, but then everybody got busy with something else or they got lazy.

But they didn't forget her. Sometimes when they were stoned and goofing, her name popped up, and everybody wondered aloud what Lenora could be doing. They started making up stories. Lenora wore red silk as she sailed in a junk with Chinese pirates on the Yangtze River. Or she was holed up in some famous artist's garret in Paris as his muse. Or she was in Marrakech scoring hashish to bring back to her pals at Westbridge. The stories got bigger and more detailed as they tried to conjure her up. Last week, Lenora was on a walkabout in the Australian outback with a tribe of Aborigines. They adopted her as their own.

Joey zipped his winter jacket. He missed the way Lenora put things right, how she got straight to the middle. If she were here, sitting with him at this table, she'd say, "Joey, you're the editor. You can do whatever you want. This isn't the best poem in the pile, but he feels things and I *really* like the part about geometry. Let's encourage him."

She did that when she was the *Westbridge Review's* editor. Snobs complained about the poems and short stories she accepted, but she told them the magazine was for everyone. Her chin would be up and her eyes dark as onyx. She never budged.

It was March. He had the spring issue to put together. He wished Lenora were here to help. Big Ray was probably right that Nixon was spraying something on the pot so they had become a bunch of unmotivated losers. None of them made the drive to see whether their exiled queen was okay. Look at him. He still was sleeping alone in an unheated attic, jumpy and broke as usual.

Joey raised his eyes from the math major's poem to the window. Blue and red lights flashed across the quadrangle. He reached for his glasses and used a finger to clean a spot on the window in front of the table. An ambulance and a police car were parked in the driveway of the philosophy department building. A large crowd was gathered near the entrance. He dropped the butt in a Coke bottle, used it to weigh down the stack of papers, and took off down the stairs. Joey sprinted across the snow-crusted quadrangle toward the philosophy department, where he quickly found Geneva, sobbing hard and doing nothing about it, so her face was red and wet as if someone slapped her hard.

"What's going on?"

Her fingers pinched Joey's upper arm.

"Ned's dead," she bawled.

Joey blinked hard.

"Ned's dead? How could that happen? He was fine when I saw him a couple of hours ago."

"Heart attack. He was in his office." She sniffed. "He was gone before anyone could help him."

The ambulance left the driveway without any sense of urgency. Girls cried. Some guys, too. Joey stared at the worn toes of his boots. His breath shook him inside out.

"Shit, shit, shit."

He met Ned this morning at Jimmy's, where they shared a window table. Coffee was on Ned, as usual. He told Joey he felt better than he had in a long time. He was pumped his book of poetry, *Flower of My Middle Age*, was coming out soon. He was supposed to have time off this year to write and travel, but that didn't happen. Westbridge couldn't spare him. It was the same old story. He and Inez definitely were going to Paris this summer though. Perhaps Joey wouldn't mind house sitting while they were gone. He could have the place to himself.

Ned stretched back in his chair at Jimmy's and grinned.

"I love the spring. The snow's nearly gone and the girls start shedding their clothes. My imagination doesn't have to work quite so hard." Ned pointed with his smooth chin. "Check out those girls in the corner." He chuckled. "Down, boy, don't stare so hard. They don't like it."

Afterward they debated the merits of Randall Jarrell's poetry as they strolled toward campus. They didn't stop exchanging ideas until they parted at the administration building's steps. Ned had a class in a few minutes. Joey asked him for a poem to print in the *Review*.

"Be glad to. Stop by the office. I'll give you something new."

Those were his last words to him.

Joey watched as Inez Burke emerged from the front door of the philosophy department. Her arm was linked with Professor Mitchell's. She was pale and tight-lipped. She did not turn toward anyone as they walked to Itch's car parked near a bank of blackened snow. Joey thought he should do or say something, but it appeared Itch had everything under control.

Mack strutted through the crowd. He wore a shirt and tie beneath his fringed jacket. His beard and hair were trimmed neatly. It was Mack's student-teaching outfit. He slapped Joey's back and steered him away from Geneva, who was too broken up to complain about the snub. Mack's smile made him look hungry.

"You want to know what Ned was doing when he kicked? He was with a girl in his office doing the dirty deed."

"What are you talking about?"

Mack pointed toward the curb.

"See that girl over there? The tall redhead?" His voice rasped with excitement. "That's the one. She had to call for help, but it was too late. Old Ned was a goner."

NON JE NE REGRETTE RIEN

The memorial service was held three days later on a Saturday. No church, Ned Burke had specified, so it was held in the auditorium of the college's administration building. On stage, gobs of daffodils and tulips were arranged in vases on either side of a large framed photo of Ned, who gave a knowing smile to his assembled mourners. Inez sat in the front with family and Professor Mitchell, who gave the eulogy, and other members of the Dirty Old Bastards Club, who grieved the loss of their leader. The ones still married sat with their stony wives, who likely hoped this was a lesson for them all. That letch Ned had it coming to him, having sex with a girl more than half his age, and after the doctors warned him about his bad heart. The Winter Streeters and their followers sat behind the Dirty Old Bastards, and behind them, the Roach Motel tribe. The rest of the auditorium was filled with friends of the Burkes, students, professors, and alum.

Wind drove a cold rain against the windows of the auditorium as Edith Piaf's voice warbled "Non Je Ne Regrette Rien" through the sound system. Even if they didn't understood its words, they knew what Piaf sang. She lived the way she wanted. She had nothing to cry about although maybe she should. Joey said Ned had requested the song be played at his funeral.

The song was done. Joey walked across the stage to the podium. He wore straight clothes, even a tie lent by the math majors downstairs who no longer used them. His hands shook as he adjusted his glasses.

"I'm going to read two poems Professor Burke wrote." He glanced down at the front row. "The first is 'Jasmine.' He wrote it for his wife, Inez Burke."

Joey's fingers grabbed at air, and he spoke in a melodic poet's voice as he recited the poem's lines, and then the next, "This Fragile Heart," which Ned finished a few days before he died. Tim knew Joey was extra-shook, but he wanted to do this for Inez who asked him to read. She sent Itch to relay the request.

Tim heard Joey say both poems at least thirty times during the past few days. He humored his friend, sitting with him in the kitchen and listening to him practice after he came home from his job at the Denton State School for the Mentally Retarded. Tim was done with his shift, and he sat back with a beer or a joint while Joey went through the poems and worked on his delivery. He kept reminding Joey to look up once in a while and not to shuffle his feet.

Denton. His mother couldn't understand why he was at that place, working with retarded adults who lived there most of their lives, although she admitted her youngest child had a caring heart. The truth was he couldn't find anything else after he graduated in January. He dodged Dean Hendrick's firing squad in June, when she learned, as she suspected during commencement, he didn't have enough credits to graduate. She made such a stink, threatening to kick him out, but it came down to the fact she couldn't prove anyone forged the list of graduates. It was a clerical error. That's what the girl in the office said. Tim owed Mack big for that, and once again, Ned Burke backed him up. He only had to take two more courses, and then he was legit. His mother never had to find out.

Joey's voice cracked on the poem's last line. *"One small tick and then another, that's all I ask these days."*

Nina sniffed beside Tim.

Papers rustled in the speakers as President Longo stepped to the podium. Confused, Joey brushed against the heavy, blue curtain and nearly knocked over Ned's picture as he went left, then right, then left again, while President Longo leaned toward the microphone to welcome everyone to a reception at Faulkner Dining Hall.

"Ned Burke was a special member of the Westbridge State College community," President Longo said.

At that moment, a baby's cry came from the rear of the hall. President Longo stopped, startled by the clear, tiny voice, out of place in this somber gathering of adults. So did Joey, who stayed still on stage as he raised his hand and squinted toward the back of the auditorium. Tim smiled. It was a new baby's cry, small and urgent. He heard his nephews and nieces cry like that plenty of times. This baby wanted to eat. Nothing else was more important. People turned in their seats. The crying stopped as quickly as it started. President Longo resumed his drone.

Joey moved hurriedly through the row, squeezing past Mack and Manny, and he practically sat on Nina as he made his way to the seat Tim saved for him. His eyes were bright behind the lenses of his glasses.

"You did great," Tim whispered.

Joey whispered back.

"Lenora."

Joey grinned like a happy idiot.

"She's here? Lenora's here?"

"Yeah, yeah, I saw her. She's way in back. And get this, she's holding a baby."

A REAL SHOCKER

Lenora leaned against the closed door of *The Hard Truth* office and waited for someone to find her. She gazed down at Isabel, asleep in her arms now that she was full. The toe of her Frye boot touched the Army Navy Surplus backpack she used in Europe, which was filled with diapers and baby clothes. She watched as the crowd filed through the open double doors and ducked beneath the cold rain dropping from the eaves onto the marble steps.

"Are you going to be all right?"

Lenora turned toward the voice. It came from the man who carried her backpack from the bus stop downtown. He offered to help when he saw her struggling with the load after she got off the bus. The man was going to Ned's funeral, too. He was a former student, in his early thirties, a high school teacher, he told her. He was wandering around the center of Westbridge to check out the place. He hadn't been back since he graduated, but the town hadn't changed much. He joked he was happy Jimmy's was open and serving the same bad coffee.

She smiled.

"Thanks. I have friends here."

She was stunned when she read about Ned's death in the *Standard Times* and terribly sorry she didn't visit him after she returned from Europe. She sent the Burkes a postcard from Paris, but she wanted to tell Ned in person about the trip, that she did make that toast to his health at a sidewalk café. She found all the places he told her about and, yes, the man at the bookstore was friendly.

Her parents tried to talk her out of coming to Ned's memorial service. Isabel was only six weeks old and too small to take out in public. But Lenora was determined to go. She told her parents that Isabel would be all fine. It wasn't a long bus ride. They'd be back the same day.

"Hurry, somebody," Lenora said to herself.

Tim was the first through the door, and then Joey and Manny, who stood in front of her. They stared with their mouths open.

She shook her head.

"Yeah, she's mine. Her name's Isabel."

Tim started to talk but stopped. Then Manny tried. Joey twisted his tie and said nothing. The last time they were together they posed for photos at graduation. She kept those photos in her room to remind her of their happy faces. It was almost a year later, and they were the same boys although Tim had let his beard grow back, and they all wore clean duds for the memorial.

She sighed when Tim came beside her.

"Gee, Lenora, you have a baby," he said.

"Uh-huh. Have a look."

She lifted the flannel blanket, then the brim of Isabel's pink, ruffled bonnet. Isabel's lips moved as if she were kissing.

"She's pretty. She looks just like you," Tim said.

"That's what my folks say."

Her voice was thin, and Lenora felt tears as Tim put his arm around her. His head touched hers.

"This is a real shocker," he said quietly.

Her breath stuttered.

"Yeah, it is."

Tim motioned to Joey and Manny, who stood with their mouths open.

"What's the matter, you morons, haven't you ever seen a baby before?" he said.

The overhead light in the foyer shined in Joey's glasses.

"I saw you from the stage," he said.

"I thought so. That was a good reading you did. I liked the last poem especially. A little prophetic, wouldn't you say?"

One corner of Joey's mouth curled upward.

"I miss you, Lenora," he said. "Why did you wait so long to let us know?"

"Maybe you guys should get a phone."

Manny called to Mack, Big Ray, Geneva, Nina, and the others.

"Come see Lenora's baby," he told them.

Lenora moved so they could see Isabel, who didn't stir despite the commotion.

Big Ray pushed through the group and kissed Lenora on the top of her head.

"We were wondering what happened to you," he said.

"Well, here I am. Sweet, isn't she?"

Then it was Mack's turn. His head swiveled around the foyer.

"Did you get married, too?"

She raised her chin. She expected something like that from Mack.

"It's Isabel and me. There's nobody else."

"So, you brought back a little souvenir from Europe?"

Lenora rolled her eyes.

"Yeah, something like that."

The janitors pushed wide brooms up the aisles of the auditorium. The Winter Street freaks were the only ones left and they talked about getting to the reception before the food ran out. They jabbered about sandwiches and cake. They would have seconds or thirds, and if they could manage, sneak some back.

"Lenora, you coming?" Tim asked.

Nina stood next to him, listening.

"Yeah, but I have to catch a bus later. The last one's at four."

"Four? So soon?" Tim said.

"I'm afraid so."

Joey whistled sharply from the open double door. He raised a black umbrella overhead, grinning as he pushed its wire innards upward until it snapped open.

"Ta-da! To keep the baby dry," he announced. "I remembered seeing it in the commuter lounge downstairs. Lenora, get under here with your baby."

They left the building together. Hairy guys joked and laughed. Their queen was back from her journey. No one could take her place although there were girls who tried.

Joey held the umbrella over Lenora and her baby. Tim wrapped his arm protectively around her while Manny carried the pack. They took their time, detouring around the largest puddles in a party mood now that the miserable stuff about Ned was over. It was time to kick back and remember their old friend.

It felt good to return to the tribe. She shouldn't have stayed away so long.

THE RECEPTION

oey's tongue stuck out between his lips as he carried a full plate of food in each hand through the dining hall. One was for him. The other was for Lenora, who sat at a back table with the baby. She asked Tim to get her food, because she needed to change Isabel's diaper, but Nina wanted to talk with him, in private, which probably meant she was going to nag him about something. Nina was a nice girl, but not the right girl for Tim, kind of bossy now that she was absorbed into the Winter Street tribe and over her initial awe. Joey volunteered to get Lenora food, drawing a few wisecracks, of course, about whether he could make it back with anything left on the plates. But Lenora was grateful.

The dining hall was full for the reception. Westbridge outdid itself for Ned Burke, as it should. He was larger than anything or anyone at this little state college. He should have been teaching at Harvard or Brown, but he confided to Joey he liked being the biggest man on campus. Dean Hendricks gave Joey a sharp eye as he moved by the table reserved for the college's top brass, including President Longo and Dean Louis March. The dean's daughter went to Westbridge last semester after she flunked out of her fancy girls college and before she could transfer to another. She was wilder than her father, a decent guy really, could imagine. She and Joey got it on a few times, part of her plan to stick it to her parents, so they had good times getting stoned, once in the dean's office, and at least he had sex for a while.

President Longo put down his coffee cup.

"Fine job today, Jim," he said.

Joey didn't correct him. He concentrated on not dropping the plates. He squeezed past the Burke family tables. He nodded to Inez, who gave him a controlled smile. Itch said she was taking downers to get through the ordeal.

Inez came toward Joey. She wore a black dress that fell in a shapeless sack to her ankles. Her cat-eyed glasses hung on a silver chain around her neck.

"Whose baby is that back there?"

"That's Lenora's baby. Her name's Isabel."

"Lenora?" Inez lifted her glasses. "Are you bringing that plate to her? Let me take it."

Joey winced when he saw the baked beans ran into the chocolate cake, but he could do nothing about it now. He handed Inez the plate and she waited for him to lead the way. He went ahead, squeezing between the tables and taking bites from his sandwich. He was famished. Behind him, Inez greeted the people she knew and accepted words of condolence from those she didn't until she finally caught up with Joey.

"Joseph, thank you for reading at Ned's service. He would have enjoyed it very much."

Joey swallowed what he was chewing.

"I was glad you asked. I looked up to Ned." He nodded to the back corner of the room. "There she is."

They cut at an angle to the table where Lenora sat. The Winter Street tribe took up three tables, and Geneva hovered near Lenora, so she could see the baby. Geneva stepped back when Inez approached.

Inez set the plate in front of Lenora.

"I believe this food is for you."

Lenora peered up at Inez.

"Inez, I'm terribly sorry about Ned."

Inez nodded solemnly.

"I'd like to see your baby." Inez sat sideways on a chair so she faced Lenora. Her silver bracelet, heavy with charms, looked as if it were in orbit around her wrist as she reached to pull back the blanket. "She's darling."

Joey took another bite of his sandwich. Inez bent toward Lenora, talking so only she could hear her. Lenora nodded, and they went back and forth in a soft hum. He heard two words clearly: "Paris" and "money." The charms on Inez's bracelet tinkled as she patted Lenora's arm.

Inez raised her head.

"Ned enjoyed his soirées at your apartment. He said it kept him younger longer. Thank you for coming to his memorial. I appreciate your thoughtfulness."

No one spoke until she returned to her table.

Joey sat in Inez's spot.

"Did I get you enough food? Sorry about the beans and cake."

"It's okay. I'm hungry enough to eat anything. Thanks."

Mack leaned in between them.

"I was thinking we should continue this back home. We'll get a bottle or two of the hard stuff to give Ned a proper wake. Anybody got any money? Come on, Tim. You got paid yesterday. Fork it over. You, too, Manny. We can forget about Joey. He doesn't have a pot to piss in. What about you Lenora? Oh, honey, don't give me that look."

SOMETHING ELSE

Tim sat between Nina and Lenora at a table in the dining hall. The crowd thinned. The college's big shots were the first to go, but the Winter Street tribe stuck around for the free food. Lenora held Isabel in the crook of her arm as she spoke with Geneva, one in a series of friends who stopped to visit. Tim listened to their conversations with interest. They all wanted to see the baby and tell Lenora what they'd been doing since they last saw her. He already knew everything they wanted to say, but he enjoyed seeing her reaction and listening to what she told each one. She wore her hair up, wound tightly on the back of her head, and he admired the smooth, long lines of her neck and jaw as she laughed.

It started when Joey was done eating the first time and he hopped up to cruise the room. Big Ray took his place. He told Lenora he was still making pizzas and living in a slummy triple-decker in Brockville, but he puffed up when he announced he was accepted into Harvard's divinity school. Tim almost lost it when Lenora said, "Tell me, Ray. When did you get so close to God?" Ray, who wore a buttoned-up white shirt beneath his overalls, told her all about it.

Now, it was Geneva's turn. She wrinkled her freckled nose.

"She's got kind of a big head. Did it hurt giving birth?"

Lenora's fingertips moved lightly in a circle over Isabel's belly. The baby's green eyes shone as if she had something to say.

"Hurt? Of course, it hurt. I didn't take anything for the pain, and it drove the nurses nuts. But it was worth it. Don't you think?"

Geneva sat.

"I suppose so. I don't want any kids unless they knock me out completely and hand me the baby when I wake up. You can do that, right?"

"You can, but I read it's better for the baby if you don't."

Geneva licked her lips as she paused.

"That was too bad about Ned, wasn't it? Christ, Lenora, I saw him only a few days before he died. He was coming out of the administration building. I wasn't gonna stop, but he called me over. Ned asked how I was doing. He seemed okay. I was shocked when I heard he died. You hear how it happened?"

"I heard. I think I remember the girl. Tall redhead?"

Geneva's head bobbed.

"Aw, Lenora, I'm bummed about this."

Lenora murmured.

"I'm sure it's been hard for those who cared about Ned, especially Inez."

"Oh," she whispered, and then in true Geneva fashion, she shook it off. "Did you hear Mack and I are going out?"

"No, I didn't. I'm happy for you, Geneva."

"We aren't living together or anything like that. Besides, I couldn't stand living in that dump with all those slobs." She flipped her hair over her shoulder. "No offense, Tim."

Tim studied Lenora as Geneva rambled on about the things she and Mack did and wanted to do, like take a road trip out West before he started his teaching job. Tim thought Lenora looked tired and a little sad, but he didn't think either was for Ned Burke. He leaned forward to interrupt Geneva.

"Mind if I hold her?" he asked Lenora.

"Have you held a baby before?" Lenora said.

"Sure, lots of times with my nieces and nephews. I'm their favorite uncle."

Nodding, she rewrapped the flannel blankets before she placed Isabel in his arms.

"That's it. Be careful of her head. Her neck muscles aren't strong yet."

Lenora pushed a hand against her hip, studying Tim until, satisfied, she sat down. Isabel was a light, little bundle in his arms. Milky spit bubbled between her lips. He knew a lot about babies. His sisters kept having them. This baby was an easy one. Fat cheeks. Sweet smelling. She didn't cry except in the auditorium when she was hungry. Lenora was taking good care of her.

"She's something else," he murmured.

Lenora leaned back in her chair. Nina stood and held her jaw as if she bit something hard. She looked that way since Joey told them Lenora was in the auditorium and they all rushed to find her before she could get away. He still couldn't believe Lenora finally showed up in Westbridge and with a baby.

Nina's arms were crossed.

"Tim, I'm gonna get something else to eat. You want anything?" she asked.

He shook his head as he let the baby's tiny hand curl around his finger. He bent to kiss it.

"No, go ahead."

Geneva got up, too.

"Wait up, Nina. I'll join you." She flashed Lenora a peace sign. "See ya."

"See you, too, Geneva."

Lenora rewound the knot in her dark hair, acting casually, but her eyes followed Nina and Geneva to the other end of the dining hall, where they stood talking near the table of food. Lenora's lips formed a crooked smile.

Tim felt his chest rise and fall.

"How's it going?" she asked.

He knew Lenora didn't mean how he was holding her baby.

"I'm hanging in there, Lenora." He pulled his finger to test the baby's grip. "I finally graduated in January. You missed the huge hassle about that, but Dean Hendricks couldn't prove a thing, so I came back and finished those two courses." He frowned. "I'm working at Denton. It's okay for now. It pays the bills."

Lenora reached into the backpack at her feet for a cloth diaper and used it to dab the drool around her daughter's mouth. She raised her face close to his. Tim decided melancholy was the best word to describe her expression.

"I know exactly what you mean," she said. "Sometimes you follow a dead end for a while."

Tim raised his boot onto the rung of the next chair so he could put the baby in a better place. It was his turn to talk with Lenora.

"We got a kick out of those postcards you sent from Europe. We couldn't believe how many words you could fit onto a small card. We all had a laugh about that." He chuckled. "It sounded like you were having a great time."

She folded the diaper into a small square.

"I did. I met some cool people and saw lots of things I wanted to see." She laughed. "I came back home with thirteen bucks. It was a good thing Ned gave me that money." She twisted the white square. "That's what Inez Burke was talking to me about just now. She apologized. I told her she didn't have to. It was only a misunderstanding."

"Misunderstanding." He paused. "I called your parents' house a couple of times this fall. I think I might've talked to your mother. Didn't she tell you?"

The corners of Lenora's mouth quivered.

"Tell me? No." She kept pulling at the cloth. "This whole thing's been hard on my folks. You should've heard them when I came back pregnant from Europe. Ai-yi-yi. They were so pissed. Their scholarship daughter gets knocked up like a high school dropout. Why in the heck did I bother going to college? They're still mad at me. When I went into labor, they dropped me off at the hospital. Do you believe that?" She shook her head slowly. "But they paid for everything, and they do love Isabel. Really, how could you not love her?"

"Lenora, if I'd known, I would've visited you. I have a car now. You should've told us you were gonna have a baby."

"A car?" Her fingers twisted over the cloth. "I wrote you a letter after I came back, Joey and Manny, too, but I didn't send any of them. I wanted to tell you, tell somebody, but another day went by and that didn't happen. Besides, I wasn't feeling too hot. After she was born, I didn't have time for anyone else." She shoved the diaper into the bag. "So, are you and Nina a couple?"

He shrugged.

"We've been seeing each other since the fall. It's nothing serious."

"I get the feeling Nina doesn't feel the same way."

Tim shrugged.

131

"Maybe," he said.

She made that crooked smile again.

Manny sat beside her. He wanted his shot. Lenora laughed, because he was shoving a hunk of chocolate cake into his mouth.

"Looks like you guys won't have to eat for at least a day," she said. "How've you been, you old Portagee?"

Manny grinned.

"I'm doing great, Lenora. I got accepted into law school at Boston University."

"Hot damn. A lawyer? You?"

"Yeah, me. Somebody's gotta protect the rights of us Portagees." His head jerked toward Isabel. "By the way, Lenora, I'm relieved to see your daughter has two brows although it may be too soon to tell. Sometimes they grow in when they get older."

She made a squealing laugh as she slapped Manny's arm.

"Very funny, wise guy."

Joey arrived. Pieces of the napkin in his hands dropped to the wooden floor.

"You're still here? I thought you said your bus left at four," he told Lenora.

She glanced at the clock above the dining hall's door and swore. It was four thirty.

"What's the matter?" Tim asked.

"That was the last bus today. Shit, what am I gonna do?"

Tim grinned. Joey and Manny did, too.

"I think we can figure something out," Tim said.

FORGOT HOW MUCH

Tim held the baby while Lenora used the payphone at Faulkner Dining Hall. Manny and Joey waited with him. Joey set the grocery bag of food he mooched off the dining hall staff on the floor. He whistled while he paced the hall. Lenora's voice rose and fell while she explained to her mother the funeral took longer than expected, which was a lie, and at the reception afterward she met so many people she lost track of time, which was true.

"No, no. You don't have to come get us. We're staying with friends. Yeah, yeah, I have enough of everything for Isabel for another day. She'll be fine. Really, Mom. I'll take the early bus tomorrow."

Lenora grabbed her neck as if she were choking.

Tim gazed down at Isabel. Her eyes peeked at him beneath her bonnet.

"You have a very silly mother," he told her.

Manny stood beside him.

"I still can't get over Lenora having a kid," he said.

"Tell me about it."

Lenora fed coins into the phone. Tim had moved his VW van to the faculty lot near Faulkner, so Lenora didn't have to walk far in the rain with the baby. Nina already split with Geneva and Mack to Winter Street. All

Nina told him was, "How about later you pay a little attention to me?" He was watching Lenora change the baby when she said that. He glanced at Nina's scowling face, and told her, "sure," although he didn't mean it.

Joey was back and bouncing in place.

"I've got an idea. Why don't we kidnap Lenora and her baby?"

Manny gave Joey's arm a chop.

"That's brilliant, Joey. Where's she gonna live?"

"She can share the attic with me."

Manny rolled his eyes.

"You're nuts. That's no place for a baby. Forget it. Lenora's not going along with that."

Joey kept bouncing.

"It's just an idea. I want her back with us. I miss her. Tim does, too. I bet even more than me." Joey made a hee-hee laugh. "Look at you. You're turning red. It's okay. We all know how you feel about her. Boy, is Nina pissed at you."

Isabel's lips made little smacking sounds. She was getting hungry again.

"Tim's not listening to you, Joey," Manny said.

"Yeah, I am. I'm just trying not to drop the baby." Isabel began bleating and turning her head toward her mother's voice. "And you're right. I'm glad to see Lenora. I forgot how much."

Lenora spun around. One finger was up.

"She'll be perfectly safe, Mom. I'll see you tomorrow. First bus. I promise. Bye."

Lenora groaned as she hung up the phone, and then she walked toward Tim with her hands out.

"Looks like she's about ready to blow. Why don't you give her to me? I can feed her in the car."

A TOAST TO NED

Mack, Joey, Tim, Manny, and Big Ray were in the kitchen of 221 Winter Street, toasting the late, great Ned Burke. They drank Irish whiskey, because the occasion merited something stronger and classier than beer. They even managed to scrounge up enough clean glasses, thanks to the math majors downstairs.

The others waited as Mack lifted his glass high.

"Here's to Ned Burke, the Dirtiest Old Bastard of them all. May we all be as lucky as him to die in the saddle. Sweet Jesus take his soul and let him have his way with the angels."

Everyone cheered and took a sip of whiskey. They were all half in the bag after polishing off a bottle, so they sent Geneva and Nina, who wouldn't touch any of it, to the package store for another.

It was Big Ray's turn. His belly pushed the edge of the table forward as he rose and cleared his throat.

"Here's to Ned Burke, a man who never sold us out. Ned walked in the front line when we protested the war. To Ned Burke, a man of his word!"

Glasses clinked above the rumble of "amen's" before they took another drink. Then they started talking about another piece of Ned, the man of words, who wrote guest columns in *The Hard Truth* about the war in

Vietnam. Joey remembered how one of them began, "*If I were of age today, I would go to jail rather than fight in a war whose cause could not be mine.*" They remembered his impassioned speech when one of his colleagues got canned. The crowd of students was stunned by his words that day.

Joey stood. He closed his eyes and held his glass of whiskey in two hands as if he were about to sing.

"*Nor shall Death brag thou wanderest in his shade/ When in eternal lines to time thou growest/ So long as men can breathe, or eyes can see/ So long lives this, and this give life to thee.*"

Everyone tipped their heads back as they drained their glasses.

"That was touching." Mack reached for the empty bottle. "Where'd you get that? Shakespeare?"

"Correct. 'Sonnet 18.' Good guess. And you're gonna be an English teacher?"

"Shut up, egghead. I'm better with the American shit," Mack said. "What in the hell's taking those girls so long?"

"They probably took the money and split," Manny joked.

Mack downed the last drops in the bottle.

"Tim, you got any pot left?"

"In my room, but Lenora's putting her baby to sleep in there. I don't wanna bother them."

"Listen to you." Mack chuckled. "I think Nina's a little ticked off about her. You should've seen her face when you told Lenora she could have your bed." He chuckled again. "It might be a little bit crowded back there if Nina sticks around."

"Let me worry about that."

Mack leaned toward the table.

"Did everybody see how big Lenora's tits got? Shit. They're freakin' huge. She's a little loose around the middle from having her kid but those tits. Mama mia. And then at the reception she whips them out to feed her baby. My God, don't tell me you all missed that."

"Missed what?"

Geneva was in the doorway, clutching a bottle of Jameson. Nina cut them all down with her eyes.

"Nothing, girls," Mack said. "You came back just in time. Our glasses were dry."

Geneva stomped to the center of the kitchen, then slammed the bottle and the change onto the Formica tabletop. Coins rolled across the floor. Joey's jiggling foot kicked a quarter against the refrigerator.

"Look, you assholes, we heard everything. You can have your precious Lenora and her freaking huge tits and that little brat of hers." She ground her fist into her side. "Nina and I are going to the VFW for some fun. Anybody want to join us?"

Mack smirked.

"Hope you find somebody with teeth, honey."

"Shut up, Mack."

Geneva raised her hand to slap his face, but Mack caught her wrist. He clicked his tongue.

"Be nice, dear."

She broke free and was out the door. Nina went with her. Tim followed, and everyone heard them yelling in the stairway. It was the fight of the week for Tim and Nina. It didn't take much. Last week, she made a fuss when he worked a double shift at Denton. There could only be one reason he still saw Nina. She was available. Tim was that lazy of a guy.

Chuckling, Mack grabbed the new bottle and twisted off the cap. He refilled their glasses.

"What's all the noise about?" Lenora said behind him.

Mack spun around. Lenora's arms were up as she twined her hair into a bun. A wet spot on her Indian print blouse spread over the nipple of one breast.

"The little one finally conk out? Finally. How about having a drink with us? Just a wee one. I hear Irish mothers do it all the time," Mack said. "Sit next to Joey there. I think Tim's gonna be a little while. He and Nina are having a little discussion downstairs."

Lenora sat. Joey handed her a glass. Mack reached across the table with the bottle.

"Just a little," she said.

"Joey, put your glass on the table. Your hand's moving around like you've got the shakes, buddy."

Mack poured their drinks. Voices still echoed in the stairwell.

"I'm glad Lorraine and Nancy aren't home." Mack held his glass. "We've been toasting Ned Burke. It was supposed to be Tim's turn. Lenora, why don't you go instead?"

"Me?"

"Why not? You two were cozy." He raised his hand as if he were stopping traffic. "I meant that in a good way. I saw Inez talking to you today."

"She did."

"Let me guess. It was about that big to-do she made last year at the party. Thought so." Mack grinned. "Hey, we're having another one this year. You should come. Manny and I are graduating. And a couple of the others. Really graduating, not like that faker Tim. I even got a job teaching in the fall. Now, that's something to celebrate." He sniffed the whiskey. "Only Joey, our scholar here, is going to linger a while at Westbridge. I believe he's on the six-year plan. Right, Joey?"

Joey played with the ends of his hair. His right knee shot up and down. "Uh-huh."

"Lenora, give us a toast."

She smiled as she thought, and then she reached for her drink. She stood and raised the glass.

She said, "Here's to Professor Groovy." The rest of them went, "Hey, hey."

ISABEL CHANGES EVERYTHING

Somewhere in the dark, Lenora heard the bedroom door open and shut. Tim said her name softly. She could make out his shape as he came toward the bed, where she sat nursing Isabel.

"You coming back later?" he whispered.

"I don't think so," she whispered back. "I'm gonna stay here with Isabel. She woke up again."

"Why don't you bring her out there?"

"That's no place for a baby. It's too smoky and loud. I wasn't expecting so many people to show up. Did you?"

"You know how it is. Any excuse for a party. Even somebody dying." Tim knelt on the mattress. "Jesus, it's dark in here. I can hardly see you."

"The lamp beside your bed's too bright."

Tim moved away.

"Wait a sec," he said from across the room.

She heard the scratch of a match, and then Tim carried a lit candle stuck in a wine bottle to the nightstand. He stood there rocking on the balls of his feet.

"That's a lot better," she told him.

The stereo boomed Traffic's "Mr. Fantasy" from the living room. Ned

Burke's wake grew into something much larger than a few toasts of Irish whiskey after the guys from downstairs showed up, and then Nancy and Lorraine across the hall. Next, the Roach Motel tribe came and a few of the Dirty Professors. They had a packie run and Tim broke out his stash of pot. Lenora danced a little with Tim and Manny, laughing at their stories, totally off the wall, because they were all stoned except her. She didn't drink either after the whiskey in the kitchen, so she ended up feeling a little like the only grownup at the party.

Tim gestured toward the wall.

"Want me to tell them to turn the music down?"

"No, no. It's okay. I don't want to spoil their fun. She'll be all right as long as I'm with her."

"You mind if I stay?"

"Course not."

Tim slipped off his boots. The bed's springs creaked as he slid beside her. He lay on his side, watching the baby nurse. Isabel watched him, too, until slowly, her lids fell, and her mouth stopped moving. Lenora smoothed the dark wisps of her daughter's hair.

"What's it like?"

"What's what like? Having a baby? It's a lot of work. I should've done this differently." Lenora stuck a finger in Isabel's mouth to loosen her grip. She buttoned her blouse, waiting to see if she stayed asleep before she lifted the baby to her shoulder to burp her. "I'm not sorry I had her. It's a real trip having a baby grow inside you from almost nothing, and then she's born, and now I'm the most important person in her life." She sighed. "Isabel changes everything."

On the other side of the wall, someone howled like a wolf. The others joined him. Lenora laughed.

"That Mack," Tim said. "The wolf thing's new. I suppose next he'll be doing the old Cossack dance routine with Manny."

"Sounds like you're missing out on a fun time. You don't want to join them?"

"Eh, I see them all the time. I'd much rather be here with you."

"Yeah?" She pushed the hair back from his forehead. "Did I tell you I liked you better without your beard?"

"Twice. This makes three times. I should go shave." He rolled on his back, rubbing his jaw. "Yup, I think I'll go do that right now."

"You don't have to."

He grinned.

"It worked the last time. Remember? Oh, Lenora Dias don't you shake your head at me."

"I'll shake my head if I want, Timothy Devlin. I'm not that easy anymore."

Mischief was in Tim's blue eyes. He and Lenora teased each other like they had done a million times, and it felt so easy to be together. She should have sent that letter to Tim. If he visited, it would have been one of the few bright moments during the past several months while she waited to give birth. All she did was stay in her room reading or venture out to the library to get more books or see the doctor or play with her sisters. But if she sent the letter, and if he never came, it would have been worse. Two phone calls to her parents' house, even if it wasn't his fault her mother didn't tell her, wasn't exactly trying.

"I missed you, Lenora. I missed you an awful lot."

"Uh-huh, so much you got yourself a girlfriend while I was gone." Her voice sounded too loud. "It doesn't look like you could've missed me that much."

"I told you it wasn't serious. Nina and I just have a thing going."

"A thing. What in the hell does that mean?"

"We go places together. See each other. Have some laughs."

"Sleep together. Have sex."

"That, too."

"Thought so."

"Come on. Forget about her. She doesn't wanna see me any more. I bet you and everybody else in the neighborhood heard her yell that from downstairs. Why don't you find a nice spot for Isabel so she's not in the way." He patted the other side of the bed. "How about over there? Then you can come over here."

"I don't think this is such a hot idea, Tim."

"Sure it is." He inched closer. "Isabel will be fine. She's sleeping."

His hand was on her thigh. He moved it lightly. She held her breath and let it go slowly.

"Tim."

"That's right. My name's Tim."

She made a place for Isabel on the bed, and then she lay beside Tim.

141

"Like this?"

"That's better."

She smiled up at him.

"I do like you better without your beard."

He chuckled.

"Stop talking about my beard and let me kiss you."

She closed her eyes. His lips reached hers. It'd been a while since she had that kind of kiss.

But in the middle of the next, there was a light knock at the door. Manny pushed it open.

"Sorry, Lenora, have you seen Tim? There you are."

Tim hurled a shoe against the door.

"Forget it, Manny. Not this time. Get lost."

Manny dodged another shoe then a pillow. His black brows formed a deep crease.

"Cut it out, asshole. Nina was in an accident. She totaled the car when she hit a pole. The Roach brothers saw it. She's okay, but she's shook up. She's asking for you."

Tim moaned.

"We're not going out anymore. You heard her tonight."

"Tim, she needs you," Manny said. "Nina had too much to drink, and the cops are there."

Tim muttered "cops" as he sat up and swung his legs over the edge of the bed. His head was in his hands.

Lenora patted his arm.

"You should go help her. It's the right thing to do," she said.

He nodded.

"Can you stay another day?"

"No, Isabel and I have to leave early tomorrow. We're taking the eight o'clock bus. I promised my mother."

"Shit." He turned toward her. "I'll be back as soon as I can. Wait up for me, will you?"

Tim kissed her so quickly she didn't even get to kiss him back. Then he and Manny were gone. Their voices followed them down the hall. Lenora got up to shut the door all the way. She returned to bed to make a safe place for Isabel before she rolled over to blow out the candle. She fell asleep listening to music through the wall. She knew the song. It was something by Janis Joplin.

A LITTLE LATE

enora woke up early. She and Isabel were alone. Something must have happened, because Tim never returned. Even Manny wasn't in his bed. She got Isabel ready and walked through the quiet apartment, a typical Sunday morning-after scene of empties, filled ashtrays, and people crashed in the living room. She thought of leaving a note but didn't. They'd figure out she was gone.

The rain stopped, but the sky was still overcast and the air had the tedious chill of early spring. She hoisted the backpack on her shoulders and carried Isabel up Winter Street through the still campus to downtown. She knew when the bus was coming, and she had enough time and money for coffee and a little something to eat at Jimmy's. She recognized a couple of the townies at the counter when she went to place her order. Her story about the cook from *The Hard Truth* was still taped near the register.

The cook wiped his hands on his apron as he came to the counter.

"Haven't seen you in a real long time, honey. That's a real cute baby you've got there," he said.

"She is, isn't she?"

His gold tooth showed.

"You alone? Why don't you take a seat? I'll bring you your order."

Lenora ate at a window table so she could see who went by. It was too early for students to be hanging around the center of Westbridge. They were sleeping off the night before. Not long ago, she would have been doing the same. She told that to Isabel, and the baby's eyes blinked beneath her bonnet as she listened to her voice. Lenora glanced at the clock then past the commons where the bus stopped for the traffic light at the corner.

"Time to go," she said.

She chose a seat toward the front of the bus. Isabel would fall asleep when the bus started as she did on the ride here, and she would want to nurse again. She loosened the ties on her daughter's bonnet and the zipper on the front of her suit. She played a fingertip along her cheek. Isabel's mouth spread apart in a smile.

"Hey, there, sweetie."

The driver shut the door. He was getting ready to steer the bus from the curb, but stopped when there was shouting outside. Tim banged at Lenora's window and called her name.

"I'll see you soon," he shouted.

Behind him, Manny and Joey stood on the sidewalk near Tim's van. Those crazy guys had their arms up and in motion. She smiled and waved.

She turned when the bus driver called over his shoulder.

"Miss, does that guy wanna ride?"

"No, he came to say bye. He's just a little late."

The driver grunted and steered the bus around the commons. Tim trotted alongside, yelling things she couldn't hear until the bus picked up speed. He stepped back off the road, and she watched him standing in the street until the bus left the center of Westbridge.

Lenora smiled to herself as she sat back in the seat. She looked down at Isabel.

"So, what do you think about that?" she asked her daughter.

LAZY ASS

Joey reached into the black, metal mailbox hanging next to the front door of 221 Winter Street. He pulled out an electric bill and a postcard. The front of the card had one of those corny beach scenes with red sunlight flashing on the water. When he flipped the card over, the backside was filled with the tiniest print in black ink. He recognized the handwriting. Lenora wrote this way when she sent them postcards from Europe. She addressed the card to Tim, but Joey felt it was fair game to read. It was late morning. Maybe Tim was up. Maybe he wasn't. He had a double shift yesterday at Denton State School for the Mentally Retarded. Joey wasn't going to wait for him to wake up to find out what Lenora wrote. It had to be important.

He shoved the bill back in the mailbox and sat on the steps. His left foot tapped a stair tread.

"Tim. I guess this is the best way to reach you since you only called that one time after Ned's funeral in March. Anyway Isabel and I are moving to New Hampshire on July 16. We'll be living in a commune called Great Meadow I found through a friend. I think it'll be a real good place for us."

Joey muttered, "Holy shit, a commune in New Hampshire."

He scanned the rest of her message quickly. It was amazing how much

Lenora could fit on the back of one small card. She wrote Isabel was five months old, a happy baby who laughed and smiled a lot. Her parents didn't want them to leave, but Lenora said living at home was a drag. She and Isabel will be going to New Hampshire by bus. It'll be a long ride for them. She gave Tim her new address and phone number. And at the end, she wrote: "Maybe some day you'll get off your lazy ass and come see me."

Joey started laughing. First, it was a little hiss of a sound, and then it grew into a shoulder-shaking, stomach-grabbing laugh that was hard to stop. It was as if Lenora's words sent a jolt of electricity through him and he couldn't let go. It was definitely the best laugh he'd had in months. *Get off your lazy ass.* He wiped away tears. All that sweetness and news from Lenora and then, kapow, she gives Tim a zinger at the end. Lenora killed him.

Lenora was correct, as usual. The last time Tim saw her, he made it in time to watch her leave on the bus. He drove the VW van like a crazed man after they left Nina behind at the hospital in Brockville. Her folks were with her anyway while she waited for a doctor to set her arm in a cast and stitch up her forehead. Nina lucked out with the cops that night. It was smart to bring Professor Mitchell to the crash, because Itch, the most sober one at Ned's wake after Lenora, had experience with these kinds of things. It looked real bad when they got there. Nina was hysterical, and Geneva, who was in the front seat, didn't help things when she began to cop that I-hate-the-pigs attitude of hers. But Itch, a tenured member of the English faculty and a regular contributor to the policemen's auxiliary fund, was able to talk the cops out of arresting Nina.

During the wild ride from Brockville to Westbridge, Tim kept muttering things like, "it was going so good, then this had to happen" and "shit, I gotta explain." Joey knew he was talking about Lenora. Everybody could tell what was happening between him and her that night. They were joking, laughing, and dancing close. When Lenora left to be with her baby, Tim followed her. Mack said, when Tim wasn't around, of course, "I hope Timmy's got a rubber or she's taking something, cause little Isabel might get a brother or sister tonight."

Joey didn't blame Nina for not sticking around that night. There was no way she could compete with Lenora.

When they got to the center of Westbridge that morning, Tim dumped the van and ran to catch Lenora's bus. Joey slapped his jerking thigh and started whooping when he remembered Lenora's shocked face as Tim knocked at her window on the bus. She just shined. After the bus left, Tim promised to see her, but then he started helping Nina, and everybody could tell what was going to happen between those two, and it did. It was like Lenora never showed up for Ned's memorial service, or Tim got knocked in the head and had amnesia, or something. Maybe it was all the pot he keeps smoking or the beer. *Get off your lazy ass.* Joey started laughing again. He ran up the steps.

He smelled coffee when he opened the door to the apartment. Tim sat in the kitchen staring at the aluminum pot perking on one of the stove's burners. His head was on the table. Bags were beneath his bloodshot eyes.

"What are you laughing about you lunatic?" he growled.

Joey raised the postcard overhead.

"Hoo-hoo. Mail call, and it's for you, Tim. Guess who it's from?"

Tim sat up, squinting at the card's picture, and when Joey turned it over, he nodded at the handwriting on the flipside.

"That's from Lenora. Give it to me."

Joey handed him the card. Tim frowned.

"You read it already?"

Joey made himself get serious.

"Course, I read it. Wait 'til you get to the last line. It's a doozy."

Tim checked the photo on the front.

"Jesus, Joey, I wouldn't read your mail."

"That's cause I never get any, but if I did and it was a postcard from Lenora, I wouldn't care if you read it first. Honest."

Tim half-listened as he read what Lenora wrote. Joey sat at the table's only other chair. They used to have more, but Big Ray broke one and Joey couldn't remember what happened to the others. Across the table, Tim bit his bottom lip as his blue eyes went back and forth over the lines. Joey waited for him to get to the end, trying not to work up another laugh. It seemed as if Tim was always down about something lately. He hated his job at Denton. He was tired of living with slobs. He and Nina had another fight. July was too damn hot, and so on.

Joey guessed Tim had gotten to the best part in Lenora's message, because he glanced away, hummed, and then he read it again. He tossed the postcard on the table.

"For Christ's sake, New Hampshire? And what does she mean calling me a *lazy ass*? I came to say bye that time. Nearly broke my neck doing it. I called her once. We talked until I ran out of money. *Lazy ass,* Lenora's got some goddamned nerve calling me that."

"That was four months ago."

Tim glared. Joey picked up a sugar-crusted spoon and began tapping it on the tabletop.

"Shit happens," Tim said.

"It happens to her, too."

"Why are you sticking up for her?"

"'Cause it's Lenora, and she's not here to do it for herself. You know she would, don't you?"

Tim didn't answer. The legs of his chair scraped into the blackened grooves on the linoleum as he got up and searched the cabinet for a clean mug. He ended up washing one from the pile of dirty dishes in the sink. He stuck his head in the fridge and slammed the door. The blue flame of the burner popped when he turned the knob on the stove. He filled the mug with coffee.

"Christ, what happened to the milk I bought the other day?"

"No clue."

"Bread's gone, too. The only thing left in the fridge are two cans of beer and a head of brown lettuce." He blew over the top of the mug before taking a sip. "I'm getting sick of this shit."

"You mean living with a bunch of pigs?"

"Bingo." He raised the mug to his lips. "Help yourself to some coffee. It probably tastes like crap, but it's all we got."

Joey was figuring whether it was worth getting up to wash a cup when he saw Tim pick up the card. He drank from the mug as he read it again. Joey dropped the spoon and pulled a pack of butts from his T-shirt. He fired up a cigarette, deciding it was too much of an effort after all for coffee. Besides he already had a cup and a refill at Jimmy's this morning, thanks to the Irish Lit professor who said he told good stories. They were talking about William Butler Yeats when Mack and Geneva stopped for some grub to go. They were heading to a beach on Cape Cod for the day. Geneva said she was dying to go swimming. The townies stared at her halter-top. Their tongues practically hung on the counter. She knew it, because she raised her arms and announced, "It's gonna be a hot one today."

Joey began to play with the book of matches. Tim concentrated on the card as if he were cramming for a final exam. Joey giggled to himself: Lenora 101.

Tim slipped the card into his T-shirt pocket and took another drink of coffee. He shook a butt from Joey's pack of Winstons on the table and held out his hand for the matches, which were still in usable condition.

"I'm thinking I'd like to see her before she goes." Tim lit the cigarette. "She wrote she's leaving July 16. When's that?"

"I think it's tomorrow. Yeah, it is." Joey pointed to the calendar on the wall. "Definitely tomorrow."

"Brother." His breath drove smoke through his mouth. "Why in the hell didn't she write me sooner?"

"Maybe she did. Who knows how long the card's been in the mailbox?"

"I guess it's today or nothing, huh?" He rubbed his beard. "I'm off two days, and remind me never to work a double shift again. I don't need the bread that much. I kept nodding off when I was driving home. I thought I was gonna crack up my van." He tapped the butt against the edge of the ashtray. "You working tonight at Angie's?"

"Yup, I'll be chained to the sink starting at five."

Tim glanced at his watch.

"Let's see. It's almost eleven now. Manny says it takes about an hour to get there. We could see her for a few hours and be back in time for your shift. What'd you say? Manny knows where she lives. We'll get him to come."

"Why don't you go by yourself? She wrote you."

"You don't wanna see her?"

"Course, I do."

"Go wake up Manny." He finished the coffee. "If you don't mind, I'd like to keep this little trip a secret between us. Nina doesn't have to hear about it. Okay? Sometimes she gets a little upset about Lenora."

Sometimes? A little? That was what Joey wanted to say. But he was smarter than that.

"There are, that resting, rise/Can I expound the skies? How still the riddle lies!"

"What are you mumbling about now?"

"Something by Emily Dickinson." Joey got to his feet. "Are you planning to call Lenora first?"

Tim stubbed the butt cold.

"Nah, let's surprise her."

ROAD TRIP

"Which street is it?" Tim asked.

The paper shook in Joey's hand.

"Hold your horses. It should be coming soon." His head swung back. "Whoops. That's the one. You'll have to turn around."

"What? Read what Manny wrote. I knew we should've made him come with us. So what if he had plans with that girl?"

Tim made a U-turn in the middle of the road and a left onto a tree-lined street of Capes, ranches, and bungalows.

"What's the number?"

Joey's head went down and up.

"It's 24. Slow down. There's 34, 32. Almost there. Here, it is. No, no, this one. See the mailbox with Dias on it?"

Tim slowed the VW van and parked in front of a Cape painted charcoal gray and with a fenced-in yard. They went to the side door, and after Tim rang the bell, a girl stood behind the closed screen door. She was a younger version of Lenora, maybe twelve or thirteen, with dark eyes and spidery arms. She wore a flowered bathing suit and carried a gray cat.

"Is Lenora here?"

The girl stared through the mesh at Joey who hopped from one foot to the other as if he were tap dancing on the grass. Tim shook his head.

"Lenora?" the girl said.

"We're her friends from college. I'm Tim and he's Joey. I think we saw you at your sister's graduation. I was graduating, too."

"She's in the backyard with the baby." She gestured through the screen door. "Go that way. You'll find her."

Tim walked with Joey until they reached the corner of the house. Lenora sat on a lawn chair in the shade with Isabel on her lap. Her back was to them as she watched a girl jump into an inflatable pool a few feet away. Then the girl was on her feet with her hands up in the air shouting "ta-da!" Lenora moved back as water flicked over her. The Dias girls were thin and dark-haired. They had sun-browned skin.

"Isabel says that was a real good one. Next time, she wants a much bigger splash. And try spinning around a little." The girl, younger than the one at the door, stood in the middle of the pool. She stared at him and Joey. "What? What is it?" Lenora craned her neck. She raised her hand to her mouth. "Oh, my God, I can't believe it. You two."

Lenora was up and walking fast-legged toward them, with Isabel tucked in the crook of her arm. The baby's legs kicked beneath her diaper. Lenora stopped open-mouthed in front of Tim, and her head swung toward Joey. She made a tinkling kind of laugh, and Tim, happy to be the cause of it, had the urge to put his hand on her shoulder or arm or any part of her to catch whatever she was feeling. What he really wanted to do was hug her. She kissed his cheek. She did the same to Joey.

Joey bent toward the baby and tugged her foot. Isabel made a gummy smile.

"Lenora, your baby got fat."

She poked Joey's chest.

"Babies are supposed to be fat, silly. She's growing."

Joey started hopping again.

"We liked your card," he said.

Her eyes were back on Tim.

"So, you got it. Is that why you came?"

Tim smoothed back his hair.

"I wanted to see you before you left. New Hampshire. Why there?"

She twirled around and smiled over her shoulder.

"I'll tell you all about it. Let's get in the shade. It's too hot in the sun for

Isabel," she said. "These are my little sisters. Teresa is in the pool. That's Silvie behind you. They're acting a little shy. We don't have any long-haired freaks with beards in *our* neighborhood."

They sat talking in the backyard. Lenora gave them sandwiches and something cold to drink, no beer, because her parents didn't keep booze in the house. They didn't smoke either. The three of them sat in the shade while Lenora's sisters entertained them by jumping into the pool. Joey rolled the bottom of his jeans so he could stand in there with the girls, adding more water with the hose when the level got low.

Lenora told them about growing up in this neighborhood and how her grandparents had a small farm at the bottom of the street until they died. Her aunt and uncle lived next door. Her father built their house, hand-mixing the cement in a wheelbarrow for the cinderblock basement. Ranches and split-levels were going up in the little lots on this street and the ones near it. She said it was beginning to look like a suburb, except when she stood in a certain part of the yard she could still see the harbor's water. She said Manny's family lived on the other side of the bay in a tri-ple-decker. She went there a couple of times on school breaks. His mother kept calling her Manny's "nice Portuguese girlfriend."

"You all packed?" Tim asked her.

"Uh-huh. I have three suitcases and a duffel bag. Most of it belongs to Isabel."

Tim put his arm around the back of Lenora's chair. She gave him a sly look.

"What's this place like you're moving to?" he asked.

"Great Meadow? I'll find out tomorrow. All I heard is that it has a big farmhouse in the middle of the state. A hippie couple with kids started it. You know back-to-earth kind of freaks. Isabel and I'll have our own room. They have a woodworking shop and the women sew quilts and other things they sell in the city. It's how I'll earn my keep." She shrugged. "We'll see how it goes. I can always come back."

"You're going to a place you've never seen?"

"My friend, Linda, used to live there. She's the one who told me about it. Remember her? She was in my dorm when I was a freshman. Tall. Brown hair down to her butt?"

"That could almost be any girl at Westbridge."

Lenora thought.

"Sometimes she hung with Ray. She had an opinion about everything."

"Maybe."

Lenora moved Isabel to her other arm.

"This seems to be the best choice for us. I love my family, but I don't wanna stay here. What else am I gonna do? Go on welfare? "

Joey kicked the water.

"I told you about my idea."

"We're not living in that attic with you. You can forget all about that."

"It's gonna get lonely," Joey said. "Manny's moving to Boston in August. Mack says he wants to live closer to his teaching job. Tim's talking about getting a place of his own."

Lenora's head tipped to the side.

"Yeah?"

"I'm looking around."

"Sounds like the old Winter Street gang's breaking up."

"Something like that."

She reached for a ball her sister kicked near her chair.

"Why didn't you call me again?"

"I got busy with work, stuff."

"Stuff." She threw the ball into the pool. "How's Nina?"

He felt heat rise up his neck.

"She's okay."

"Is that why you didn't call?"

"Jesus, Lenora why are you giving me the third degree?"

She kissed the top of Isabel's head.

"I dunno. I think about you and ... well, I think about you sometimes."

Tim studied Lenora. Everything about her got quiet.

"Oh, yeah, and you called me *lazy ass.*"

"You didn't like that, huh?" She smiled. "Well, it got you here."

AT ANGIE'S

Tim sat at the end of the bar at Angie's, dipping a chunk of bread into the plate of spaghetti and pushing the greasy sauce around the rim. He shoved the bread into his mouth. He watched Joey through the order window as he worked in the kitchen. Joey was hunched over the double sink. His elbows moved as he scrubbed a big pot.

They got back from Lenora's as Tim promised in time for Joey's shift although halfway through their visit he wished he hadn't brought him. He wanted to stay longer. Maybe he could have taken Lenora out to eat. They could have had a nice talk. He didn't know why he insisted on bringing Joey, but seeing her did make the nut happy. Joey kept jabbering about Lenora and Isabel all the way back to Westbridge. Lenora's sisters got a kick out of him. Her parents, who showed up later, weren't so sure, but Joey laughed at all her father's jokes, which helped.

Tim kept an eye on the Red Sox game on the black-and-white TV set on a shelf above the bartender's head. Angie's was packed tonight. It always was on Saturday night. He glanced over his shoulder, where Nina waited on a table of townie rednecks. They were giving her a hard time, but they didn't know who they were messing with, or maybe they did, and they liked a woman with rough spots. Maybe that was the attraction

154

between him and her.

"Okay, boys, how about I see some ID from everybody," she said as she held a tray against her waist.

The townies pulled out their wallets, but they joked about it. Nina was a good waitress. She got her customers' orders fast and flirted enough so she got big tips. The owners loved her. She was the main reason Joey worked as the dishwasher, a job he had last summer. One of the owners swore up and down he would never hire him again. He said Joey had to be the lousiest dishwasher they ever hired. His dog could do a better job. But after the last drunk quit in the middle of the shift, Joey didn't seem quite so bad. At least that's what Nina told the owners. It was decent of Nina to stick up for Joey, especially since she didn't see him the way Tim did. Nina said Joey was a complete spaz and the poetry he spouted was dumb. One time when they were all stoned, she told Joey that, and he answered her back, "I believe calling me a dumb poet might be considered by some to be an oxymoron." Nina didn't respond. Tim bet she didn't even know what an oxymoron meant.

Tim glanced at the TV set. The Sox were up two in the fourth against the Orioles. Yaz was having a good game. Nina set her tray on the bar beside Tim as she told the bartender she needed six beers. She winked when Tim said her name.

"Didn't see you come in." She waited while the bartender reached inside the cooler. "What'd you do today? I stopped by, but the place was deserted."

He shoved the plate forward.

"Not too much. Slept late. That double shift was murder. Joey and I went for a long ride."

She nodded.

"Ride. Where'd you go?"

"No place special. Just goofing around."

She arranged the bottles on the tray.

"I'll talk with you later," she said.

He hated lying to Nina, but he knew what would happen if he didn't. She would totally flip out. He couldn't even mention Lenora's name in front of her. If somebody else did, she'd snap, "Big deal. She's not so special if you ask me." That was it, though. Lenora was a big deal. She was special if you asked anybody else.

155

"Hey, there, Tim, how's it hanging?"

Tim looked to his left as Mack took the stool beside him. The skin on his face not covered by hair was red and raw as if somebody took a blowtorch to it.

"You fall asleep in the sun or something?"

Mack raised himself so he could check his reflection in the mirror behind the bar.

"As a matter of fact, I did. You should see Geneva. She got fried, man. Poor girl was in some serious pain when I dropped her off at her place."

"Gee, Mack, that was mighty thoughtful of you," Tim said.

Mack waggled his finger at the bartender.

"When I stopped in the kitchen earlier, our friend the dishwashing poet told me all about your little visit to Lenora. Stupid freak got so excited he dropped a couple of plates. There were pieces all over the floor. Good thing the owner wasn't around." Mack grunted when the beer was set in front of him. "Joey said Lenora was moving to a commune in New Hampshire. Way out in the middle of nowhere. Making quilts and shit like that." He gulped his beer and wiped his mouth with his hand. "So, how's our lovely queen doing these days?"

Tim checked behind him. Nina was taking an order at another table. Now that Mack knew, it was only a matter of time before she did.

"Great. So's the baby. She's a cute little thing. Smiles all the time."

Tim lifted the beer bottle to his lips. Manny came through the side door. He punched Tim's shoulder as he made his way to the stool beside Mack.

"What's the score?" he asked.

"Sox are up two," Tim said. "I thought you were going out with that girl."

"Don't ask."

Mack signaled the bartender. He wanted to buy a beer for Manny.

"You ready for another, Tim?"

"Sure, if you're paying."

They drank and swapped stories. Mack told them all the guys at the beach ogled Geneva in her bikini. Afterward they stopped for the greasiest fried clams ever at a joint near the bridge. Tim told them about Lenora and the baby, about her little sisters playing with Joey, and the place in New Hampshire she was moving to tomorrow. They howled when he repeated what Lenora's father said about Joey, "Doesn't that hairy boy ever sit still?"

Manny leaned forward over the bar.

"I called the woman Inez Burke knows in Boston. I got that room she's renting out. I have to mail her the deposit this week. I'll be outta here the end of July." He grabbed the beer. "Tim, I heard there's going to be an opening at the Roach Motel. One of the studios, so it's dirt cheap. Itch told me about it."

Mack made a roaring laugh as he slapped the edge of the bar.

"Roach Motel? No fuckin' way. Bro, you can't go over to the other side."

Tim ignored Mack. He watched Joey through the kitchen window. Most of his hair was bunched in a hairnet. The owner's wife insisted. Joey leaned his backside against the sink and his nose was stuck in a slim book Lenora gave him. It was by one of the Beat poets. Lenora said she wasn't taking it with her to New Hampshire. Tim frowned. New Hampshire sounded so far away. Maybe she'd meet somebody at that commune. Maybe she'd forget all about them.

Tim felt a poke in his side. Mack talked out of the side of his mouth.

"You got anything on you?"

"In the van."

"Why don't we finish these beers and take a little ride through town. We're not gonna have too many more nights like this. What'd you say?"

"Sounds good to me. Let me pay for my dinner."

Mack downed his beer.

"I've been thinking maybe we should have one last party before we all split. We had one for graduation a few weeks ago, but it was kind of a bust. The best freaks split early for the summer and most of the Dirty Old Bastards were a no-show. I think Ned dropping dead bummed them all out. I heard the professor from the drama department got a case of the guilts and went back to his old lady and kids." He reached into his jeans pocket for his wallet. "You like the idea?"

"Eh, Mack, nothing we do can do now could possibly ever top the last weekend bash."

"You've got a point there." Mack left dollar bills on the bar top. "Let's take that ride. Manny, you ready? We'll come back for Joey later."

SO FAR SO GOOD

enora held a cardboard template in the shape of a triangle as she studied the fabric on the worktable in front of her. It was a blue calico, with maple leaves caught in a perfect wind that kept them aloft and evenly spaced. She was figuring the best way to get the most pieces from the material while beside her Alyce unrolled a bolt of yellow fabric. It was for an order of baby quilts for a boutique in Boston, and Alyce told Lenora this morning this was a good first project for her.

Alyce wore her brown hair bound up in a bandana, peasant style. She had a way of smiling all the while she talked. She and Alyce were in a small room off the kitchen. Through the window she saw one of the men drive a red tractor with its chug-a-chug engine in the field. Everybody was out there weeding, except her and Alyce, who said it'd be too much for the baby.

She and Isabel arrived three days ago at Great Meadow, named that by Alyce and Matthew Sinclair for the large clearing around the farmhouse he inherited from a great aunt he hardly knew. She and Isabel had a small room on the second floor. There was even a crib that had been used by Matthew and Alyce's four children, who were now school-aged. Isabel guessed the couple was in their late thirties, maybe older, because Matthew's long hair and beard had gray. There was a young couple with one small child, but most of the people who lived at the commune were single men and women who came to live the good life in the country. In all, there were twenty-two people including Isabel, who was the only baby, and Alyce announced when Lenora stepped off the bus she was happy to have someone so new in the house again.

Lenora picked up the marking pencil to trace the outlines. She thought about what she'll write Tim. She'll tell him yesterday a storm came too fast when she took a walk with Isabel. They were getting soaked when a farmer, their closest neighbor, stopped his pickup truck to offer them a ride. The man had a sparse way of speaking. "I'll give you a ride" were the most words he said at one time. She'll tell Tim about the rules in the house, how the chores are divided, and how they all eat dinner together. Matthew says the blessing, and after the meal most sit around, smoking a joint, and talking politics and planting. So far, so good, she'll write.

Lenora lifted the template to another part of the fabric. Isabel slept in a playpen beside the worktable. All the while, Alyce talked about the life she used to have as the wife of a successful businessman and the one she preferred now. The farm came just in time to save them from the suburbs. Their friends thought they were insane to leave it all behind.

"What shocked them was when we said, 'Leaving what?' We were bored out of our minds. We didn't belong anymore." She stuck out her tongue. "Some of the people who come here don't last. It's not the work but the hang-ups. They think it's going to be a free-for-all, and they start getting themselves into trouble. Either they split or we ask them to go. Matthew calls Great Meadow his great experiment in civilization. I think that about sums it up."

Alyce stood when somebody knocked at the kitchen door and a man's voice sounded hello. She came back moments later.

"You have a visitor, Lenora."

"Me? I don't know anybody here."

"Our neighbor George Evans says he does."

"Oh, the farmer."

Lenora glanced down at Isabel asleep on her side. She followed Alyce into the kitchen, where George Evans blocked the screen door. He wore a brown canvas coat over his overalls. His tractor cap was bunched in one hand while he used the other to smooth the strands of hair crossing his scalp's shiny, pink skin. His cheeks pushed his eyes upward so they looked as if he were pleased about something. Lenora thought he must be older than her parents.

"Where's your baby?"

"Isabel's sleeping in the other room. Did I forget something in your truck?" He cleared his throat.

"No. I'm here to offer you a job. Part-time. I need a housekeeper."

"A housekeeper. You don't know anything about me."

"I believe I know you well enough."

The corners of Lenora's mouth twitched.

"I have Isabel to take care of, too."

"Bring her along. I'd say Mondays and Thursdays would be the best." His large farmer fingers crushed the cap. "It involves cleaning, laundry, and some cooking. I'm not good at any of those things. Mother used to do all of it until she passed away last year." He cleared his throat again. "Pay is three dollars an hour to start."

Lenora glanced at Alyce, who checked the dough rising for tonight's bread. The woman gave her a slight nod, but Lenora had already made up her mind. She had a hundred dollars stashed in her room, a gift from her parents, emergency money.

"Mr. Evans, why don't we try it?"

"I prefer George."

"Okay, George. Today is Wednesday. Isabel and I can be there tomorrow morning, say eight."

"I will look for you."

George said his byes to her and Alyce. The woman clucked as she watched him back the pickup from the driveway.

"We've been here three years, and this is the first time George Evans has stopped by. Wait 'til I tell Matthew." She clucked again. "I guess old Yankees can be friendly after all."

Lenora returned to the sewing room. Isabel was still asleep. She lifted the template to mark more triangles. She was cutting pieces for a saw-toothed pattern called Bear Paw. She thought she'd like to make a quilt like it for Isabel. She hummed to herself as she marked another piece. A year ago, she graduated from Westbridge and left everybody she loved to travel in Europe. Now she was on her own with a baby and living in the country. A farmer she only met for fifteen minutes wanted her to cook and clean for him. She bet Tim would laugh about that. She didn't stop humming.

SIDESHOW FREAK

Mack stood in front of his third-period class, the last one today because this was the half-day before Thanksgiving. He wore a pained teacher face while he waited for the kids to stop fooling around. Joey sat to his left at his desk. Mack asked him to talk to his classes about *Beowulf*, because the students in his three morning classes couldn't make sense of it. He agreed with them this great Anglo-Saxon epic poem was a great Anglo-Saxon bore. All these years he managed to escape reading *Beowulf*. Now, he was forced to teach it to sophomores who likely wouldn't remember anything except that they were forced to read it in high school. If there were anyone who could pump some life into a poem written a thousand years ago, it would be Joey.

Mack shook his head. The kids still hadn't quieted down. They were hopped up about having a few days off for the holiday. He didn't blame them. He looked forward to it, too. Plus he bet they all knew why the nervous guy with the long hair and beard sat in the front of the classroom. Word gets around fast in school, and Joey did such a bang-up performance for the first two classes, they were psyched it was their turn.

Mack stuck two fingers in his mouth and whistled sharply. He pointed at the left corner of the room where the troublemakers sat.

"How about settling down back there. Look, people, the longer you keep talking and messing around, the shorter the time Mr. Franklin here will have." He glanced around the room and then at Joey, whose brows bounced above his glasses at being called mister. Slowly the kids shut up. "That's better." He cleared his throat. "People, this is Mr. Joseph Franklin. He's about the smartest guy I know, and he's going to tell you something about *Beowulf*. Ready, Joey?"

Joey was on his feet. Mack gave him a nod before he walked toward the back of the room, making eye contact with the class' worst offenders as he slid into a desk in the last row. Mack frowned. Somebody carved the words on the desk's top: "This class sucks." The carving was new. Stupid kids. *This class sucks.* What a goddamn nerve. He was the cool teacher in this school.

He folded his arms behind his head and stretched his feet into the aisle. Joey stood in front of the blackboard, making a nervous laugh as he talked a little about himself and how much he loved poetry. Everything about Joey moved although he stayed in the same spot on the floor. His right leg did the Joey dance while he tossed a piece of yellow chalk and caught it in the same hand. Chalk dust was smeared in a wide stripe against the back of his pants from where he leaned against the blackboard's tray.

Mack lent Joey the shirt and pants, two sizes too big for the skinny freak, but he didn't have anything clean or decent enough to wear to class. Mack told him to keep them. They didn't fit since he put on a few pounds after he started teaching. He blamed his roll on getting stuck in a building all day and eating cafeteria food. Those ladies liked to pile it on his plate. A few extra pounds. Big deal. His new girlfriend, one of the teachers in the foreign language department, certainly didn't mind. He started going out with her after he broke up with Geneva this summer. Things were getting too sticky between them. She started talking about living together, and Mack didn't see how that was ever going to work. It was time for a breakup anyway. New job. New pad. He wanted to see who else was out there, and as usual, he didn't have to look too far, four doors down from his classroom, to be specific. Geneva was a real pain in the ass about it for a while, calling him up and sobbing over the phone. Once he caught her parked outside his house, spying on him. Finally, she seemed to be over him, or at least she left him alone.

Joey gave the kids in the class a big smile as if he expected some great news from them. He pointed to the blackboard where he wrote, "*Da wases on burgum Beowulf Scyldinga/ loef leodcyning, longe prage.*"

Chalk passed from one hand to another. It disintegrated in his twisting, twitching fingers and dropped yellow dust onto the front of his shirt and pants.

"You think reading *Beowulf*'s tough? Try it in Old English. That's the way it was written." Joey pointed toward the blackboard. "It means *Now Beowulf bode in the burg of the Scyldings, leader beloved, and long he ruled.*"

Mack looked around the room. Every kid studied Joey like he was side-show freak. Good for Joey keeping these monkeys interested. He sure wasn't getting anywhere with *Beowulf*. He was tired of the blank looks and moans of protest when he told them to open their books. He didn't understand why in the hell the head of the English department insisted these kids read *Beowulf*, but he did, and next week the old fart was going to observe his class to see how they handled it. That's why Mack asked Joey to come. Actually it was Tim who came up with the idea during the last time they were together. They were smoking pot and shooting the shit at Tim's crappy place in the Roach Motel. Tim was right. It didn't matter if it was new or old poetry. Joey would understand it.

"Scholars guess *Beowulf* was written before the tenth century. There's only one copy, and it survived a fire in some rich lord's mansion, and so it's locked up in the British Library in London because it's a national treasure." He made a nervous laugh. "So, why in November 1973 should any of us care about what somebody we don't know wrote in a language hardly anyone understands?" He shrugged. "Because it's an epic poem. That means it's a story bigger than any other story and it's written in a beautiful language. Another example of an epic poem is the *Odyssey* by Homer."

"We didn't like that one either," a wise guy said from the back of the room.

"Oh, yeah?" Joey dropped the chalk and grinned as he picked it up. "Well, *Beowulf* has a great warrior, two monsters, and a dragon that kills him at the end in a big battle. There's lots of gore and a magic sword. Pretty cool, eh?" He raised his arms. "Believe it or not, some people spend their whole lives studying *Beowulf*. Mack, eh, Mr. Mackenzie gave me thirty-five minutes. So, let's get started."

Poor Joey. The three of them deserted him at 221 Winter Street. First, Manny left for Boston, and Mack moved in with a couple of grad students on the lake to be closer to his teaching job. Tim left after him, renting a studio apartment at the Roach Motel. The students who took over Winter Street inherited Joey, who didn't have enough bread to go anywhere else. They were the next generation of freaks at Westbridge: kids who never had to worry about getting drafted. They came to Westbridge looking like hippies, with long hair and beards, using counter-culture lingo, so none of them ever underwent the big mind-blowing change in consciousness. They already did drugs in high school. They didn't care too much about politics or injustice although they said all the right things. They were like that plastic tie-a-yellow-ribbon-shit playing on the radio. Mack frowned. It was a bloody shame. The freak bloodline definitely was thinning.

Joey told Mack he felt like a spook haunting Winter Street. After the first few weeks, he stopped trying to be buddy-buddy with the new guys. He stayed in the attic, running an extension cord up there, so he could have a light to read and listen to a ballgame, first the Red Sox, then the Celtics. He was able to chip in toward the rent, thanks to Dean March who gave him an advance on his state scholarship. For a while, he scrounged food at the dining hall, faking he was on the meal plan until Westbridge State College cracked down and made everyone show IDs at the door. He still had his dishwashing job at Angie's on the weekends and sometimes he did odd jobs for Inez Burke, who was putting her house up for sale.

He watched as Joey picked up a book from the desk and turned the page. He lifted a finger.

"He has done his worst but the wound will end him. He is hasped and hoped and hirpling with pain, limping and looped in it." Joey put a lot of energy in his voice. "Ah-ha, now Beowulf has killed Grendel."

Mack remembered when he was student teaching, the old coot who was his advisor told him to never turn his back on the kids and don't smile until Christmas. But Mack wanted to be the hip teacher all the kids liked. He had a beard and wore his hair longer than any man on the faculty. He had lots of stories about peace and love to share, G-rated, of course, but they got the idea. Too bad he had to actually teach them something like *Beowulf* although Joey was doing a damn good job of it. A couple of the kids, the girls who always did their work on time and that nerd boy, had their hands up for questions. Joey spoke at their level about the mighty warrior who showed up at the king's great hall and how his people freaked out because a monster kept breaking in and killing them.

"After Grendel, Beowulf had to fight his mother, and you all know how mothers can be if they're really mad." He paused while the kids laughed, and then he recited, *"Grendel's mother, monstrous hell-bride, brooded on her wrongs."*

Joey paced in front of the room. He was up and down the aisles as he gave them a crash course in *Beowulf*. He was better than *Classic Comics* or *Cliff Notes*. He was almost as good as having the answers to the test. The little punks knew that. For once they shut up as Joey made them see *Beowulf* was a damn, great story about a warrior fighting monsters instead of some dull piece of crap in Old English. Of course, it was a bummer when Beowulf gets bumped off at the end, but he has a mighty funeral. The kids would talk about Joey for weeks. They would think he was a genius. They would be right, of course.

Joey jumped a little when the warning bell rang. Some of the kids groaned.

"That's all the time I have, so one more thing." The chalk flew from Joey's hand across the room as he spoke, *"They said that of all the kings upon the earth/ he was the man most gracious and fair-minded/ kindest to his people and keenest to win fame."*

KNOCK THREE TIMES

y time Tim arrived at the Westbridge VFW, Mack, Manny, and Joey were already at the back corner table next to the jukebox. The place was half-filled with townies, only a couple of women tonight, because the rest of them were probably home getting ready for the big Thanksgiving meal tomorrow. Tim knew that's what his mother was doing, baking pies and cranberry bread. She'll be in her glory when he and the rest of the family sit down for dinner.

A full beer stood in front of the empty chair on Joey's side of the table.

"It's about time you showed. I was thinking I might have to drink that beer before it got warm," Mack said. "What happened? Did one of the retards make a break for it?"

Tim ignored Mack as Manny offered his hand for a soul brother shake. This visit was only a pit stop for Manny. Tonight he was crashing at Tim's place before he took the bus to his folks' house tomorrow. He wanted to check in with the tribe. Tim said "hey" to Joey as he sat beside him and raised the bottle.

"Who do I thank for the beer?"

"Me," Manny said. "Where's Nina?"

"She left this morning to see her parents."

166

What Tim didn't say was Nina hinted all last week for an invitation to his mother's, but he didn't go for it. Bringing a girl to a holiday dinner was asking for trouble. He could see his sisters pulling him into the kitchen and pestering him with questions about their relationship. His mother would give Nina a close eye to see whether she was daughter-in-law material. So, no thanks, he wasn't ready for anything like that with Nina. Of course, they had a big fight about it, too.

Mack belched.

"I'm looking forward to a good meal tomorrow. My mother can sure roast a bird." Mack toggled his thumb at Joey. "Get this. Old Joey is eating with Inez Burke and Itch."

"Inez cooks?" Tim asked.

Joey grinned.

"She says not if she can help it. We're going to a restaurant. Some place fancy. I've gotta wear a tie and suit, so Inez is giving me something from Ned."

Mack hooted.

"My advice, Joey, is to not eat with your hands, and if food drops on the floor, it's definitely not cool to eat it no matter how long it's been there," Mack said. "Also, use the napkin a lot, but keep it on your lap. Course, if the place is that ritzy it should be made of cloth, so you won't have to worry about making a mess." He took a swig of beer. "Shit, I wish I could be a fly on the wall for that."

Tim's head swiveled toward Joey on his left.

"How'd did it go today in Mack's classroom? You know the *Beowulf* thing."

"*Lo, praise of the prowess of people-kings/ of spear-armed Danes, in days long sped,/ we have heard, and what honor the athelings won!*"

"I take it you did okay," Tim said.

Mack bent forward.

"You should've seen him. It was like Joey cast a spell over the kids. They just sat there with their fuckin' mouths open." He turned toward Joey, who was tearing the label off his bottle. "I think they learned something, too. What did that girl in my last class ask? Oh, yeah, she asked how much of *Beowulf* was history."

Joey grinned.

"What can I tell you? I was a hit."

The bottles shook when Mack slapped the table.

"You should've seen him talking in Old English. Say some of that shit, Joey."

"*Hwaet!*"

The music in the jukebox stopped, and another forty-five dropped onto its turntable. The song began.

Tim cocked his head when Joey began to giggle as "Knock Three Times" played.

"Don't tell me you picked this dumb song."

Joey shrugged.

"What can I tell you? The song's so dumb it's great."

Manny leaned across the table.

"You won't believe it, but this is the fourth time tonight he's played it. See those townies over there? They're getting pretty pissed having to listen to it again." Manny shook a finger toward their table. "Watch. One of those assholes will get up and stick some money in the jukebox and play something country. It's kinda been the battle of the bands here at the VFW."

Tim could tell the three of them were way ahead of him. They probably smoked a joint and drank a couple of rounds of beer. Funny how things seemed when you're on the outside. Mack still hogged the conversation as usual. Tim would rather hear Joey's version of what happened in his classroom. He wanted Manny to talk about law school and living in Boston.

Mack tipped his head toward Manny.

"The Portagee here was telling us about his visit to Lenora."

Tim set his bottle down. He heard some of the story over the phone. Manny rode the bus to New Hampshire during the Veterans Day weekend. He said they put him to work stacking firewood, which he said was just the thing to give his overworked mind a rest, that and a hike in the woods along an old logging road with Lenora and the baby.

"Lenora's real cool. Her baby's cute. She's crawling around. Real playful. I had a blast there."

Mack smirked.

"You two sleep together?"

"Jesus, Mack, it'd be none of your business if we did. But for the record, no, we didn't."

Mack waved his hand.

"Don't get so bent out of shape. It's not like you two don't have a history. So, is she shacking up with somebody there?"

"It didn't look like it. I could tell a couple of the guys want to. What else is new?" Air puffed through Manny's nose. "She's awfully busy taking care of that baby anyway."

Tim nodded. This was more than he had heard, but then Nina was there when Manny called, and she wouldn't have appreciated a lot of questions about Lenora in New Hampshire. Lenora wrote him a three-page letter at the end of summer about her new life at Great Meadow. She went on about the people who lived there and the farmer she works for. She wasn't planning to see her family until Christmas. Of course, she expected a letter back, but he hadn't written yet. What could he tell Lenora? I'm happy you're happy? I hate my job. I live in a junky apartment. By the way, Nina moved in.

Beside him, Joey sat sideways on the chair and leaned against the wall's knotty pine paneling while he sang with the music and knocked on the table at the right parts.

Manny's head jerked forward.

"Shit, here comes trouble," he mouthed.

Tim watched out of the corner of his eye as a townie marched across the room to the jukebox. Nobody at the table said a word, but they kept locking onto each other's gaze when the townie dumped a fistful of change into the machine and began punching its buttons. The juke's lights shined on his scowling face. Their mouths quivered with suppressed laughter. It'd be a while before they heard "Knock Three Times" again.

Joey half stood as he reached into his jeans pocket and put whatever coins he had onto the table. Tim picked up one of the quarters. Joey must have emptied his change jar.

"You're not thinking of playing that song again, are you?"

Joey glanced toward the townies' table. One of them flipped him a middle finger.

"Nope. I'm thinking we should call her," he said.

"Call who?"

"Lenora. I wanna tell her about Mack's class today." Joey pushed his glasses back up his nose. "Don't you ever think about her, Tim? Don't you ever miss her?"

The words "sure do" were out of his mouth without him thinking about it. Joey grinned and pointed toward the men's room.

"There's the payphone. I probably have enough. Come on."

Tim smiled as he raised the bottle to his lips. Lenora wouldn't expect a call.

"Maybe after a coupla more beers."

"I wouldn't wait too long," Manny said. "They all go to sleep with the chickens."

Mack shot upright in his chair and swore when Geneva walked through the front door of the VFW. She hustled toward their table.

"Fuck, she better not make a scene here. I told you about some of the crap she pulled on me," Mack muttered.

Geneva stopped at the end of the table, listening to their hellos. Mack was the last to say anything. She jammed her hands into the pockets of her long wool coat.

"Don't worry, Mack. I'm not here to bug you. I only came to say bye cause I'm leaving this weekend for the West Coast." She glanced around the room. "I sure as hell can't wait to get outta this dump."

Tim heard all about the trip from Nina and Geneva, when she came by the other night. She was driving cross-country by herself, stopping to visit a couple of people along the way. She still felt lousy about Mack dumping her. Geneva said she should have known better to fall for a guy like him, but they were together long enough she thought maybe he changed. Why not get the hell out of Westbridge? Nothing held her here.

"Be real careful out there, Geneva," Tim told her.

Geneva dragged the edge of her top front teeth over her bottom lip.

"Ain't you gonna say something, Mack?"

Mack gave her one of his stud smiles.

"Honey, it's been real nice knowing you. Send me a postcard when you get there, will ya?"

Her head swung back and forth.

"Maybe I will."

Tim, Manny, and Joey got up to hug the girl, because she looked like she was ready to cry when Mack went to the bar to get them another round of beer.

THE CALL

enora opened the oven door to check the pies. Juice from the apples began to bubble through the slits in the crust.

"Probably five or ten more minutes more," she told Alyce who kneaded dough for the rolls.

The women in the house had been baking and cooking since this afternoon. Everyone who lived at Great Meadow would be here for Thanksgiving, and they invited a few friends from town, including George Evans, the farmer next door. He supplied the turkey, one he delivered yesterday, plucked and cleaned. Dinner was done and the guys, who were splitting firewood most of the day, hung out in the kitchen. They brought their guitars and were jamming, mostly old folkie tunes, but some of it they had made up.

Lenora stooped. Isabel was beneath the kitchen table with Alyce and Matthew's youngest girl. She rubbed her eyes and whimpered.

"Hang on, sweetie," she told her.

Alyce waved her flour-coated hand.

"Put the baby to sleep. We'll take care of the pies. "

Lenora crouched beneath the table and wiggled her fingers so Isabel would crawl toward her. She scooped up the baby, and people called goodnight as she carried her from the kitchen. She was at the bottom of the stairs when the phone rang in the hallway, and Matthew, who answered it, said, "Lenora, it's for you. You want me to tell them to call back?"

"No, I'll get it."

She held Isabel in one arm as she took the phone from Matthew. It was probably her mother. She was disappointed she and Isabel weren't coming tomorrow, but she promised to see them at Christmas. She would stay as long as she could.

Instead of her mother's voice, she heard the jangling noise of a barroom.

"Lenora, it's me. You surprised?"

"Yeah, Joey, I'm surprised. What's going on?"

"Tomorrow's Thanksgiving."

"I know that, silly."

"I'm here with the guys at the VFW. Even Manny. We had a little bit to drink."

"Sounds like more than a little bit to me."

Joey's laugh exploded in her ear.

"You're so funny. Hold on. Somebody here wants to talk with you." She heard Joey say, "Take the phone. It's your turn."

Lenora shifted Isabel in her arm. Tim said in the receiver, "Hi, Lenora. How are you? Is that Isabel making that noise?"

Isabel babbled ma-ma-ma because she wanted to nurse.

"Uh-huh, that's her. You should see how big she is. She crawls all over the place. I have to keep an eye on her all the time, so she doesn't get into trouble."

"Cool." Coins dropped into the payphone's box on the other side of the line. Lenora sat on the chair beside the hall table. "I'm sorry I didn't write back. I guess I don't have much to tell you. I live a pretty boring life these days."

"Boring. Are you still working at Denton?"

"Yeah, but I wanna do something else."

Isabel tugged the phone's cord.

"What's stopping you?" The other end of the line was silent except for the background noise. "Tim, you there?"

"I'm still here. I'd like working for a newspaper. You know, reporting."

"I thought you were real good at it. Remember your story about Dean Hendricks? I liked the one about the custodians wanting a raise and the one about how many books get stolen from the library in a year. You wrote a lot of stories like that for *The Hard Truth*. You could do it again and get paid this time."

"That'd be nice." She heard Tim talk to Joey. "Take this. Ask the bartender for more change for the phone." He was back with Lenora. "You think I'd have a shot?"

"You have your clippings, don't you? You could go to the *Enterprise* in Brockville or even the *Standard Times*."

Lenora let Isabel settle into the crook of her arm. She lifted her blouse so the baby could take a nipple. In the kitchen, the guys played something by Jerry Jeff Walker. He came to Westbridge during her sophomore year. She went with Tim and Manny to the concert. Tim knew somebody at the door so they didn't have to pay.

"Thanks, Joey." Tim fed more coins into the phone. "That should last us a while. Sounds like you're having a party there."

"Party? No, some of the guys are playing music. We're all getting ready for the big feast here, and you know how guys get excited about food." She laughed. "You going to your mother's?"

"You know my mom. She wouldn't allow me to go anywhere else."

"I guess not. I mean what kind of son fakes graduation so his mother won't be disappointed? By the way, did she ever find out?"

Tim chuckled.

"Not so far. Maybe I'll tell her when she's real old and can't catch me."

She switched Isabel to the other breast. Tim said one of his sisters, Lenora met her a few times, had another baby. The boy was her fourth. The baby should keep his mother occupied. She wouldn't complain about what he was doing or his long hair and beard. Tomorrow, he'd end up drinking beer and watching football. He might take a walk around the neighborhood. Then Tim talked about the people they both knew from Westbridge. He told her about Geneva stopping by and what an ass Mack was to her.

"Are you still seeing Nina?"

He paused.

"Yeah, I am." He paused again. "She's moved in."

"Moved in?" She tried to keep her voice even and light. "It's getting serious?"

"I dunno."

"You don't know?"

"Please deposit eighty-five cents for the next three minutes."

"Shoot. I'm outta change. Where in the hell's Joey? Lenora, I'll call you again soon. I promise"

"Okay, Tim," she said before the line went dead.

She put the phone onto its cradle and stroked her sleeping daughter's head. She glanced at the phone and sighed. It wouldn't ring again tonight for her.

Matthew came from the kitchen. He held his youngest daughter's hand. The toes of her bare feet stuck out beneath her nightgown.

"Something wrong, Lenora?"

"No," she said softly.

Then she was on her feet and carrying Isabel up to their room.

DO WHAT I DO

The next afternoon, Inez Burke held a sports jacket as Joey worked his arms into the sleeves. The brown tweed belonged to Ned when he was younger and fitter, and before he reinvented himself into the grooviest professor at Westbridge State College. Inez stepped back to see the effect as Joey's eyes flitted around the room of Persian rugs, Tiffany lamps, and Pueblo pottery. He made a point of staying clear of all of them. He stood near the baby grand piano, where he felt semi-safe although the propped top made him nervous.

"Turn around, Joseph." Inez's charm bracelet clinked as her fingers wiggled, and Joey did as he was told. "I think he looks quite distinguished. What do you think, Mitchell?"

"Let me see."

Itch's ponytail hung over the back of his black suit as if he were an undercover nark ready to testify in court. He leaned forward to straighten Joey's paisley printed tie, which also belonged to Ned. So had the trousers. The scuffed brown boots were Joey's.

"Ned wore the jacket and pants when he got the job at Westbridge." She folded her arms. "I found it in the back of the closet."

Itch looked sideways at Inez. His lips lifted into a smile.

"Inez, I'll think we might be able to fool the maitre d' after all if we divert him from the footwear." He checked the grandfather clock beside the bookcase. "We should leave. It'll take an hour to get there."

Joey sat in the back seat as Itch drove them to an old inn west of Boston. Inez extended the invitation two weeks ago when he helped her clean the basement. She planned to move into a home she owned in Boston's Back Bay as soon as the lease ended with the tenant, a musician with the symphony. She was deciding what was worth taking and what to give away. Since Ned died, Joey went to her house most Saturdays to mow her lawn, rake leaves, or do whatever chore Inez needed. Sometimes she gave him a book from Ned's collection when she paid him.

The first time he protested, Inez clicked her tongue and said, "It's one less book to move. Don't worry. I'm keeping all the signed first editions. Did I ever show you the ones by Henry Miller? You should see what he wrote Ned."

Then as she paused over some kerosene lanterns and Mason jars in a corner shelf, she said, "Do you have plans for Thanksgiving? No? Would you like to join Mitchell and me for dinner? We'll dine at a very nice restaurant. My treat, of course." She pressed her lips. "Please. You will be doing me a great favor. I don't look forward to spending the day without Ned. He was a man who loved holidays."

Joey's foot tapped the car's floor as he watched the scenery. At Inez's request they were taking the back way. The trees went bare after Columbus Day weekend, and his room in the attic had been cold ever since. There was no insulation in the rafters, and whatever heat came up from the apartment got sucked through cracks in the roof's shingles and the gaps around the windows. He'd have to scrounge up some more blankets.

"Joey, do you have a book of matches back there?"

Itch held a joint. Joey sat forward and fished through the pants, surprising himself because there were no holes in the pockets. He tossed the half-twisted book to the front seat.

"To whet our appetites," Itch joked. "Do you mind, Inez?"

Inez shook her head as she rolled down her window. Joey never saw Inez smoke pot although Ned never let a joint pass without taking a hit. Inez's high of preference came from a bottle, preferably very old and very expensive.

Itch inhaled, and then held the joint for Joey. He took his turn. It didn't taste top shelf, but most of the pot you got through the Roach Brothers, Itch's regular suppliers, wasn't. He stuck the joint back between Itch's fingers.

"Thanks," he said as he exhaled.

"I hope you two don't break into fits of foolish laughter for no reason at the inn," Inez said flatly.

"Don't worry. Joey and I know how to behave in mixed company. We're seasoned potheads."

"I see." Sunlight glinted on the shoulders of Inez's fur coat. "I'm glad I'm not dining with a couple of amateurs."

When the joint was spent, Inez and Itch talked quietly in the front seat. Joey thought he dozed for a while, because the scenery changed remarkably and he couldn't remember how it happened. Last night, they didn't leave the VFW until last call. They were having too much fun. He made a snorting laugh, thinking about how he fooled Tim into talking with Lenora on the phone.

After he hung up, Tim said, "I told her about Nina living with me."

"You did? What for?"

Tim scrunched his lips and said, "She asked about her, and what could I do? Lie? She'd find out anyways, and then she'd really be mad at me."

"How'd she take it?"

"She sounded kind of funny. You know how her voice gets high and soft sometimes?"

The rest of the night Tim didn't say much. Even Mack noticed.

"Gee, Tim, did your mother die or something?"

Tim didn't answer.

Joey sat up when Itch pulled the car into the inn's driveway, and Inez was telling him she saw a parking space straight ahead. Inside the inn, they sat beside a fireplace where logs burned brightly behind a metal screen. Joey studied the well-dressed crowd and the table set with china while Inez talked with the waiter about the choices in wine.

Across the table, Itch winked.

"Just do what I do. You'll be fine," he told Joey.

PART THREE
ALL TOGETHER NOW

LEAN ON ME

Mack studied Joey as he slept in his hospital bed. His chest was the only part of him that moved beneath the white sheet, and it flipped him out to see his friend lie so still. Mack wanted to say shake that leg Joey, goddamn it. Twist something like a matchbook or napkin until there's nothing left but atoms. Get up. Walk around. Say some poetry, man, I've never heard before and don't understand. Knock me out with that big brain of yours.

But instead Joey breathed through his open mouth. His full beard hanging over the top of the sheet couldn't disguise how thin his face had gotten. Joey looked like one of those POWs they kept showing last year on the TV news, like he'd been living in a Vietcong prison and wasting away with nothing to eat but spoiled rice and bugs instead of the attic at 221 Winter Street. When Joey got up to use the toilet, now that the nurses let him out of bed, his legs were sticks beneath his hospital gown. His butt was flat and bony where the back came apart.

Joey had double pneumonia, and he could have died. It was unbelievable.

A nurse walked sneaky-shoed into the room. She was one of the young nurses, all in white, even her seamed stockings, with a perky little cap

181

stuck to her dark hair with bobby pins. She was the best looking of the bunch, and Mack had been here enough times visiting Joey to see them all. Mack eased himself upright in the chair and pulled his boots back so the nurse could get to the other side of the bed. Sunlight, bleached and useless because it was January, made a sweet spotlight on her ass as she fussed over her patient.

"How's he doing, Beth? It's Beth, right?"

The nurse flashed him a smile. Joey's eyes opened beneath her pointy tits.

"He does look better." Her attention was back on Joey. "Hello, Mr. Franklin. I'd like to take your temperature."

Joey had been a patient at St. Anne's Hospital in Brockville for over a week, ever since Tim found him beneath a heap of raggedy blankets in the attic. He stopped to check on Joey, because he hadn't heard from him since New Year's. Tim said Joey was so out of it he didn't wake up until he shook him hard and yelled in his ear. He got scared Joey was close to dying. One of the windows in the attic was missing, so Joey replaced it with cardboard, but wind forced enough dry flakes around the edges, snow formed piles beneath the eaves. Tim said his own breath came out white when he spoke to Joey.

Tim said he almost lost it finding Joey like that. He knew he had to get him to the hospital, but he couldn't carry him even though he was only skin and bones. Joey was too weak to make it downstairs, even with his help. He asked the kids who lived at the apartment when they last saw Joey, and they all shrugged. They thought he was away somewhere. Tim went next door to where Nancy and Lorraine used to live to use the phone to call an ambulance. The new girls let him.

Mack watched the nurse shake the thermometer before she stuck it beneath Joey's tongue. She talked to Joey, but her back was to Mack, so he couldn't hear what she was saying. He got up from his chair and stared out the window at the dirty snow in the alley below.

He got choked up when he first saw Joey lying in bed. They all did. The three of them felt like shit, like they had abandoned the guy. Sure, Joey should take care of himself, like Nina said, but Joey was Joey.

"Normal," the nurse said brightly. "I think you'll be leaving us soon, Mr. Franklin."

Mack looked over his shoulder. Joey tried to smile, but Mack read the worried expression on his face. The doctor said he wouldn't release Joey unless he had a good place to go, one where he was guaranteed three squares, a heated room, and someone to look out for him until he recovered. This was serious.

Joey couldn't go back to 221 Winter Street anyway. The Westbridge Board of Health condemned the place after one of the reporters from *The Hard Truth* wrote a front-page story about student slumlords, using what happened to Joey as an example. It stirred things up. The *Brockville Enterprise* did a story, and then a Boston TV station picked it up, complete with footage of Joey's attic bedroom, the blackened bathtub, and the stack of empties next to the fridge. Mack was sitting on a bar stool when he saw it on TV. He almost dropped his beer. Their old landlord squinted into the camera as he growled "I can't help it if those college boys lived like pigs." But the health inspectors found more than that: Bad wiring and plumbing, rats in the basement, leaky sewer pipes. The health board said it wasn't fit for humans and kicked everybody out. Mack and the others should be proud about the stink the new reporters at *The Hard Truth* made, but the do-gooders put Joey in a fix. He didn't have anywhere to go.

When they broke the news to Joey two days ago, the poor guy started crying.

"Don't worry, Joey, we'll figure out something," Tim had told him.

The three of them talked over Joey's situation and went over the list of possibilities. Joey's mom had moved to Florida and couldn't afford to fly him there. His old man went MIA years ago. Manny rented a room in a house in Boston, so he couldn't take him. There wasn't any space for Joey at the cabin Mack rented with a couple of grad students, and besides even if they had, they lived so far from Westbridge, Joey would have to hitch to get anywhere. Tim couldn't take Joey. He lived in a hole of a place at the Roach Motel with Nina, who wasn't exactly the Earth Mother type. What did Manny say about Nina? He hoped she and Tim didn't have any kids, because she'd be the type of mother to eat her young.

The three of them talked about who would be willing and able to take in Joey, but they came up empty. Big Ray, who loved Joey like a brother, was at divinity school. Anyway, Ray had become one of those pious pains in the ass, not quite as bad as a Born Again Jesus freak, but still annoying as hell. They even thought of calling Inez Burke since she had a soft spot for Joey, but she was on a trip somewhere in Europe. Itch was out of town.

At least Mack talked the cops into letting him inside 221 Winter Street so he could clear out Joey's things. The place didn't look that much worse than when they all lived there, except someone had ripped the sink out of the bathroom. The room reeked, but it always did. When he and Tim went to Joey's attic all they found were books, his old Remington typewriter, and papers. His clothes fit in one cardboard box. They didn't bother taking any of the blankets, because it smelled like poor Joey pissed himself when he was sick. All of his possessions fit in the trunk of Mack's Ford Fairlane.

The nurse smiled again at Mack. He could have run over and kissed her.

"Your friend's doing so much better."

Joey's squinting eyes reached Mack across the room.

"Where's Tim and Manny?" he rasped.

"I dunno. I thought they'd be here by now."

Joey smiled weakly as Manny appeared at the door. He had the guerilla grad look going with his trimmed beard, black clothing, and a Ché Guevara beret.

"Speak of the devil," Mack said.

Manny laughed as if he had just heard a joke.

"Joey, have I got a huge surprise for you. Are you ready?"

"Ready for what?"

Joey reached for his glasses on the nightstand. Manny waited until he had them on before he stepped aside.

"Come on in, mystery woman," he announced.

Manny's arm swung wide as Lenora walked through the doorway. She held out her arms and made such a big smile, the dimples on her face popped. Her brown woolen cape swirled over her laced-up boots as she charged toward Joey's bed. Her dark hair dropped down her back into one dark swell.

Joey raised his head from his pillow.

"Lenora, you came."

"Uh-huh. Tim called last night. Isabel and I took the bus from New Hampshire early this morning." She swooped forward, kissing the skinny freak's face. "Jesus, Joey, look at you."

Joey grinned the most Mack had seen all week. He, too, grinned. No one told him about Lenora.

"Where's the baby?" Joey asked.

"Isabel's downstairs with Tim. The nurses wouldn't let me bring her up. She's sitting on Tim's lap and having a great time pulling his beard, but I don't know how long that'll last. I told Tim to call the room if he runs into trouble." She whipped off her cape, letting it fly over Joey's blanket. Her Indian print skirt hung over her hips. She had gotten thin again. Their queen smiled at Mack as if all were forgiven between them. "Hey, Mack, how're you doing?"

"Nice that you came all the way to see old Joey."

"See Joey? Nobody told you?"

Mack stepped to the other side of the bed.

Joey kept grinning.

"Told me what?" he asked.

Lenora patted the hair back from Joey's forehead.

"I've come to spring you from this joint."

Joey blinked beneath his thick lenses.

"Spring me? Where am I going?"

"You're gonna come with Isabel and me to New Hampshire. The doctor said it was okay." She glanced back at Manny. "He almost changed his mind when I told him we were taking the bus, but then Tim said he'd drive us in his van."

Manny stood beside Lenora.

"You should've seen Lenora in the doctor's office," he told Joey. "All she had to do was flash that smile of hers and he was totally sold."

"New Hampshire. To the commune?" Joey said.

Lenora smiled at Joey.

"Tim told me about 221 Winter Street getting condemned. Bummer." She glanced across the bed at Mack, but her attention was back on Joey. "Matthew and Alyce said it was all right. You'll like Matthew. He went to Harvard. He's real smart so you can talk about books all you want. When you get better, they'll put you to work so you won't feel like you're freeloading."

"You sure about this, Lenora?"

"Yeah, you big goof. You can leave Great Meadow and come back to Westbridge when you're feeling better."

Joey gazed up at Mack.

"You gonna come with us tomorrow, Mack?"

Mack sniggered.

"Course, I will. I'll call in sick and let the little bastards make some poor substitute teacher's life miserable."

DIRTY RAGGED EDGES

enora and Manny walked together in the hallway outside Joey's hospital room. Most of her hair fell over one shoulder as she gave him a sideways look.

"Boy, Joey looks bad," she said.

"You should've seen him when Tim first found him. He was like death warmed over. It's a good thing Tim stopped by to check on him that day or he would've been a goner. The guys living there didn't give a rat's ass about Joey."

She sighed.

"Don't worry. I'll take care of him." She slowed her pace and Manny did the same. "Aren't you supposed to be in school?"

"I took a few days off."

She nodded.

"How's that going?"

"Fine. I work a lot harder than I ever did at Westbridge."

"I bet you do. You're a real good friend to come down from Boston."

"Hey, it's Joey."

She touched his beret.

"I like this thing you've got going."

"You do?"

"Uh-huh. Meet anybody?"

"Nah. You?"

"No."

They reached the door to the stairwell, Lenora playfully rushing ahead, using the handrails to vault the steps a few at a time. Manny chased her. Their voices echoed inside the hollow of cinderblocks. She glanced back, her eyes bright, as she kept a few steps ahead of him. He did catch her at the bottom, but she was through the door and into the corridor, slipping past his extended hand. Lenora halted, breathing a little hard. She looked down the hall where Tim walked Isabel. His back was to them, and he was singing and moving his elbows while he jiggled the baby. He spun slowly near the hospital's front door and broke into a grin. He came toward her.

Lenora laughed when her baby grabbed at the air and chirped, "Mama."

Later, she held Isabel as she waited for Tim to turn on a light in his apartment. A lamp covered with a red, silky cloth gave the small room a rosy glow. Tim threw his keys on the kitchen table.

"This is it. Not much, eh?" he said.

Lenora gazed around the room. A table with a Formica top, the one that used to be at 221 Winter Street, was in the kitchen corner next to a bed topped by satiny pillows and an Indian spread. A ratty couch and a bookcase jammed with textbooks and paperbacks were arranged in another part of the room. Roach clips, rolling papers, and candles were strewn on the wooden spool table in front of the couch. Janis Joplin smiled from a poster on the wall above the stereo as if she didn't care what she was doing. Beside her, Clint Eastwood wore his *Fistful of Dollars* serape and had a lit cheroot stuck between the thin lips of his poker face. Nina's things were everywhere: Her clothes, her jewelry, and a hat with a feathered plume.

"Looks cozy enough to me."

Lenora sat on the couch so she could get Isabel out of her snowsuit. The baby's eyes were all over the room. Tim stood near them.

"How old is she now?"

"She'll be one next month." Lenora worked the zipper of Isabel's suit. "Is it okay we stay here? Nina won't mind? You did ask her, right?"

"Course, I told her. Where else you gonna stay tonight?"

Lenora's mouth curled into a smile as she undressed the baby.

"That's not exactly the right answer, Tim."

He grunted.

"It'll be fine."

Lenora folded the snowsuit then patted her daughter's stomach as she lay on Tim's couch. Isabel plucked the air and kicked her feet. She wanted to crawl around the apartment, but all Lenora saw were dirty, jagged edges.

"Where are we gonna sleep?"

"The couch pulls out."

"That'll work." She lifted Isabel as she reached into her backpack. "I need to fix her some cereal. Do you mind holding her again?"

His hands were out.

"Let me have her."

Tim had Isabel in his lap when Nina came home later. Lenora sat beside them at the kitchen table. She whipped the spoon around the inside of the bowl to get the last of the cereal, but Isabel stuck out her tongue and rubbed the back of her head against Tim's chest in protest. Lenora laughed with Tim.

"I guess she's had enough," he said.

Nina shut the door too fast, letting frigid air shoot across the small room.

Lenora put the bowl on the table.

"Nina, come check out the baby," Tim called.

Nina took her time getting to the kitchen. She studied Isabel as she unzipped her jacket.

"She's got green eyes. She didn't get those from you. Your eyes are dark brown."

"No, she didn't." Lenora raised her chin. "How have you been Nina?"

"Tim and I are great. Aren't we, honey?"

She kissed the top of Tim's head. His nod was so slight it couldn't count as one as far as Lenora was concerned. She bent forward to clean Isabel's face before she untied her bib.

"That's good, Nina," she said without looking at her. "Tim, if you turn her around, she'll stand and jump. Hold onto her waist. That's the way. See how much she likes it?" She giggled. "Oh, you have cereal on your beard. Stay still. I'll wipe it off."

Tim chuckled as Isabel bounced and went "ba-ba." Nina threw her coat onto the bed. She was wearing all black, her waitress uniform for Angie's.

Tim said on the ride from the hospital Nina had dropped out of West-bridge. She was a full-time waitress at the restaurant.

Nina went to the dresser. She pulled the silver hoops off her ears.

Tim called to her.

"Nina, I'm gonna drive Joey up to New Hampshire tomorrow. He's staying with Lenora until he gets better. The doctor said it was a bad idea for him to take the bus. He wouldn't release him if he did." He paused as Nina kept her back to him. "Manny and Mack are coming, too. We'll be back the next day."

The bands of Nina's silver bracelets rattled as she dropped them in a heap onto the dresser top. Lenora saw the girl's reflection in the mirror. Her lips were a tight, white line as she listened to what Tim had to say.

HALF IN DREAMS

Lenora woke in the middle of the night. She had gotten up once already when Isabel wanted to eat, and she lay half in dreams listening to the windows shake in their frames. Beside her, Isabel was warm inside the sleeping bag. Lenora thought she heard the wind again, but Nina was crying in bed. Tim whispered to her.

She knew what it was all about. Ever since Nina came home, she sat on the other side of Tim, her arms crossed as she weighed what they said and didn't say. She gave a little dig of her own here or there in the conversation. "Oh, really," she said, rolling her eyes, after Lenora talked about the farmer next door teaching her to drive his tractor and how she drove in circles until she got the hang of it. Nina headed to the bathroom when Tim and she talked about the time they went fishing with Joey and none of them could catch a thing because he kept talking. She stayed in the bathroom so long, Tim knocked on the door until he got a muffled response telling him to stay the hell away. Tim shrugged when he sat down, but his neck was blotched red.

Lenora tried to block their voices with her hand, and then afterward the rustle of clothes and sheets. She pulled the pillow over her head when she heard the box spring move. She shut her eyes and focused on the wind.

A PROPER BUZZ

Tim sat up in bed. Lenora and the baby were gone. The sleeping bag she used was rolled on the open mattress of the couch. She had stacked the pillows and the sheet beside it. Next to him, Nina opened one eye. "Did you hear her leave?" he asked.

"She's gone? Good riddance." Nina patted the space beside her. "Get back in bed."

Tim listened for noise in the bathroom while he dug a clean pair of briefs from the dresser drawer and sat on the mattress to put them on. Nina crept toward him, wrapping her arms around his waist. Her breasts flattened against his back.

"Cut it out, Nina. She might come back." He pointed toward the door. "She couldn't have gotten very far. Her bag's over there. See?"

Nina flopped back naked onto the bed.

"So what."

Tim started for the bathroom.

Afterward he followed Lenora's boot prints in the dust of snow that fell last night. She got as far as three apartments down, Professor Mitchell's bachelor pad. Tim knocked on his door. Itch, dressed in a silky, blue robe, and slippers, answered with a mug in his hand.

"Just in time, neighbor. I've made another pot of coffee. I warn you it's only marginally better than Jimmy's, but it'll give you a proper buzz and stunt your growth." Itch shut the door behind Tim. "I suppose you're looking for my breakfast guests. Heard they snuck out without you knowing."

Through the living room's opening, Tim saw Lenora sitting on Itch's black leather couch. She held Isabel on her lap, and the baby peeped when she recognized him. Lenora nodded. Her hair was pulled into two braids she pinned around her head, giving her that Madonna of Westbridge look she sometimes wore way back when.

"I'll take that cup. A little milk would be great if you have it," he said.

Itch shuffled in his slippers to the kitchen.

"Have a seat. I'll be back," he shouted from the kitchen.

Tim sat next to Lenora. Isabel bounced forward in her lap, her hands stretched out as she babbled "ba-ba." Lenora let the baby crawl over the couch to his lap. Tim chuckled when she tugged the hairs of his beard. He gave her a little hug.

"She likes you," Lenora said quietly. "I don't know why. You're such a bastard."

"Lenora."

Before he could say more, Itch was back with his coffee.

"Lenora was telling me about Joey getting sick and how the Board of Health condemned Winter Street. I sure hope the board doesn't take a close look at the Roach Motel." Itch clicked his tongue. "I'm sorry I didn't know about any of this. I got back yesterday from a conference." He handed Tim his coffee. "I'll certainly see what I can do with the administration for Joey."

Tim sipped the coffee, holding the mug away from Isabel. He winced. Itch wasn't kidding. It was horrible.

"We're taking Joey to where Lenora lives," Tim said.

"She told me all about that. You might want to postpone your trip a day or two. I hear a bad storm's coming."

"How bad?"

"A foot of snow. Maybe more. How are the van's tires?"

Tim eyes kept traveling toward Lenora. Nina definitely wouldn't put up with her and the baby staying another day. And Lenora acted like she was fed up about something.

"Decent. Besides, it rides okay in snow. That little engine doesn't have much power, but at least it sits in the back, and we'll have a lot of weight with all those people. I think we'll be all right." He nodded at Lenora. "We should go. Joey's supposed to get discharged at eleven. Mack and Manny should be here soon."

Lenora grabbed the baby's snowsuit from the back of the couch.

"Come here, Isabel, so I can dress you."

Tim downed the rest of the coffee. Itch scrambled toward a desk. He raised a finger.

"Wait a minute." He scribbled on a piece of paper he tore from a pad. He gave it to Lenora. "This is Inez's address in Boston. She'd love to hear from you. She'd want to know how Joey's doing. She's quite fond of that boy. We all are."

Lenora stuck the paper in her coat pocket. She reached for Isabel.

"Thanks. I'll write her."

Minutes later, outside Professor Itch's door, Tim grabbed Lenora's arm. Her eyes were sharp when she spun around.

"You're mad at me."

"Brilliant conclusion, Mr. Devlin." The words chopped in her mouth like bits of ice. "Can you guess why?"

Tim moaned.

"Shit, you heard us."

"It didn't sound like Nina was making any effort to keep quiet." She squeezed her voice as she imitated the girl badly. "Oh, Tim, that's the way. I love you, Tim. Oh, Tim. Oh, Tim."

"Lenora, stop. Please."

She pulled the baby's mittens tightly on her hands. Isabel's cheeks were pinked by the cold.

"I can see what's going on." She shifted the baby onto her hip. She blinked back tears. "Congratulations to the both of you. I hope you'll be very happy together."

"How about you? At the party, you, me, and Manny. Then, you went off with Joey and who knows who else."

"You're right. I was a complete slut that weekend. Here, you go, Tim. I forgive you."

But Tim didn't hear any forgiveness in her voice. He had witnessed Lenora fling anger at other guys who crossed her, but never against him.

Maybe, they didn't care, but he did. He blew air through his mouth. Damn that girl and her X-ray mind.

"For Christ's sake, Lenora."

Tim spied Nina standing in the open door of their apartment, barefoot and wearing a red kimono with yellow flowers as she watched Manny and Mack carry boxes from the trunk of Mack's Fairlane to the back of his VW van. Nina played with the robe's sash.

Lenora saw her, too. She wiped tears from her cheeks.

"Let's get Joey," she told Tim.

THE RIDE

Tim checked the rear-view mirror of his VW van. Joey sat wrapped in a blanket in the middle seat because the heater was useless. Lenora insisted he wear her cap, crocheted with purple yarn and a big yellow flower off to the side, which he pulled down to his glasses, so he looked as if they picked him up at a soup kitchen instead of St. Anne's Hospital in Brockville. Lenora sat beside him with Isabel. Manny was in the very back seat. Mack rode shotgun.

"Everybody all set?" Tim asked.

Manny leaned against the pile of sleeping bags and stretched his legs over the seat.

"Ready to roll, captain," he said.

Lenora stared out the side window of the van's sliding door.

"Damn the torpedoes. Full speed ahead," Tim said

Mack fiddled with the radio, trying to pull in a rock station from Boston. He wore a watch cap, heavy wool jacket, and boots. He said it felt great to dress like a man instead of a teacher.

"Got it," Mack said, pounding the beat on the dashboard and throwing his head back as he sang off-key to "Cisco Kid."

Tim backed the VW from the parking space in the hospital's lot.

"Lenora, is Joey comfortable enough?"

Her dark eyes met Tim's briefly in the mirror before she asked Joey, "How are you doing?"

Joey grinned as he raised a thumb.

"A-okay."

Lenora's gaze swept toward the side window. Tim swore under his breath as he put the van in first. She was killing him.

They drove north from Brockville, detouring around Boston. They still hadn't met the storm although the sky's belly was gray and full. All the way, Mack fiddled with the radio, switching channels for the songs he liked. He yakked about the good times at Westbridge, asking Tim whatever happened to so-and-so, as if they hadn't spent most of the last week together in Joey's hospital room. Tim listened only enough to keep the talk going. Mack's conversations seemed to spin in small loops these days. Now, he talked about his ex, Geneva, and how her car broke down in Las Vegas when she was driving cross-country, and that's as far as she got. Tim had heard this one at least four times. She was dealing blackjack at one of the casinos. Geneva sent Mack a postcard, claiming she met the old has-been Elvis with his white jumpsuits and cape. Mack pretended he didn't care.

"I wonder how Geneva's doing in Vegas. I don't think she'd cut it as one of those dancers who only wears a couple of feathers and some sequins. She doesn't have the bod for it. But she's got big tits. That's probably why the casino hired her to deal blackjack. I bet she wears one of those getups that squeezes her tits so tight they look ready to pop from her top."

"Why don't you go see her and find out?" Tim said.

"Vegas? Eh, too plastic."

Manny was zonked out in the back seat. He told Tim he and Mack went to the Westbridge VFW after visiting hours were over at the hospital. It was Wednesday. Draft beer was a dime. They nearly got into it with a couple of vets over goddamn Nixon and Watergate so they decided to haul ass before they got thrown out of the joint.

Behind him, Lenora talked quietly with Joey until he fell asleep. So did the baby as Lenora nursed her. In the rear-view mirror, Tim stared at her breasts, white and full, her nipples a brownish pink, as Isabel pushed up her blouse. Lenora hummed as she fed her. He recognized the tune. His mother sang it. His sisters, too. The baby's eyes closed slowly.

"Does she ever bite you?"

Mack was half-turned around his seat.

Lenora yanked down her blouse.

"Only once on purpose, when she got her first tooth. It scared her when I cried, so she didn't do it again. Sometimes it happens when she falls asleep and her jaw shuts, but she doesn't mean to do it. Any other questions about breastfeeding?"

"Not now," Mack said as his head swung forward.

They stopped at a diner after they reached New Hampshire. Tim parked the VW in front of a bank of dirty snow. They walked in a pack, Mack leading the way, to the door. The guys lit cigarettes, except for Joey, who was dying for one, but thought it'd be a bad idea considering he had pneumonia. They stamped their feet on the snow and joked about the cold. Lenora and the baby brought up the rear.

Inside the diner, the truck drivers at the counter were busy with their food, but they raised their heads above their plates when the group filed toward the window booths. Tim was glad Mack made Joey take off Lenora's hat. Now, he looked like a sick, skinny freak instead of a sick, skinny lunatic. Tim, Manny, and Mack slid into one booth. Joey and Lenora sat in the one beside it. The waitress brought menus.

"Coffee all around?"

"Yeah, honey, except for the baby. She's drinking mother's milk," Mack told her.

The waitress, whose hair was dyed an unnatural shade of red, cackled.

Lenora stood, lifting Isabel to her hip as she stooped for her backpack. She was going to change Isabel's diaper, and she told Joey what she wanted before she headed toward the back of the restaurant for the women's room. Lenora's hips had a nice wiggle when she walked, and the truck drivers all made a point of watching.

Tim moved to Joey's booth.

"You hanging in there, Joey?"

"Yup, I have a great nurse." Joey grabbed a napkin from the holder as he removed his glasses. "I really appreciate everything, bro."

"You'd do the same for me, bro."

"Anywhere. Anytime. Any place." Joey breathed on the lenses and wiped them clean. "What's wrong with Lenora?"

"What do you mean? She seems okay to me."

"She's uptight about something. Every time you ask her a question she barely answers. You two have a fight or something?"

Tim checked the back of the restaurant. Lenora wasn't returning yet.

"Nina and I did something that definitely wasn't cool. It really ticked Lenora off." He shook his head. "Man, I feel like crap."

"It couldn't have been that bad."

Tim sighed.

"Yeah, it was. And Lenora's not letting me off the hook."

Joey made a snorting laugh.

"I wonder why."

"What do you mean?"

"Shit, Tim, you figure it out."

"Figure out what?"

Joey shook his head. *"Give all to love;/ Obey thy heart."*

"Jesus, I'd slug you if you weren't so fucking sick."

Joey grinned.

"Go ahead. I dare you." The waitress set cups of coffee on the table. Joey reached for the sugar. "Emerson wrote it by the way."

The waitress tapped her pen against her pad.

"You boys ready to order?" she asked.

Joey hadn't opened the menu. Tim wondered how much dough he could have. He thought maybe nothing.

"I'm gonna have the tuna fish sandwich with French fries. Could you toast the bread? Sound okay, Joey?" He waited for Joey's nod. "Make it two. What did Lenora tell you she wanted? Oh, yeah. Dry toast and the vegetable soup." The waitress scooped up the menus. "Lunch is on me, Joey."

"Thanks, Tim." Joey stirred his coffee. "Watch out. Here she comes. Ooh, I see steam coming out of her ears. No, no, don't get up. Stay here."

Tim glanced over his shoulder. The hem of Lenora's patchwork skirt rippled as she came toward them. She stopped at the end of the table.

"I believe you're in my seat."

He moved toward the window.

"No, I'm not."

Joey plucked a napkin from the table.

"Your order's coming, Lenora," Joey said. "Watch out behind you."

She sat beside Tim as the waitress set the bowl of soup and toast on the table. Lenora broke off a piece for Isabel, who said "ba-ba" when she took it.

"I thought I was ba-ba," Tim said.

"Everything's ba-ba right now, except me." Lenora reached toward the floor for her bag. She handed Tim a jar filled with applesauce. "Could you open it for me? Please? It's for Isabel."

Tim twisted off the top and set the jar on the table. Isabel's lips made little smacking sounds.

"Boy, she likes that."

Lenora lifted the jar to his nose.

"Smell. It's homemade."

Joey stood.

"I'm gonna use the john," he said.

Lenora kept feeding the baby. She hadn't touched her soup.

"Lenora, stop for a minute."

She held the empty spoon.

"What is it?"

"Please don't be mad at me. I hate it." He paused when she raised one eye. "I messed up big time last night. Those things I said. I'm sorry. I'm really, really sorry."

Lenora sighed. "I'm sorry, too."

"Then we're friends again?"

"Sure, Tim, if that's what you want."

The snow started falling several miles later. The wind drove small dry flakes across the road in waves. The waitress warned them they were expecting at least a foot, likely more as they headed north and west, so they'd better get going before it got too bad. The road stayed decent until Concord, where they stopped briefly at a pay phone so Lenora could call ahead to Great Meadow.

"Matthew said they've already plowed once," she said when she slid the side door back.

Mack piped up.

"Who in the hell is Matthew? Is he the leader of the ashram? Your guru?"

"How many times do I have to tell you it's a commune and not an ashram?" Her hands were out. "Here, Manny, I'll take her back."

Manny, who had switched places with Mack for the front seat, handed her Isabel. Lenora and Joey stayed in the middle.

After a while, Manny switched off the radio. All it could get was a crappy easy listening station anyway. Before that, they listened to news on the public radio station, and Manny kept getting agitated about Watergate. He sounded a little like Big Ray when he muttered, "The little bastard's not going to get away with it this time," but then, they lost the channel, which was fine with Tim. He was trying to concentrate on the road.

Mack hung over the middle seat between Lenora and Joey as he fired questions about Great Meadow. What was it like living in a commune? Was it a cult like the Mansons? Did they wear clothes? Each time, Lenora made a face before she answered. Tim laughed. Mack was getting a rise out of her, and he enjoyed hearing Lenora talk her way out of it. So did Joey, who wore a shit-eating grin, and Manny who made braying laughs. The baby was wide-eyed at the noise. Lenora was being Lenora again, sassy and smart, fending off any remark as if she were the winning contestant on some TV quiz show. Their queen was happy, so all was well in their freaking little world again.

"No, we wear clothes. It's too cold in New Hampshire to go around naked," she said.

She waited for Mack to come up with another crazy question.

"Do you have group sex?"

They all hooted when she answered, "Only the farm animals, Mack."

"Got any boyfriends up there?"

"Boyfriends? No, and that's the end of that one."

"Are you vegetarians?"

"Mostly. We eat what we raise."

"Hot damn, you've gone native on us, Lenora," Mack said.

The banter helped Tim stay loose as he followed the tracks in the snow made by the cars and trucks that went ahead. The wipers moved the snow so two wide wedges were the only cleared glass on the windshield. When he squinted through the falling snow, he saw red taillights in the distance. He kept the speed steady, and the tires made a zipper-like noise as they gripped the snow. He hummed in the back of his throat. The banks along the road reached the windows of the van. Westbridge never had this much snow.

"This is the fucking sticks, Lenora. Why in the hell did you move all the way up here?" Mack asked.

"It's a good place to live. You'll see when we get there," she said.

"Where's the closest bar?"

"About twenty miles. Wilbur doesn't have one."

"Jesus, Joey, it's like you're moving to a monastery," Mack said.

"The guys try brewing beer," Lenora said. "It's not too good, but we do grow our own weed. Matthew calls it Great Meadow Gold."

"Far out," Mack said.

It was nearly dark when they crossed the line into Wilbur, founded in 1807, elevation 843 feet and population 350, according to the road sign, and then they didn't see a building again until they passed the town's general store, which was already closed.

Lenora leaned forward. Her breath was warm on Tim's neck.

"You're gonna take the next left," she told him.

"How much farther do we have to go?"

"About four miles." She thrust her hand forward. "Slow down. You're turning there. Tim, keep it in second."

Tim liked having her voice close to his ear.

"Lenora, I'm positive she means me when she says ba-ba."

"You can believe it if you want, but I heard her say it to one of the dogs. Maybe it's cause you're both so hairy."

He laughed with her.

"She might have a point there," Tim said.

The snowy road followed a small river through the woods before it wound around a large pasture.

"Is that it?" Manny asked.

"No, that's George Evans' farm. He's the bachelor farmer who pays me to clean his house and cook for him. Don't say anything, Mack. He's sort of old." She laughed. "We're almost there. We're gonna take a right and head up a hill. Stay in the middle of the road, so we don't go off the side."

"You're shitting me," Tim said.

"No, I'm not. Oh, look. Someone plowed. I bet they brought the tractor down."

They were three-quarters of the way up the hill when the wheels spun and dug a little. Tim swore, but he kept the van moving forward, and they all cheered when they reached the top. Several yards ahead, a farmhouse glowed through the falling snow. A sign said: GREAT MEADOW.

"That's it. Don't stop. Just pull through the gate. See. They plowed the driveway for us," Lenora said as the baby began to cry. "Shhh, Isabel. They're only happy we made it."

A man wearing coveralls strolled from a barn toward the van. His gray hair stuck out beneath a red woolen cap. Snow collected on the ends of his beard.

Tim rolled down the window.

"You must be Tim. Hi, I'm Matthew. A long, hard trip, eh?" He pulled off his woolen gloves and the bottom side of his hand was rough when he shook Tim's. Grinning he peeked inside the VW van. "There's Lenora and little Isabel. Welcome back, you two."

AT GREAT MEADOV

Lenora studied Joey as he slept in the bed set up for him in the library. She pushed back his hair and placed her hand on his forehead. His skin felt slightly warm.

Beside her, Tim whispered, "Is he okay?"

"He's just beat. You saw him at dinner. He could barely keep his eyes open."

She glanced toward the windows. The wind had picked up, and now snow pummeled the glass. Tim noticed it, too.

"Looks like we got here just in time," he said. "I'd hate to be driving in that mess in the dark."

"That'd be awful."

She rearranged the blankets so Joey's shoulders were covered. This was his room for now. It was Alyce's idea. Eventually he'd move in with one of the guys when he was stronger. Tonight, Tim, Manny, and Mack would sack out on the mattresses they dragged down from the attic.

"Will we be able to get out tomorrow?"

"No, Tim, I'm afraid you're gonna be stuck here with us until the snow melts." She smiled to herself. "You'll have to call your girlfriend and tell her you're not gonna make it back any time soon. Your boss, too."

"You're pulling my leg, aren't you?"

"Course, I am. Don't worry. We'll get you dug out and send you on your merry way to Westbridge."

"You're such a funny girl."

He grabbed her wrist, but she wriggled away.

"That's what I am all right." She saw his grin in the dim light. "We should let him sleep."

She shut the door behind them. She heard Mack's voice in the kitchen. One of the girls laughed hysterically. Manny and a couple of the guys were in there with them.

"You can join them if you want," she said.

Tim shrugged.

"Only if you do."

"Watch Mack in action? No thanks." She stuck out her tongue. "Follow me."

Tim followed Lenora upstairs to the second floor and along the hallway, past the door to her room where Isabel was asleep, to a small space beside a large window where there was a short couch and a table with a reading lamp. She sometimes sat here with Isabel, daydreaming and getting away for a while.

She sat and reached for the lamp's switch.

"What do you think of Great Meadow?"

"People seem cool, especially Alyce and Matthew. Joey's gonna be all right here." He rubbed his beard. "But."

"But what?"

"It seems so far away."

"Far away from what?"

"The people you care about. Like your family and us."

"Us." She paused. "I've got Joey here. Manny's in Boston. Geneva's in Vegas. You're not thinking about Mack, are you?" Her eyes narrowed. "I didn't think so. You can't be talking about the Roach Brothers or the Dirty Old Bastards. Oh. Did you mean you?" She made a soft "huh" in the back of her throat. "I'm not sure your girlfriend would like that. I can hear Nina now." She raised the pitch of her voice. "'What the hell's she doing here, Tim? Huh, Tim?' "

"Lenora, stop that."

Lenora pressed her lips.

"Did you finally get ahold of her?"

"No. She must've gone out. She said she might."

"She *did*?"

Tim frowned.

"Lenora, let it go, will ya?"

"Sorry. I can't help it." She peeked over her shoulder as snow slammed against the window. "What *do* you want to talk about? What's safe? I know. Work. You still at Denton?"

"Yeah, but I did stop by the *Brockville Enterprise*. I talked with the editor-in-chief and showed him my clippings." The corner of Tim's mouth curled upward. "He remembered the Dean Hendricks profile. I guess his wife took a night course there, and she used to bring home *The Hard Truth*. But he didn't have anything. He told me to check back in a couple of months. Something might open up then."

"He's interested. I knew it."

"He only said maybe."

"A maybe is a lot better than a flat-out no. You'll see."

Tim sat back.

"What about you? How long are you planning to stay down on the farm?"

She shrugged.

"I dunno. I like it here."

He stretched his arm along the back of the couch.

"If you didn't have the baby, what would you be doing?"

She thought for a moment. It was hard to imagine life without Isabel, but Tim wanted an answer.

"Probably living in a big city, saving up enough to travel some more. I'd fall hard for another jerk who doesn't deserve me and I'd get all bent out of shape when he splits. Just like the old days at Westbridge." She laughed. "Thank goodness for Isabel."

"Man, you sure could pick 'em."

"What do you mean?"

"Manny and I joked about it. We'd see a group of guys and choose which one you'd want. We were usually right. You seemed to like 'em tall. Long hair, of course. It didn't matter the color. Always good looking although that guy in your junior year sure wasn't." He snorted. "You're always a sucker for guys who say they're writers."

"Sounds like you and Manny have me all figured out."

"Ha, you were our case study for four years. By the way, Manny and I looked over this bunch. We couldn't figure it out though. Maybe that guy, Joshua. Or was it James? What's with all the long names anyway? Are they monks or something?" He snickered. "Course, we haven't met the farmer yet."

She threw her head back as she laughed.

"George? No way. It's nothing like that. And, no, I don't have anything going with anybody here." She poked his chest playfully. "Why are you so interested? You have a girlfriend. Yeah, yeah, you don't wanna talk about her."

Tim's arms and legs spread open. He chuckled and smiled at whatever Lenora said. He showed all the signs. Not this time, she told herself. She decided that earlier tonight when Tim sat beside her at dinner and spoke only to her unless somebody asked him a question. At one point, his hand held hers beneath the table. If Tim wanted to be with her, he was going to have to work harder than this. She wasn't up for any of this love on the fly.

"Sometimes you drive me crazy, Lenora, like today. First, you act like you want to murder me. Now, you're being real nice again. What's with that?"

"I dunno. You tell me." Loud laughter from the kitchen funneled its way up the stairway. She glanced toward her bedroom door. "Do you hear Isabel?" She listened. "I better check on her. The kitchen's below my room." She nodded at Tim. "Maybe you should get to sleep now. It's awfully late, and you have another long trip tomorrow." She patted his knee. "Your bed's ready in Joey's room."

Tim's smile faded fast.

"I suppose you're right."

She followed Tim to the top of the landing and watched him walk downstairs. He turned once, but she didn't call him back. She went to the room she shared with Isabel.

FAREWELL TO THE NORTH

T im let the VW van's engine get warm. The sky broke blue between the ragged bits of cloud left by the storm that cleared this morning. He woke once when he heard Joey talking in his sleep and realized the storm had passed. He went to the window and watched the last, fat flakes float downward. He lay back on the mattress and thought of Lenora sleeping in the room above him. He wished he could stay. He wanted more time with her, but that wasn't going to happen. He fell asleep listening to Joey talk nonsense.

Tim shoved his bare hands inside his coat pockets and lifted one cold foot then the other on the snow-packed driveway. Matthew was out before breakfast using the tractor to plow the snow that fell last night, eighteen inches by the man's estimation. Manny and Mack loaded their things into the van. The redheaded girl who slept with Mack last night tailed them. Tim watched as Lenora came through the front door with her baby in one arm and a grocery bag in the other. Joey, bundled in somebody else's warm clothing, was beside her, looking pale and pinched as he blinked in the sunlight.

Lenora stepped off the porch. She handed Tim the bag.

"Here's some food for the road. Alyce was afraid you'd starve or something."

"Manny, put this somewhere safe."

He sniffed the bag.

"Food."

It was going to be another long ride, especially since they were dropping Manny in Boston. Matthew gave Tim advice on how to drive the hill to the main road, which basically was to keep the van in low gear and stay in the middle unless someone comes the other way. He said the road from Wilbur to Concord should be decent. It'd be a piece of cake after that on the interstate.

Tim and Matthew shook hands. Behind him, Manny hugged Joey, and then Lenora. Mack was somewhere with the redhead.

"We'll take care of your friend. Right, Lenora?" Matthew said behind him.

"Uh-huh," she said.

Tim walked toward Joey and tugged his woolen cap to the top of his glasses. Joey made his most idiotic grin.

"Get better, bro. I'm gonna miss you."

"Farewell to the highlands, farewell to the North/ The birthplace of Valor, the country of Worth."

Matthew nodded at Joey.

"Robert Burns?" he asked.

Joey raised a finger.

"Bingo."

Tim went toward Lenora and her rosy-cheeked baby.

"Have a safe trip back," she told him.

He ran his finger beneath the baby's chin.

"Be good, Izzie."

"Ba-ba."

Lenora's red, woolen mitten tapped the front of Tim's jacket.

"Tim. His name is Tim." She shifted Isabel in her arms. "She'll say it the next time we see you."

"I dunno when that'll be."

Lenora tipped her head to the side as if she had to think it over.

"Now you know where to find us."

Everything about Lenora was still. It seemed as if she were standing with her baby in the center as everything else spun around her. Tim wanted to share that spot or pull her out of there with him so they moved together. She was too beautiful to leave behind. So without thinking more or even asking, he kissed her quickly but softly on the lips, and afterward Lenora made a breathy little laugh as she said his name.

"I guess I'll have to surprise you some day," he told her.

She laughed again and told him back, "Why don't you do that."

URGE FOR GOING

Lenora was stacking dishes in the cupboard when George Evans stamped the barn muck off his boots at the back door. He greeted her as he padded in his white socks, heels first, into the kitchen, and then he was at the sink, washing his rough farmer's hands.

"You're done already, George?"

"No, but I wouldn't mind having a cup of tea and some more of that pumpkin pie you made. How about taking a break, Lenora?" He spoke over the running water, and then he whistled a tune she supposed he made for his cows when he milked. "I see you beside the icebox, Isabel. Come have pie with me."

Isabel chugged forward, stiff-legged and with her hands out for balance. She said George's name although not quite all of the last G. He picked her up and held her hands under the water with a tenderness you wouldn't expect from a man who never had children. Lenora smiled as Isabel watched the water flow over her hands.

"Isabel, you have nice long fingers. You'll make a good milker when you get bigger." George used a dishtowel to wipe her small hands. "Okay, all clean. Let's eat."

"Pie," Isabel said.

"Ayuh, let's have some pie."

Lenora lit the burner beneath the kettle before she reached for two small plates of pink glass. She figured George must be around sixty-five. She was certain he never smoked pot although he drank, because there were bottles in the trash. He also bought dirty magazines, because she found them when she put his laundry away. She wondered whether he ever had a serious romance since he never mentioned a woman. His father died in a tractor accident when George was a junior in high school, so he didn't get to finish. He needed to work the farm. He was the oldest of three sisters and one brother, the baby. Lenora wondered at what point George gave up having his own family.

George sat with Isabel on his lap, bright-eyed and ready for anything. She took her nap earlier on the couch, a relic of burgundy velvet, horsehair, and carved wood that belonged to George's mother who died two years ago. Both watched Lenora move around the kitchen, cutting wedges of pie, a large one for George and a small one for her to share with Isabel. She poured the hot water into the cups and set them on the table out of Isabel's grab. George liked his tea with milk. She took hers plain.

Lenora sat.

"George, let me have her."

Isabel opened her mouth for the first piece. Across the table, George hummed in the back of his throat then swallowed.

"Good pie."

Lenora smiled. George could have been in church, the way he spoke so softly.

She came here twice a week, on Mondays and Thursdays, to clean, wash, and make enough food to last George until she returned. She usually walked the few miles. Today, she pulled Isabel in a red wagon with fat wheels that belonged to George when he was a boy. In the winter, she used a sled with red runners he found in the barn's loft. If the weather was stormy, George drove them. He whistled the same cow-milking tune there and back.

George wrapped the string of his teabag around the spoon to squeeze it dry.

"Lenora, you're supposed to be back Thursday, but I'm hoping you'd come an extra day this week to wash the windows on the first floor." He cleared his throat. "I'd pay you extra, of course."

"I can do that."

He cleared his throat again.

"I have some other chores. Nothing hard. I should box up mother's clothes for the church's Indian mission. They're in her room. Someone could put them to better use. Maybe there are some things you'd like although she had a bigger … I mean she was a bigger woman than you."

Lenora smiled, but not too much, because George's clean-shaven face was pink to his hairline.

"That'll be fine, George. I can come Saturday. Isabel, have the last bite. Open up. We have to get going."

Later, the wheels of the red wagon rattled over the dirt and stones of the farm's driveway as Lenora towed Isabel back to Great Meadow. It was late in the day, and although it stayed lighter longer, there was a chill in the air fed by the wetlands beside George's farm. Spring came so much later to Wilbur than any other place she lived. Isabel sat in the wagon, saying "Mama, look" as something small stirred the dead leaves along the road or at a stubborn drift of dirty snow or the gaudy green of skunk cabbage that popped on the banks of the stream. They made the turn and started up the hill. It was a game to see how far up Lenora could take the wagon before she had to ask Isabel to walk, now that she could, or she carried her piggyback.

Lenora heard a sharp whistle from the hilltop. Joey stood there with two fingers in his mouth. Isabel shouted "Joey" as if there was a W in his name, and he joked the first time he heard her say it he should change the spelling.

Joey used his full arm to wave. Lenora couldn't remember when he was this healthy, not even when he arrived at Westbridge as a freshman. He filled out on good food and when he was strong enough, farm and shop work. He kept himself clean. He even trimmed his beard and tied his hair back. Joey said it was because of her, but she thought it was Matthew's influence. The two hit it off from the start. Both loved shooting the shit and literature.

Lenora stopped the wagon, and Isabel climbed out with much effort.

"Take my hand, Isabel. We're in the road."

The wagon rattled behind them as Lenora shortened her steps to match her daughter's. Joey came jogging toward them, and Isabel hid behind Lenora, all giggles, clutching the back of her long skirt until Joey swooped her up.

"I've got you, Izzie."

"Jo-wey."

He spun Isabel around as she squealed his name. He stopped and blew on her neck. He grinned at Lenora when he held up both hands.

"I see you had another good day in the woodshop," she joked.

"It's a miracle I haven't lost a finger yet. They actually let me use the table saw today. It scared the crap outta me."

Joey bounced Isabel in his arms as they walked together up the road.

"You packed?" she asked him.

"Getting there." He chuckled when Isabel placed her hand on his mouth, and then he said, "What are you doing, Izzie?"

"Jo-wey talk."

He shook his head.

"I'm gonna miss you both so much," he said.

"We're gonna miss you, too, Joey. You could stay if you want. Matthew said it was okay."

"Lenora, do you think I'm cut out to be a farmer or a carpenter?"

"Nope."

"Besides, it's too far to the next smoky bar or greasy spoon. I can only take this clean living for so long."

They laughed together as they reached the open gate of Great Meadow. Two mutts came bounding off the porch of the house to greet them. Isabel reached toward them and said, "Dog."

PEACE OF THE PLACE

Joey sat with Matthew by the woodstove in the living room, recliners side by side, with the footrests up, as he listened to the sounds the house made: the clatter of plates, the laughter of kids, and above them on the second floor, a guitar. He and Matthew went outside after dinner to share a joint of homegrown, and now the peace of the place seemed profound. He noticed it immediately when he arrived in Great Meadow. People spoke quieter and slower. The night sky was darker, the stars brighter. The silence sometimes buzzed in his ears. It was as if all the hard stuff was rubbed off. Mack said it was because everyone was spaced out from doing so much pot, but that was Mack. He couldn't believe anyone could be nice all the time.

Tim was right. Lenora took him on like a project. "Here, try this," she'd say as she brought him a bowl of stew or bread that Alyce, Earth Mother Superior, baked. She made food he had never eaten like brown rice, winter squash, and greens. On sunny days, she took him outside, bundled in clothes she borrowed from one of the other guys who lived there. When he was strong enough, she went with him on short walks around the farm. Isabel came with them, playing with her mother's hair as she rode her hip.

He was well enough weeks ago to leave, but he waited out the winter, and half the cold spring. He lingered because of Lenora and Isabel, but if Mack or the others thought anything would happen between him and her, they were mistaken. She was strictly his angel of mercy.

Joey opened his eyes when Matthew spoke in a soft rumble.

"I like to do the very same thing, just listen to what's happening in the house. I especially enjoy the voices of the children in the study."

"Those are happy sounds." Joey hooked his thumb toward the ceiling. "Think he'll ever get the song down?"

Matthew laughed softly.

"When you came here you were such a nervous fellow. Lenora warned us, but it was something to see. Sometimes at dinner you were like a one-man band the way the parts of you moved. Look at you now."

"Yeah."

Through the far doorway, he saw Lenora step quickly down the hall, her arms around Isabel as the baby cried about something. Joey chuckled. Isabel's problems were so solvable. It always came down to something she wanted, and usually Lenora fixed it. His own life should be so easy.

"When are you leaving?" Matthew asked.

"Friday. Lenora's borrowing George's pickup to drive me to White River Junction to catch the bus." Joey dug into the breast pocket of his denim shirt. "I was meaning to show you this. I copied it. You dig William Carlos Williams? Here's 'The Red Wheelbarrow.' It sort of sums it up, don't you think?"

Matthew unfolded the paper and read its words aloud. He chuckled.

"Joey, you aren't much of a farmer or a carpenter, but you know poetry."

Later, Joey went upstairs to bed. The single guys lived in a room converted from the attic, but it was a hell of a lot nicer than the one at 221 Winter Street. He had the room to himself tonight. The others made the drive to Hanover to go to the movies after they picked up parts for the tractor and some supplies for the woodshop. Joey could have gone, but he skipped the trip. He didn't have many days left at Great Meadow.

He sat at his writing table, his hand resting on the stack of papers beside his typewriter. It was Lenora who told him to stop telling her other people's poetry and to make his own. He went to his room that night to start the first, called "Last Snow." When he read it to her the next day, she closed her eyes as she listened, and afterward she whispered, "Joey, I love it."

He had 28 poems, each one written at Great Meadow. He mailed copies last week to Professor Mitchell, an agreement between the two for an independent study to fulfill his last requirements to graduate. It was a stretch Itch was letting him do all this for credit, but the man's status rose at Westbridge after his smash speech at commencement in '72. A big-shot reporter from the *Boston Globe* whose kid graduated that year wrote about it in a column. Then Itch was named head of the English department. Suddenly, he was BMOC.

Outside, the dogs barked. Joey peered through the window. Matthew walked in the moonlight, chucking sticks for the dogs to fetch on his way to check the barns and livestock. Through the floor he heard a baby's cry, Isabel, of course, but it didn't last.

THE ASSIGNMENT

Nina passed the phone to Tim.

"It's Manny," she said without any interest in her voice.

Tim twisted the phone's cord while he watched the Celtics play on the tube with the sound off.

"How's it going?" Tim hesitated. "Everything okay?"

"Yeah."

Tim was relieved. It seemed like every time they talked somebody had a hassle. Joey was in the hospital. Manny's landlady wanted him out of her house, so he had to find another place fast. Tim hated his job at Denton. Then he got hired as a sports reporter at the *Brockville Enterprise*, not his field of expertise, but it was the only opening at the paper. Now he had to write stories about high school jocks for a son of a bitch of an editor whose idea of a compliment was, "You're getting closer, kid." Or Manny felt like he was pissing fire after he picked up a dirty girl at a club. Or Tim had a big fight with Nina, but that one Manny had to drag out of him. Tim didn't talk about him and Nina. He knew better. Manny would tell him to dump her.

"Manny, I don't have long to talk. I gotta cover a story. A high school coach is retiring after a million years or something. One of his old players went onto the majors and he'll be there. It's actually at Mack's school."

"You're liking this job. I hear it in your voice."

"Pay's crappy and my editor thinks I write nothing but crap, but, yeah, I love going into a coffee shop and seeing the guys read my stories."

Manny hummed.

"Is Joey still coming Friday? I can make it if he is."

"As far as I know," Tim said. "It'll be great to see that nervous nut. He sends me postcards, but there's almost nothing on them. Just some pretty poetry about goats and trees."

"He lucked out house sitting for Inez. Then Itch finds him that job on campus. Somebody's always watching out for Joey."

Nina stood next to Tim. She buttoned her coat.

"Hang on a minute, Manny." Tim turned toward Nina. "You're leaving now? Have a fun time at the movies." Tim was back on the phone. "What'd you say?"

"Never mind. I'll see you soon," Manny told him.

Later that night, Tim leaned against the wall of a school auditorium jammed with fans of Tony Madrid, who was going out with a bang after coaching three sports at the high school for over forty years. The man was a local legend, Tim's editor told him as he lit a cigarette at his desk. This piece better be damn good.

"I want you to squeeze as much as you can out of this for a profile for the Sunday edition," the editor wheezed.

Tim already sat down with Coach Madrid for an interview in his office, a closet of a place lined with plaques and team photos. It only had enough room for a desk and two wooden chairs, one for the coach and one for a visitor. He supposed countless assistant coaches sat on the chair, and kids sweated out whether they were still on the team after getting caught smoking, drinking, or something worse. Yesterday, he watched the guy coach a playoff baseball game, his last. His team got creamed, but he hugged each ballplayer afterward.

The lights dimmed and the school band on the stage began a John Philip Souza march. The crowd stood as Coach Tony Madrid, wearing his trademark cowboy hat and blue parka, strolled down the center aisle through two lines of cheerleaders who pumped pompoms into the air. It was quite a show.

Tim looked up from his notebook when he felt a slap on his upper arm.

218

Mack said hello. He had put on weight, at least twenty pounds since he moved out, so Mack had a paunch beneath his wide, plaid teacher tie. He shaved his beard except for two ridiculous muttonchops. Tim shaved, too, after he got sick of being hounded by his editor. "No one's gonna take a caveman seriously, kid," he growled, and after Tim shaved it off, the son of a bitch grunted but didn't say a word.

"Nice to see you," Mack whispered. "Working, eh?"

Tim raised his pen and notebook. He listened to the principal's speech, a predictable yawner.

"What can you tell me about the coach?"

"Let's see." Mack rubbed one of his chops. "He gives all his players a nickname. Something nutty like *crazy legs* or *rabbit ears*. The parents who didn't play for Coach Madrid shake their heads. The kids love it."

"Nice guy?"

"Yeah, not my kind of nice guy, too straight, but he's friendly as hell."

"Does he call you *muttonchops*?"

"Nah, wise ass, he calls me *rookie*."

The crowd was on their feet and applauding as the coach was called to the microphone.

"Thanks. I'll catch you later." He nodded toward the stage. "I gotta pay attention."

Tim met Mack later in the cafeteria. He got a chance to meet the big leaguer and some of the other alum. He scribbled without looking as they talked about the coach. "What nickname did he give you?" he asked, and then the guy giggled like a silly boy as he told him. He had half a notebook filled with those quick interviews and what he heard on stage. He couldn't possibly know any more about the man unless he moved into his house.

Mack brought him a cup of lukewarm coffee in a white paper cup. He jerked his head toward one of the tables.

"How about sitting?" he asked.

Tim stuck his pen behind his ear. They took chairs at an empty table. A high school girl offered them large squares of chocolate cake with white frosting. Mack raised his brows.

"Sometimes I have to remind myself I'm a teacher."

"Jesus, Mack, she's only a kid."

"Yeah, yeah, jail bait." He leaned on his hand. "I hear Joey's on his way back to civilization."

"Friday."

"We should give him the big Westbridge welcome home. What do you say?"

Tim closed his notebook, and then stood.

"Sounds like a plan. I'm off this weekend."

"Why don't you stick around? I know a bar near here. We can have a coupla beers and shoot pool."

"Not this time. I gotta write this up early tomorrow. See you, bro."

Tim squeezed through the crowd. In the corner of the cafeteria, near the spread of food, Coach Tony Madrid shook hands with his fans. His wife, three daughters, and son stood beside him. Everybody in the room smiled.

Tim's head was full as he drove back to Westbridge. He thought about the story he had to write, how he wanted to get this one right. He was low man in the sports department. His editor once said in a fit of meanness he hired Tim because he left fog on a mirror. He said he didn't want to lose the reporting position to the goddamn features department.

"You take any journalism classes? No? Good. I won't have to break you of any bad habits." He grunted. "I saw your clips from that shitty rag at your school. You can write. Let's see if you can report." He cleared his throat. "Congratulations. You're hired. Go see the girl in the office."

It wasn't the welcome he expected, but it was better than working as an attendant at Denton. The newsroom didn't smell like piss although sometimes he had more enlightening conversations and certainly more love with the clients at Denton than from some of his co-workers at the *Brockville Enterprise*. Being the new guy, his job was to take scores over the phone from gruff-voiced coaches and do small write-ups on the more important games. He wrote whatever his editor told him to write, and after he handed in his copy, he watched him tear it apart.

This story about Coach Tony Madrid should have gone to the top reporter, but he was on vacation. The other guy in the sports department had something else to cover. His editor, stinking of cigarette smoke, sat on the corner of his desk to give him the news.

"I have my doubts you're ready for this, kid but I've got no choice. It's your chance. Don't blow it or you'll be writing agate for the rest of your life."

The man flashed his yellow teeth in a grin that could be mistaken for a frown. It didn't make any difference to Tim.

Tim rolled down the window of his VW van and reached for his pack of cigarettes on the seat. He was feeling a little wound up but not just about the story. He looked forward to seeing Joey again. For starters, they'd have a few laughs over his job at the paper. Joey would tell stories about the people at the commune, especially Lenora and Isabel. He got a letter from Lenora a month after Joey moved there to say he was getting better. Tim meant to write her back this time, but he didn't. The new job and Nina took up his time.

Tim jammed the lighter into the socket. He was a few miles from West-bridge when he decided he needed a beer. He didn't want to have one with Mack, watching him drool over some girl at a bar. Mack was a lot more fun when they were all stupid kids and nothing mattered.

He saw the neon lights of the bar on the edge of the tracks. It was a totally townie place, but as he pulled into the lot, he recognized Nina's blue Mustang parked on the lit side. Nina and her girlfriends must have stopped here after the movies. He parked his van beside it.

A couple of drunks at the bar turned their worn-out faces when Tim walked through the side door. The joint was nearly empty and an old country tune by Patsy Cline played on the juke. It was easy to spot Nina in a corner booth. She was making out with a guy, not being shy about it, and when Tim stepped forward he saw it was Roach Brother Bob. Tim felt his hands tighten. He stood at the table until Nina opened her eyes and pushed Bob away. Both looked guilty as hell, and now everything about the past couple of months made sense.

"Jesus, Nina, what the hell are you doing?"

DONE WITH THE CURE

On Friday, Mack smoked a butt and leaned against the front window of Jimmy's Coffee Shop while he waited for Joey's bus. He lifted his head as he blew smoke. He wore his teaching clothes although he loosened the tie. He drove here after school, watching the minutes of the last period drag. He let the kids take over today and sat in the back row, asking dumb questions and cracking jokes like the clowns in his classes. During the last period, he chose one his top students, a girl with an especially fine pair of titties although she hid them under heavy sweaters or blouses buttoned to the collar. She'd be pretty if she did a little more with her hair and stood straight. She was definitely a virgin. He doubted she'd ever been French-kissed.

Mack grinned as a group of college girls walked past Jimmy's, heading, he bet, to one of the bars to fake their way inside.

"Hey, there, ladies," he crooned.

They giggled but didn't stop. Two glanced back and snickered. Mack burned from the neck up. Jesus, one year out of Westbridge and he had lost his touch. These girls were probably freshmen sneaking into last year's graduation party at Winter Street. Maybe they'd been at the last weekend bash. He checked his reflection in Jimmy's window. Shit, no wonder. He looked like a goddamned English teacher from some regional high school. He ripped off the tie and stuck it in his back pocket. He touched his jaw, deciding the chops must go. It was bad enough being called Mr. Mackenzie by kids not much younger than him, but then these girls shot him down.

He tossed the butt into the gutter. Screw it. Screw them all. He'd been looking forward to this weekend ever since Manny called to say Joey was done with the cure and heading home. Joey wasn't going back to Winter Street, of course. When Mack drove by there today, the place was boarded up, and two signs were nailed to the building. One said no trespassing and the other, for sale. But Joey lucked out again, watching Inez Burke's home until it sells. It'll be nice to have him around again.

Mack and Manny cooked up a plan. Tim said he'd do whatever. The guy was bummed about Nina. That's what happens when you get too attached to a woman, and especially one like Nina, who makes a stink every time a guy tries to break up. But in the end she was the one to do him wrong, and in this case, with Roach Brother Bob no less. When Mack called him Wednesday night, Tim told him not to make a big deal about it, but he gave him advice anyway. Forget about her. Find somebody else. This weekend would do Tim good. It would do them all good.

After Joey shows up, they'll head to Tim's place at the Roach Motel, drink beer, and smoke joints while Manny made them spaghetti. It was his Portagee mother's recipe for homemade sauce with linguiça sausage. Manny used to make it at Winter Street, the ingredients cheap enough so they could make pigs of themselves and belch for hours afterward from the grease. Later, they'll go to the VFW. And that was only Friday night. They'll hang together all weekend having laughs, maybe getting laid. He checked himself again in the glass. He definitely had to shave.

Mack turned when he heard a bus make the turn near the sub shop and drive the loop around the commons before it braked in front of Jimmy's. The door hissed open. Joey knocked on a back window and gave him a thumbs-up as he followed the line of people down the aisle. He clutched his typewriter under one arm when he came down the steps.

Mack rushed forward.

"Jesus, Joey, you look great."

A grin was plastered on Joey's hairy face. He glanced around. "Thanks. Hold on."

The driver opened the door to the bus' compartment. Joey pointed to a suitcase and two boxes Mack guessed were filled with books.

"You parked nearby? These are heavy."

Mack nodded toward the cobbler's shop beside Jimmy's.

"Just over there. Let me get those."

They walked along the sidewalk side by side.

"I see you still have the Fairlane."

"It's getting a little rusty, but the engine runs great."

They dumped Joey's things in the trunk beside a case of beer and got into the front seat. Mack poked the key into the ignition.

"Shit, Lenora did a great job nursing you back to health."

"Yeah, she did."

Mack raised his eyebrows.

"You two get it on?"

Joey shook his head.

"How about one of the other girls? The redhead was real friendly."

"No, on all accounts."

Mack cranked the engine.

"Well, that's a fucking shame."

Joey shook his head again.

THE HOMECOMING

The four friends sat around the kitchen table at Tim's apartment. They were feeling full and working on a beer buzz. Dishes were dumped in the sink, and the joke was they would arm-wrestle later to see who had to clean up the mess. Or maybe they'd let it all pile up until it got so disgusting like they did once at 221 Winter Street. That time they ended up throwing everything into the trash and passing the hat so they could buy new stuff at the Five and Dime. Of course, Manny was excused from washing dishes, because he cooked tonight's grease fest. Joey's insides burned when he burped. This was nothing like the food he'd been eating at Great Meadow the past few months.

Mack stretched his legs with his arms crossed behind his head. He shaved at Tim's, and now he had pink, smooth skin where there used to be furry cheeks. All agreed it was an improvement.

Manny cracked, "Which president do you think Mack looks like now?"

Mack put up with the jokes, because he was stoked to be at the center of attention. He called to Tim who rolled a joint of Great Meadow Gold, a parting gift to Joey from Matthew.

"This place is sure empty," Mack said. "Nina clean you out or did you get robbed? You don't even have a TV or a real bed. Just a bunch of mattresses on the floor."

Tim licked the paper's glue to seal the joint.

"After we split, she showed up with her two brothers and took whatever she wanted. She tried nabbing my stereo, but I reminded her it was a graduation present from my mother, and we all remember how much trouble I went through for that. I held onto the kitchen set from Winter Street and the couch at least. The posters, too."

Their heads swung toward Clint Eastwood looking lean and mean in his serape and Janis Joplin, happy but out of it. They all nodded reverently, except Mack who bent backward in his chair to check the alarm clock on the floor.

"Are we gonna sit around here all night or are we going out? I heard they have a band at the VFW."

Tim held the unlit joint aloft.

"Hold your horses, Mack. It's early," he said. "You know what the scene's gonna be like up there. A bunch of old drunk vets checking out the girls. Horny college guys. The band will be loud and lousy. They'll play oldies or country music or both. Then one of the townies will try to pick a fight. Jesus, we did that for how many years?"

Manny nodded.

"Besides, if we go later the girls'll be drunker and you'd have a better shot."

"Very funny, Manny," Mack said.

Joey sat back taking it all in, the jokes and jabs, all in fun, although he detected something sharp in the talk between Mack and Tim. Mack would go off on some old story, like when one of the freak friends ended up in a state mental hospital because he did too much acid. Tim rolled his eyes and said, "Yup, those were the days," and Mack gave Tim a look like he was guilty of breaking ranks. Then Manny made some remark to put it all in perspective: the guy needed help, and besides he escaped from the joint to 221 Winter Street a couple of days later. Manny might make a lawyer after all.

Joey glanced up when Tim called his name.

"Hey, dreamer, you want another beer?"

Joey shook his bottle. He still had more than half left. He lost count how many he drank, three, maybe four.

"I'm cool."

A knock was at the door. Mack was on his feet, looking hopeful as he yanked it open. Professor Mitchell was on the other side, and he chortled when they all gave him a little cheer.

"Now, the party can get going," Mack greeted him.

Itch's ponytail swung as he came forward to shake Joey's hand.

"Joey, I'm glad to see you've risen from the dead." Itch took a chair as Tim offered him the lit joint. "Don't mind if I do."

The stereo played something folksy, another sad song about hitting the road and leaving someone behind. Joey didn't mind. He was feeling sentimental. If he were back in Great Meadow, he'd be enjoying another after-dinner chat with Matthew about the farm or something more ethereal. Isabel might be on his lap, her dark curls damp from her bath, and then Lenora would stroll in, laughing about something one of the girls in the kitchen said as she scooped up her baby. This morning, Lenora smiled and cried at the same time when she said goodbye at the station in White River Junction. During the bus trip, when he wasn't napping, he felt himself pulled farther from that clean, simple life. Matthew told him he could move back although he knew he wouldn't.

Lenora gave him a copy of Ginsburg's *Howl*, with the inscription, "To Jo-wey, our favorite poet. Love, Lenora and Isabel." He hugged them both, and it broke him up when Isabel kept saying "Jo-wey go."

Joey glanced up when Itch blew across the top of his bottle to get their attention.

"Gentlemen, I have some news. I wasn't going to say anything until it was a done deal, but guess who's buying 221 Winter Street?" He pointed toward his chest. "Yours truly. After I get the place fixed, I'll take over the second floor and rent out the first. Good investment, don't you think?"

Mack, who sulked on the couch, got to his feet.

"This is freakin' unbelievable," he said. "I drove by there today, and it bummed me out when I saw the for-sale sign. Now it's gonna stay in the family." Mack raised his fist in a power salute. "Hot damn, Mitchell, you're a freakin' genius."

The rest nodded and made happy grunts. Itch beamed. Next week, he was taking Joey to Inez Burke's house to get him settled. He was the one who suggested that Joey live at the house until it sold although it was Inez who called him at Great Meadow. She thanked Joey for his note about Ned's book that came out in March and his apology he couldn't make it to the reading in Boston. She also called with a business proposition. Joey did a little dance when he hung up the phone, and then he went to find Lenora.

Itch's eyes focused on Joey.

"I can't get over how great you look. You don't even twitch anymore. Maybe you should've stayed in New Hampshire. From those poems you sent, I am guessing it was the good life up there."

"You get a chance to read them?"

"I did." He murmured. "I was impressed. So were my colleagues in the department. You really focused in New Hampshire."

"Am I all set with Westbridge?"

"I'd say you came out ahead."

Joey sighed.

"That's a relief."

"Will you be coming to commencement?" Itch asked.

"I wasn't planning to."

"You might want to change your mind. I have a regular gig now." Itch glanced up when he heard the fridge door open and the clink of bottles as Mack reached for another round. He popped the tops before setting them on the table. "How is Lenora?"

"Lenora? She's really into her baby. I miss them already," Joey said.

Tim was up and searching though a stack of newspapers on the floor next to his mattress. He stood between Itch and Joey as he spread a newspaper on the table. It was the front page of the *Brockville Enterprise*. Tim's piece about Coach Tony Madrid was smack in the middle, the centerpiece. Joey quickly scanned the print, and then he turned the paper so Itch and Manny could read it.

"This is great," Joey said. "What did your editor say?"

"He said I did a half-way decent job. Believe me. It's a compliment from that guy. I actually think he liked it. He didn't change too much, and at the last minute he lobbied to put it on the front page." Tim wiped beer foam from his lips. "I'm gonna mail it to Lenora. She's the one who got on my case about wasting my time at Denton."

"You should do that," Joey said. "She was happy when she heard you got that job."

Tim lit a cigarette, and then shook the pack at Joey.

"Nah, I gave it up."

"Is she seeing somebody up there?" Tim asked.

Joey felt the edges of a smile.

"A guy? No." He nodded at Mack who changed the record to something harder and faster. "Mack asked me if she and I did it. One time, soon after I got there, we talked about her last weekend in Westbridge. She was the one who brought it up. She said, 'Joey, we had a lot of fun that night, but just so you know, it's not gonna happen again. I don't want you to get the wrong idea why I brought you up here.' I mean what could I say? She was sweet about it though."

"Sweet about what?" Mack said as he sat at the table.

"We're talking about Lenora," Tim said.

Manny set his beer on the table and pointed a finger toward the center of the group.

"Any of you ever wonder about Lenora's baby?" he asked.

"What's the big deal?" Mack said. "She came back from Europe knocked up." He snorted. "Do I have to explain how these things happen? Jesus, didn't Manny Sr. ever give you the talk?"

"Shut up, Mack. I did a little math one night and figured out she could've gotten pregnant during that last weekend blowout two years ago." Manny paused. "If that's so, I can think of five potential fathers. Remember, our Lenora was a busy little girl that weekend."

No one said a word. Tim's head was cocked to one side. Itch sat back, chuckling to himself.

"Shoot. I never thought about it." Mack shook his head. "I did ask her at Ned's funeral if she came back pregnant from Europe. She didn't say she got that way there."

Manny counted his fingers.

"There's Tim, then me, then Tim again, but, Tim, that only counts for one, then Mack, and maybe Ned, and then Joey."

Mack raised his hands.

"Count me out. The kid can't be mine. I didn't touch Lenora."

Manny's dark brows formed a thick, woolly V.

"You told me you screwed her in the woods at the pond," he said. "You sure went into a lot of detail as I recall. You're saying it never happened?"

"I tried, but Lenora definitely wasn't interested. She practically kneed me in the balls."

"What in the hell did you do that for?" Manny's voice cracked.

"I was feeling left out. This was after your threesome. Remember?"

"Left out! Left out! You fucking asshole!" Tim yelled.

Tim reached across the table and dragged Mack forward by the neck of his T-shirt until they were chin-to-chin. Bottles rolled to the floor. Beer spilled over the linoleum. Manny, Itch, and Joey got to their feet.

"Get your hands off me," Mack croaked.

"You fucking pervert." Tim's head moved in small tremors. "Trying to force yourself on Lenora, then lying about it. No wonder she's always so pissed off about you."

Mack's mouth hung open as Tim went nuts about Lenora and all the stupid things Mack did, like the way he treated women and the guys who were supposed to be his friends. Mack made little choking sounds as Tim twisted the top of his T-shirt tighter. Joey rushed forward to break them up, but Manny beat him to it.

"Whoa, whoa," Manny said. "Take it easy, Tim. Let him go. Look at his face."

Mack bucked back into his chair, nearly falling after Tim let him go. Everyone stared at Mack, who rubbed his neck, acting like he was almost killed. A minute later, though, after he recovered, he made another snorting laugh. His eyes were crushed into two slits.

"I know why you're so pissed off, Timmy boy," Mack said. "You've got the hots bad for Lenora, always have, and you keep fucking it up."

Tim crashed into the corner of the table as he went after Mack, hitting his jaw, and when Mack tried to swing back, both fell against the table, toppling the chair beside it, as Tim got in another shot, this time harder. Mack cursed as he fought back, but Tim was faster. He was ready to pop Mack again when Manny wedged between them.

"Do something, Joey," Manny yelled, and Joey tugged Tim's arm while Manny shielded Mack.

"You okay, Mack?" Manny asked.

"Keep that fucking maniac away from me," he yelled.

Joey backed Tim to the bathroom door, blocking his way back. He wondered how this was going to end, and he hoped Mack kept his big mouth shut.

"Chill out, Tim," Joey said quietly.

Tim nodded as Manny helped Mack to his feet, but he shook off the gesture, and muttering, he grabbed his jacket off the back of the couch.

He glared at Tim.

"You're a fucking loser, Tim," Mack said. "You always were."

Mack was out the door, giving it a hard slam to make his point. No one spoke. Joey glanced at Tim, who scowled at the closed door.

"Lock it," Tim said.

"You don't mean it," Manny said.

"Sure I do. He can sleep in his car."

Manny didn't lock the door. Neither did Tim. They helped Itch right the chairs. Manny picked up the bottles.

"Great homecoming, eh?" he joked.

Joey laughed as he reached for a beer bottle that rolled near the couch. It still had a third left so he swiped the top of the neck clean with the bottom of his shirt and took a swig.

"It hasn't been boring so far."

Tim was on his knees using a bath towel to mop beer off the floor. His jaw was tight as he swirled the dirt over the linoleum.

Itch dropped onto one of the chairs.

"As ugly as that was, it does eliminate one possibility concerning paternity," he said. "Actually two. Even if Ned went off with Lenora, and he swore he didn't, I can say with certainty little Isabel can't be his. The man was sterile. That's why he and Inez didn't have kids. And that's why there are no love children of Ned Burke running around Westbridge." He cleared his throat. "Has Lenora ever spoken to any of you about this?"

The three of them took a chair. Manny and Tim shook their heads. Both stared at Joey. He shrugged.

"I asked her one time if she shouldn't get Isabel's father to help her out with money," Joey said. "She got awfully quiet and said he didn't know about her. She said it was better this way. She knew how to take care of her daughter. He wouldn't."

"That's all?" Tim asked.

"If I had any idea Isabel could be mine, I certainly would've asked more questions," Joey said. "Lenora was done talking about it. You know how she is."

"What's Isabel look like now?" Tim asked.

Joey thought. He saw her walking with Lenora outside Great Meadow. Isabel wore a bonnet, Lenora liked dressing her in them, so her eyes were big beneath its brim. She searched for something interesting to pick up, a white quartz stone or a feather. He wrote a poem about it called "What Izzie Finds." He felt himself smile.

"There's a lot of Lenora in her face. But she has the greenest eyes and this cleft to her chin. Her coloring is lighter than Lenora's. I guess she looks like Lenora and somebody else."

Manny nodded solemnly.

"Somebody else. Like one of us?" he said.

"Shoot. I dunno."

Tim and Manny groaned.

"Wait a sec." He reached into his back pocket for his wallet. "I've got a picture from her first birthday party. Here. See for yourself."

Manny and Tim bent over the photo. Lenora held Isabel in her lap, laughing as the baby reached toward the camera.

"I can't tell," Tim said. "Can any of you?"

"If Lenora's baby has green eyes, I seriously doubt she's mine," Manny said. "Everybody in my family has brown."

"Good point, Manny," Tim said. "Maybe it's down to Joey and me."

"Me a father?" Joey said, choking on the words.

"There's one definite way to find out." Itch coughed. "I know from personal experience. It's a blood test. But it's usually a last resort kind of thing. I think it's better you talk first with Lenora. Don't you agree?"

The light was dim, but Joey saw the way Tim's eyes looked through the walls of the apartment to some place far away. Tim smiled, but it wasn't for any of them. Beside him, Manny blew air in one long stream. Tim and Manny were thinking what he was thinking, about being Isabel's father, and now Joey's leg started to kick.

"Why didn't Lenora say something?" Tim asked for all of them.

GIRL OF THE NORTH COUNTRY

Tim raised his head from his pillow and let it drop. The alarm clock's face said it was five, and he hadn't slept much since he, Manny, and Joey finally called it a night. For hours, Tim tried to find the spot on his mattress that let him finally rest. He couldn't stop thinking about Lenora and the baby. What if he was the father? What if he wasn't? Jesus, Lenora shouldn't have kept this to herself.

His head was up again to check on Manny, who lay on a mattress beside his. Tim poked him lightly with his bare foot.

"Manny, Manny," he whispered hoarsely. "Wake up."

Manny moaned.

"I am awake. I don't think I slept at all."

"You, too?" Tim sat up. "I've been thinking we should go to New Hampshire to see Lenora."

"Yeah, yeah, we talked about it."

"I mean today. We can drive up and be back in one day."

"You're nuts, Tim. Can't it wait?"

"No, it can't wait. You gonna come?"

Manny rolled on his side toward Tim.

"Course, but I'm positive Isabel's not mine. I told you last night all the babies in my family come out looking like little monkeys. It's genetics, man. The odds of me producing a green-eyed kid with fair skin are pretty much impossible. I think you or Joey stand a better chance."

"Who the hell knows?"

Manny shut his eyes.

"What time do you wanna leave?"

"Now."

Manny moaned again.

"What about Joey?" he asked.

"What about me?" Joey's voice came from across the room. "I hear you guys talking over there."

"You didn't sleep either?" Tim asked.

"No." Joey threw off his blanket and swung his legs around, so he sat in his shorts on the couch. He rubbed his eyes and yawned. "What time is it? Oh, shit."

Manny glanced over his shoulder.

"Should we call her first?" Manny asked.

"Now? It's too early." Tim nodded at Joey. "Was Lenora planning to go anywhere today?"

"She should be there," Joey said. "We could call her on the way to make sure."

"You're gonna go?" Tim asked.

"Heck, I'm not missing this."

Tim was on his feet.

"All right," he said.

They counted their cash, and typical, Joey had five bucks. They figured they had enough for gas there and back, plus stops for coffee and chow. They took sleeping bags, and Manny his suitcase, just in case.

Tim stopped at the front door. He nodded at Mack's duffle bag on the floor, but no one mentioned his name. Their former leader was in permanent exile as far as they were concerned. Tim chucked the bag outside the front door, and then they filed past Mack's Fairlane toward his VW van. Mack was asleep in the back seat of his car. A hand hung over the purpled skin on his face. The corner of Tim's mouth quivered.

Manny saw him, too.

"Guess he wasn't so lucky after all," he cracked.

"I hope he froze his ass off," Tim said. "Serves him right."

Jimmy's had just opened when they stopped for the biggest cups of coffee the cook could pour and ordered the two-egg special before taking stools at the counter where the townies usually sat. They were the coffee shop's first customers, followed by a truck driver who was heading south through town. The cook went about his business, ignoring them all. The only noise in the place was the hiss of grease from the grill and the radio behind the counter with the news. The eggs glistened when the cook set down their plates.

Manny reached for the salt.

"You sure you wanna do this, Tim?"

Tim set his mug onto the counter.

"What do you think?"

"Just checking," Manny answered.

Later, Tim drove while the other two dozed in the VW van, Manny in the front and Joey in the middle. Both promised to take over when Tim needed a break, but he didn't mind the drive. He smoked with the window open and let his thoughts fuel him forward. He remembered when Lenora came back for Ned's funeral with her baby and how she cried when she saw them all. He thought of the letters he didn't write or the calls he didn't make. Who could she count on?

Traffic at this hour on Saturday was light even around Boston and to the New Hampshire border, where the landscape thickened with trees. He half-listened to the radio as he followed the backside of a tractor-trailer for miles until it lost him, and then he concentrated on the highway.

Manny's head swung back against the seat. He blinked at the road sign for the next exit. Tim took the turn.

"We're here already?" Manny asked. "Want me to take over?"

Tim shook his head at both questions.

"Nah, I'm gonna stop at a gas station. I gotta take a leak and get some smokes. Why don't you wake Joey?"

AYUH

enora opened the closet door and held her hands on her hips as she studied the dresses inside. It appeared George's mother didn't wear anything else. She was in this room only once before, when George asked her to dust and mop. The furniture was likely in the same spot his mother left it, but the room, located on the south side of the farmhouse, was stripped of her personal things. George said he gave them to his sisters and his brother's wife. All that was left were her clothes, and they were going to be boxed for the church's Indian mission.

Isabel climbed onto the bed and sat in the center of its quilt. Lenora went to untie her shoes.

"Jump?"

"No, you can't jump here. The bed's too high. You might fall off, and I don't want you to get hurt."

George's heavy footsteps were in the hall. Isabel's dimples showed.

"George?"

"I'm here, Isabel," he called.

Lenora placed her daughter's white high-top shoes on the braided rug beside the bed.

"Isabel, George isn't going to let you jump either."

He stopped in the doorway. His arms were filled with cardboard boxes.

"Isabel, listen to your mother." He spoke in a fake-gruff voice. "Don't get me in trouble with her."

George set the boxes on the floor. Lenora already folded his mother's nightgowns, underwear, and support hose stored in the dresser drawers. He kept telling her to take whatever she liked, his sisters already had what they wanted, but everything the woman wore was too large.

She pointed toward the closet.

"All of it?"

"Ayuh."

She started on the dresses. Many of them were made of cotton or rayon, in small prints, except for one black dress, which Lenora supposed she wore to funerals, and a pale yellow linen, for special occasions. Most were homemade. It was a shame they didn't fit.

"Ma, see." Isabel made little marching steps on the quilt as she pointed toward her reflection in the dresser mirror. "Izzie."

"Yes, that's you."

Lenora reached for a dress and carefully folded it into a square. George stood by, watching each one she took from the closet.

"Your mother had nice things, George."

She filled one carton and knelt to arrange the flaps. She peered up at George. He wore his best flannel shirt and the jeans she washed Thursday. He looked as if he didn't know where to put his hands.

"I heard your boyfriend left yesterday."

"Boyfriend? Joey? He's not my boyfriend." She slid the box to the side and grabbed another. "We're just friends. I took care of him when he got sick."

"I thought it was more than that."

"More? No. We went to college together."

He took the filled box and stacked it on the one in the corner. She rose.

"College. So, he's not Isabel's father?" he asked her.

"George."

Pink spread slowly above the collar of his flannel shirt.

"I'm sorry, Lenora. I didn't mean to stick my nose where it doesn't belong."

Isabel lowered herself from the bed, and now she poked through the shoes and bags on the closet floor until she found a red purse, which snapped at the top. She held it for her mother to open. Lenora did it without looking.

"That's okay. I can be nosy, too."

Red-faced still, George reached into his jeans pocket and filled Isabel's small palm with coins.

"Here's money for your pocketbook."

Isabel's green eyes got busy as she fingered the coins and dropped them inside the purse.

"Mine," she said.

"You're supposed to say thank you to George."

"George," her little voice said.

"I'll gladly settle for that." George's boots shuffled over the rug. "Lenora, have you thought any more about my offer?"

"About being your live-in housekeeper? That might not be a good idea, George. It might start tongues wagging in town."

"Are you worried about something like that?"

She reached for a short-sleeved blue dress with white polka dots.

"Me? No. But I haven't lived in Wilbur all my life."

"Anyone who knows me will know better. I have a big, empty house and lots of work that needs to be done. And I like having you both here."

Lenora gazed down at Isabel as she worked the purse's clasp. She knew what George meant. There was nothing between them, given the distance in their age. She felt as if she were the grown daughter who never moved too far away. George, who lived all his life with his mother, welcomed their company, especially Isabel's.

"Let me think about it some more. Okay?" She pointed toward the filled boxes. "Why don't you carry these to the truck?" She turned toward her daughter. "Isabel, get me your shoes. We're going to help George bring the clothes to the church hall."

George nodded. Lenora went back to work as he left the room. She took the last dress off its hanger then a housecoat and what must have been the woman's winter going-to-church coat. It was a dark tweed with a double row of silver buttons. All that remained inside the whitewashed closet were hats on the top shelf. Lenora took a black wool trimmed with long feathers to the mirror. Its veil reached the tip of her nose when she tried it on. She decided it was a good look with her hair up like that, and Isabel clapped when she saw her turn her head this way and that.

"I think I'll keep this one," Lenora told her daughter.

MAN WITH A MISSION

J oey listened as Matthew explained over the phone that Lenora left early that morning with George Evans.

"Something I can do for you?"

Joey watched Tim smoke and pace outside the phone booth. His head was down as if he were dodging a strong wind. Manny was inside the diner.

"I'm in Concord."

"Concord? You change your mind about leaving?"

"No, no. I'm with my friends, Tim and Manny. You remember them? It's important we see Lenora."

"It must be, since you left only yesterday." Matthew paused. "Why don't you come here and wait for her. I can't imagine she'll be all day with George."

Tim tossed his cigarette when Joey pushed open the door.

"Did you talk with her?" he asked

"No, she's with that farmer. She should be back sometime today. It'll be easy to find her. I mean there aren't many places to go in Wilbur."

Tim's head bobbed. He wouldn't let it go ever since Manny brought up the idea one of them could be Isabel's father. Last night, he kept studying

239

the photo Joey had of Lenora and Isabel, and saying things like, "Look at her chin. That's definitely a Devlin chin." Or "See those eyes. My niece, Maggie, has the same color eyes."

Like Manny, Joey figured he was out of the running. He loved Isabel, but decided he should have felt something stronger for the girl when he lived at Great Meadow. Besides, Lenora never gave any signs he could be her baby's father and she had plenty of chances. When he first came, she stayed with him for hours, playing cards, reading, or talking when he was too sick to do anything else. But he never heard any midnight confessions from Lenora.

Joey slapped Tim on the back.

"Take it easy. We'll get a chance to talk with her. Let's get coffee and something to eat."

Tim groaned.

"Eat? I thought we were only stopping for coffee. That'll take too long."

"I dunno about you, but I'm starving. I used up those eggs and toast from Jimmy's hours ago."

"All right, all right. But no dessert."

They reached Great Meadow an hour and a half later. The commune's mutts came bounding from behind the barns as Tim pulled the VW into the driveway. Matthew called the dogs to him when he stepped from the front porch. He gave Joey a big hug and shook hands with the others after they got out of the van.

"Sorry. She's not back yet. She's still helping George with something. That's what Alyce told me." Matthew scratched beneath his beard. "Why don't you drive to his farm? She might be there. You're welcome to stay here and wait. Although it looks like your friend there is kind of anxious to see her."

Joey chuckled as Tim watched the road.

"Yeah, he is."

Tim drove the VW van to George's farm, and when no one was there, they went back to Great Meadow, and then toward town, what there was of Wilbur. They passed the white Congregational church, elementary school, and town hall as they rode through the main village, searching for Lenora. Joey didn't spot George's pickup anywhere.

"Where in the hell could she be?" Tim complained.

They stopped at the Wilbur General Store for Cokes. The three of them stood in the parking lot, drinking from their bottles as they leaned against the van.

"Man, this place would drive me nuts. Too damn quiet. How could you stand it?" Manny asked.

"It was a good place for a while," Joey said.

Manny tipped his bottle toward Tim, who moved away to watch the traffic.

"Boy, I've never seen Tim this worked up before, have you?"

"Oh you are coming, coming, coming/ How will hungry Time put by the hours till then?"

"What'd you say?"

"It's from Sara Teasdale." Joey shrugged. "Tim's kinda taking the load off me in the nervous department."

Manny dropped his empty bottle into the trashcan near the store's door.

"Suppose Isabel is your kid? What are you gonna do about it?"

"Hell, if I know." Joey drained the Coke then burped. "What do I have to offer Lenora? I barely had enough to make the bus fare."

"Some things don't change." Manny snorted. "What I want to know is who's gonna ask Lenora?"

"I vote for Tim."

"Me, too." Manny jabbed Joey's arm. "What's he so excited about now?" Tim whistled for their attention.

"What color is that guy's truck?" he hollered.

"What guy?"

"The farmer, for Christ's sake."

"Blue."

"Get in the van. I think I saw Lenora go by."

Joey was yelling "hey" and still trying to shut the van's sliding door when Tim put the VW in first. The van sped from the general store's driveway, and Tim called over his shoulder to Joey when they got closer to the pickup truck.

"That it?"

"I think so. That sure looks like the back of Lenora's head. What's she got on the top? Are those feathers?" Joey leaned behind Tim. "He's making the next left. It's gotta be them."

They followed the truck as it made the turn onto a dirt road, along the river, then past George Evans' farm and up the hill where Tim's van almost got stuck in the snowstorm that time in January. The VW van's wheels kicked up stones as Tim gunned the engine.

Manny howled.

"The freak's gone loco."

"Certifiable," Joey piped up.

Tim ignored them. He parked the van beside the blue pickup when they reached Great Meadow. Through the truck's windshield Joey saw Lenora sitting beside the farmer. She wore a hat with pheasant feathers coiled over the top. She wound down her window and stuck her head outside. Her eyes widened when she lifted the hat's veil.

"I can't believe you guys. What in the heck are you doing all the way up here?"

Tim trotted toward the truck, yanking open her door and saying Lenora's name with a hoarse whisper. His eyes went from her to the baby sleeping in her lap, then her again. Manny stepped beside him. Joey came, too, the three of them forming a tight knot in front of the truck's open door. Lenora laughed and shook her head like someone pulled a fast one on her and got away with it, though anyone who knew Lenora also knew that was nearly impossible.

"You're all too much," she said.

The hat's veil dropped to the bridge of Lenora's nose.

"George, this is my friend, Tim. That's Manny. You know Joey."

George grunted.

"I'll get your things, Lenora," he said.

Tim's hands moved forward to help Lenora down.

"Nice hat."

Lenora peered through the veil as she bent toward Tim.

"Pretty neat, huh? It belonged to George's mom. You should see the others I got."

Isabel snuffled and sighed, but she didn't wake as Lenora settled her against her shoulder. George circled the back of the truck, carrying a cardboard box and Lenora's bag, which he handed to Manny.

She turned toward Joey.

"Why are you back so soon?" Lenora asked. "You change your mind?"

Joey's feet began to dance.

"Tell you later," he said. "Let's get inside. I bet she's heavy."

Lenora waved and called to George as he walked toward his truck. Tim was beside her.

"You want me to take her?"

Lenora made a squinty smile.

"It's okay. I'm gonna put her down in her crib, and then you can tell me what's going on here."

Joey and Manny exchanged glances as Lenora shifted Isabel into a better place before she walked toward the house with Tim. They followed behind, watching her laugh at Tim's story about driving all around town trying to find her. Tim gave them a quick peek over his shoulder. The guy was nervous as hell.

The air smelled like baking bread inside the house. Classical music played on the stereo.

"Wait here," Lenora said.

She said it so sweetly no one protested. Instead, they watched Lenora's skirt sway across the back of her legs as she went upstairs to her room.

Manny set the box and bag on the hallway floor.

"Um, Tim, we voted two to nothing you get to ask her," he said.

Tim looked at Manny then Joey from the corner of his eyes.

"All right, you little cowards."

Joey snickered.

"Cowards. You got that right, Timmy boy."

DO THE RIGHT THING

Tim waited on the wicker couch of the house's front porch. Lenora opened the door.

"There you are. I searched all over the house. Where's Manny and Joey?"

"Joey took him to the barn. Something about going to see a workshop." He patted the spot next to his. "Sit next to me, Lenora."

She had taken off the hat and pins so her hair fell behind her back. She dropped onto the cushion, her shoulder bumping Tim's as she sat close to him. One of the barn cats blinked and crouched on the porch railing in the far corner.

"Hey, Tim."

"Hey, Lenora. Nice to see you." His mouth stretched into a grin. "Isabel wake up?"

"No, she's still asleep. She played hard today. I had to change her diaper first."

He nodded.

"You're a great mom."

Lenora waved her hand.

"Cut the crap, Tim. What happened that made you three drive all the way up here?"

"Huh?"

"Something's up. I can see it all over your faces. It must be something big or Manny and Joey wouldn't have run off like that."

She stared at Tim as if she could draw the question from him telepathically. Of course, she was suspicious. Joey left yesterday, and now he was back. Manny wouldn't even look her in the eye. She hadn't seen or heard from Tim since January. The three of them weren't here for a long ride in the country.

Tim made a loud sigh.

"Well ..."

"Did somebody die and you want to tell me yourself? It isn't one of the guys from Westbridge? It wasn't Ray? Itch?"

"No, Ray's fine. So's Itch. We saw him last night. It's nothing like that."

Tim's hands rubbed his thighs.

"I'll make it easy for you," she said. "Go ahead. Say what you've got to say. Just spit it out. I can take it."

Tim cleared his throat.

"Could one of us be Isabel's father?" The corners of his lips jerked out a nervous grin. "There, I said it."

"Isabel's father! Whatever gave you that idea?"

"Manny brought it up last night. He said it could've happened on that last weekend in Westbridge before you graduated. Remember? When ... when you slept with all of us? Well, not at the same time. Well ... you did with Manny and me."

She crossed her arms while Tim mumbled and skipped over his words. He tried to explain what they had talked about last night, telling her about the Devlin chin and the color of his niece Maggie's eyes. He stopped when he found himself in the middle again.

Lenora's eyes drilled holes straight through him.

"So, you three got stoned last night and decided you could have some claim on my daughter." She spoke so slowly she could have been giving him directions. "You're all wrong. You're not her father, and neither is Manny or Joey."

Tim's brow thickened.

"Manny did the math."

"Manny's wrong. Isabel was born a couple of weeks early."

Tim shook his head.

"But Itch said we should ask."

"Professor Mitchell knows about this? Jesus. Who else?"

"Mack. But we're not talking to him anymore. We had a big fight about this and something else."

"Look, you stupid pothead. Don't you think if you, Manny, or Joey were Isabel's father I would've told you? I wouldn't have kept something that important to myself."

He grabbed her wrist.

"I swear she looks like me."

Lenora yanked her hand away.

"I'm afraid Isabel looks more like the man who fathered her."

"You sure? You're absolutely sure?"

She paused.

"Her father's French. We hitched together for a while in Europe. Then he skipped out in the middle of the night and stiffed me with the hotel bill. Nice guy, huh? He doesn't know anything about Isabel, and I don't know where in the hell he is to tell him. I bet he didn't even give me his real name." She tightened her crossed arms. "I don't think he'd be very good father material, do you?"

"Jesus, Lenora, lighten up. I just wanted to do the right thing."

The heels of her boots clacked against the porch's floorboards as she got to her feet. The cat scrambled off the railing and shot past Lenora.

"Lighten up?" She raised her voice. "Isabel's over a year now. I'm sure glad I didn't wait for any of you to do the right thing."

"Please, Lenora."

"Please, what? Think about it, Timothy Devlin. Why should you get to be her father? You never do a damn thing you say you're gonna do. You just want things easy. You live with a girl you don't love until she cheats on you." She planted her fists on her hips. "Joey told me all about that. Nina doesn't want you any more so you think you can come up here and I'll throw myself at you. Ha." Her hands went everywhere, punishing the air. "*Lighten up?* Isabel deserves more than that. And I sure as hell do, too. So, turn around and go back to Westbridge. I don't want to see you ever again. Ever. Do you understand? Maybe if you're lucky, Nina will change her mind. Or you'll find somebody else who doesn't care about being with such a lazy bastard."

Lenora glared at Tim. He felt his face burn and his mouth stayed open as if she had slapped anything smart from him. Manny and Joey stood beside the porch's front steps. Lenora gave each of them one of her killer looks, and without a word, she marched back inside the house and let the door slam hard behind her.

MESSING UP

Tim stepped off the porch toward the van. Manny and Joey followed. "Wow, that didn't go very well. We could hear her yelling from the barn. What ..." Manny said, but he didn't finish his words. Tim looked as if he was ready to punch him out, and they saw what he did to Mack last night, so he shut his trap.

"Let's get the hell outta here," Tim said through clenched teeth.

None of them spoke in the van, not even when they passed two deer alongside the road near the bachelor farmer's barn. Manny sat in the middle seat. Joey, who road shotgun, reached for the knob on the radio, but stopped when he caught the corner of Tim's sharp, blue eye. Instead, he stared ahead and listened to the stroke of the VW's engine. He felt his empty stomach churn.

"Tim, could I bum one of your smokes?"

"I thought you gave it up," Tim's snapped.

"I did but I'm thinking about starting again." Joey pushed his glasses back in place. "The pressure's killing me."

"What pressure? People keep giving you stuff. You have to be the luckiest mooch in the world."

"Yeah, but I hate it when my friends mess up."

"We sure messed up coming to see Lenora." He squinted into the rear-view mirror. "Thanks a lot, Manny, for that one."

"What can I tell you?" Manny shrugged. "I was wrong."

"No shit." He shook a cigarette from his pack for himself and tossed one to Joey. He shoved the lighter in its socket. "You should've seen her. I swear she was breathing fire."

"We both heard her from the barn," Joey said.

Tim reached for the lighter.

"You gonna smoke that or what?"

"I'm still thinking about it."

Tim exhaled as Joey giggled.

"What in the hell are you laughing about? I don't see one fucking thing funny about what happened today."

Joey kept laughing.

"You gotta look at it another way, Tim. Dr. Manny here tells us the moment he thinks Lenora conceived Isabel, and we all listen to him. Manny and I had our doubts, but you, Tim, man, you acted like a man possessed."

"Yeah, so what? I had the right to know if I was a father."

"Then you decide we had to drive all the way to New Hampshire to ask Lenora. As I recall, we left pretty damn early. I mean we opened Jimmy's, and the only time we ever did that was when we pulled an all-nighter. Right, Manny?"

"Hey, keep me out of this conversation."

Bits of tobacco fell as Joey's fingers jabbed the cigarette in the air.

"And then when Tim gets his moment, Lenora shoots him down big time. Pow! Right in the kisser! The man is totally crushed."

Tim blew smoke in one noisy stream.

"What's your point, Joey?"

"It's the other mistake that's slaying me."

"What mistake?"

"The one you're making now. If I were you, I'd dump Manny and me in Boston, then turn around and tell Lenora how you really feel about her."

"What are you talking about?"

"This is it, Timothy Devlin. There'll be no more chances with Lenora, who I'm convinced is the absolute love of your life. Caput. Fini. The end." Joey shook the mangled cigarette. "What'll it be, Tim? Lose your pride or make what undoubtedly will be the biggest mistake you ever make."

Tim tossed the lit butt out the window. He gave Joey a sideways glance. Manny's interested face moved closer.

"You know, Joey. You can be such a fucking pain in the ass," Tim growled.

Joey's hand shook what was left of the cigarette.

"Her lips/ I can't live without her sweet lips/ say those words, I love you."

"Who's that now?" Tim asked Joey.

He grinned.

"Joey Franklin."

ONE MINUTE

Tim let the VW van coast into the driveway of Great Meadow. He cut the lights. The best he could figure it had to be way after ten. He dropped Manny and Joey at the curb in Boston, and except for a quick stop for gas and coffee, he'd been on the road ever since. He sat in the front seat, listening to the peepers in the woods. Joey told him he slept with the window open, so he could hear what he said had to be the greenest sound ever. Of course, Joey would say something like that. Everything the guy thought came out like poetry, even something about frogs.

The house was mostly dark except for two lit windows on the first floor and one on the second. The dogs must be inside although he saw the glowing eyes of a cat on patrol beside the barn. Maybe nobody was up or they were all out. He'd knock, and if no one answered or he got sent away, he'd crash in the van in a sleeping bag and haul himself back to Westbridge in the morning. He wished he thought to stop for food, because his gut howled from hunger.

He studied the windows on the first floor. Someone was in the kitchen. He eased himself from the van's seat and shut the door as quietly as he could, feeling a little criminal as he walked toward that part of the house. He stood back a few feet from the house, peering into the lit room. He released the air from his lungs in one strong blow. Lenora sat at a table, reading a book, and her thick braids hung over the pages as her head bent forward. Her left hand was curled around a mug. The window didn't have a screen so he could see her clearly through the pane. She finished a page and sat back, nodding and thinking, before she read the next.

Tim rose on the balls of his feet. Lenora was alone in the kitchen. He smiled at his luck. He could use some now. All the way back, when he no longer had to listen to Joey and Manny egging him on, he thought of what he would tell Lenora and how he should say it, but as he stood outside the window, it all seemed too canned. Now, he hoped she'd be willing to see him. The words would have to come.

"What are you waiting for, Tim? Let's go," he whispered.

Lenora's head bobbed up when he knocked lightly on the glass. He knocked again, and she squinted at the window.

"Lenora. It's me. Tim."

She came to the glass, crouching so her face was level with his. Her brown eyes squinted as if she still couldn't see him well. She stood to raise the window.

"What are you doing here?"

"I need to talk with you."

"What for? I told you, Tim, I'm not gonna see you anymore."

"I know what you said. I came back to change your mind."

She glared down at him.

"This isn't a good idea."

"Aw, Lenora, it's the only one I have."

Her face was back at his level. She looked past him toward the VW van.

"Where's Manny and Joey?"

"I left them in Boston."

She blinked quickly.

"Boston. You drove all the way from there?"

"Yeah, I did." He raised a finger. "One minute. That's all I ask. Just one. Please, Lenora."

She pressed her lips together.

"Meet me at the front door."

Tim sprinted to the porch and waited until Lenora opened the door. Her white nightgown hung to her bare feet. She held onto the door's edge.

"I suppose you drove all this way and didn't get anything to eat. Come inside and I'll make you something."

"It'll take me longer than a minute to eat."

"You said you only wanted to *talk* for one minute."

He followed Lenora into the kitchen, where she told him to sit at the table. She heated soup in a pan and spread butter on thick slices of brown bread.

She glanced back and said, "That's Ned's book. Inez sent it." She set the bowl in front of him and the plate with the slices of bread. "I hope you like vegetable bean soup."

He thanked her as she sat across from him. Tim ate, because he was hungry, and because he needed time to get this right.

"Where's Isabel?'

"Asleep in her crib where she belongs. It's nearly midnight."

"Why are you still up? I thought you country folk went to bed early."

"Some of us do. I couldn't sleep."

He dipped his spoon into the soup.

"This is great."

"Yes, it is." She glanced at the wall clock. "I'm afraid you're using up your minute."

"You're keeping track?"

She made a quick smile.

"You bet I am."

He lifted the spoon to his mouth.

"You're not gonna cut me a break, are you?"

"That's right, Tim. Tick-tick-tick. You'd better hurry up."

Tim swallowed. The soup was good. So was the bread. Lenora leaned back in her chair. Her eyes and mouth were relaxed. He thought about her teasing jokes. These were hopeful signs.

"How's the book?"

She slid it across the tabletop.

"I like it. Ned read most of the poems at the coffeehouse. They brought back memories of him in black and wowing us with his words. He was like a rock star at Westbridge."

"Ned did have his groupies."

He opened the book to the page Lenora last read, a poem called "Round the Sound." She was holding her place with a photo. He felt Lenora's eyes on him when he recognized her and him together in the picture.

"My mother took it. That's behind the administration building." She leaned forward. "Remember my father making those horrible jokes about you guys?"

"How can I forget? He called us all whackos and weirdoes. He wasn't too far off there."

The photo was from their graduation, her real one and his fake. They were in robes and his arm was around her. They smiled at each other like no one else mattered.

"It captures the moment, don't you think?" she said.

He chuckled softly.

"I was ready to freak out. If it wasn't for you and Ned, I don't know what I would've done." He lifted the photo. "Look at us together."

She took it from him.

"Just kids. We're not kids anymore. You've got a real job. I've got a baby." Her voice dropped. "I still can't believe you drove here from Boston. I was sure I'd never see you again after what I said. I was so mad at you."

She set the photo down.

"I know you were." He made a nervous laugh. "I must've been out of my mind to believe Manny, but it did make perfect sense when we were stoned." He shook his head. "I wouldn't mind if Isabel was mine. But she isn't. Maybe I was just looking for an excuse to be close to you."

Lenora thought that over.

"An excuse. You thought you needed an excuse."

"I've used up my minute, but I'm gonna say something else. The first time I really noticed you, we were in American history our freshman year. It was cold and you had a scarf wrapped around your head, and you smiled at me when you took it off like you wanted to tell me a secret. If I had any guts, I would've gone up and kissed you in front of everybody. You were that beautiful. I didn't have the nerve then, and I didn't have it most of the time at Westbridge."

Lenora opened and shut her mouth.

"Either you were been madly in love with somebody else or sad about him, or I was too scared or lazy or fucked up or with some other girl or whatever to tell you. Joey got on my case about it when we were driving back today. Then Manny jumped in. They told me I was making the biggest mistake of my life." He squeezed her wrist. "I'm telling you now, Lenora, this is the new, improved Tim Devlin, the one who knows what he wants and does something about it."

His heart chugged harder.

"What does the new, improved Tim Devlin want?"

"I want a kiss."

She smiled that smile for him.

"A kiss? That's all?"

"A kiss for now. But a long kiss this time. Real long. The kind you don't forget."

He stood and pulled her up with him, her feet so light they could have been dancing in the kitchen at Great Meadow. Lenora laughed with her head slightly back. She was happy he was here, and he couldn't ask for anything else right now.

VERY BEST MEN

Joey sat next to Manny on the couch in the Rev. Big Ray's office at the Mayfield Congregational Church while they waited for the wedding to begin. Mack slept off his hangover on the other side. The three of them were dressed in the most god-awful suits of pure polyester, in tangerine of all colors, but it's what Janice, his bride, wanted. Big Ray, who was thrilled to get married, let her do that to the very best men he knew. She also chose white, ruffled shirts with tangerine trim, fruity pants flared at the bottoms, pointy white shoes with Cuban heels, and puffy black bowties. Manny quipped behind Ray's back, "I feel like I'm in somebody's acid trip."

Janice picked out a three-piece white suit for the Rev. Big Ray, so he looked as if he had the lead role in a Tennessee Williams play. Manny joked they should start calling him the Rev. Big Daddy Ray. Ray still had his walrus mustache, but he cleaned up his act after he left for divinity school. He cut his hair and slicked it back. They were certain he got rid of his funky collection of hog farm overalls.

The man was still big, maybe even bigger, if it were possible. So, it was a bit of a shock yesterday, although they tried not to show it, when they met Janice, a skinny little thing who on tiptoes reached the middle of

Ray's chest. It got them all talking later when Ray was someplace else what Janice saw in the man. Of course, Mack asked aloud whether they thought Ray finally got laid despite the Westbridge legend he and one of the girls from the Roach Motel tribe got it on one night in a mercy screw, or now that he was a minister, if he was waiting for his wedding night. And then, Mack wondered how he would manage not to crush his little bride.

Joey shrugged, and Manny told Mack, "Why don't you ask him if you're so interested."

Of course, Mack didn't.

Big Ray was the first of the Winter Street tribe to get married. Who would have thought? Certainly not Joey when Ray asked him to be one of the best men at his wedding. He also asked Tim, Manny, and Mack, who predicted Big Ray's wedding would be a bodacious reunion of the Westbridge freaks. The two tribes, Winter Street and Roach Motel, were invited. So were the Dirty Old Bastards. Even Geneva was coming from Las Vegas with that rhinestone cowboy singer she was seeing. He was supposed to be a star because he had a couple of hits on the country charts, which meant none of them ever heard him sing unless they were drinking in a redneck townie bar.

Ray was now the Rev. Ray, pastor of the Mayfield Congregational Church in the western part of the state, and his wife-to-be was a member. They met at a church supper. Ray told Joey over the phone, after a long wheeze, "Janice is straight, so don't tell her anything about me, if you know what I mean." It explained why no one had seen or heard from Ray for months. Big Ray was in big love. When Joey and Manny talked it over, they said in unison, "Good for him."

Sweat trickled beneath Joey's ruffled shirt. His leg was in first gear while Manny suffered in the heat beside him. Early August was a bad time to be wearing a polyester suit in a small church office with no open windows. Ray's wide body blocked the fan as he sat behind his desk and muttered the vows he and Janice had written. He glanced at Mack, who had started to snore. Mack's head was angled back and his mouth gaped beneath his full mustache.

The three of them showed up at Ray's apartment yesterday. Manny arrived by bus from Boston. Joey rode with Mack, who took the day off from his summer job painting houses. Joey had seen Mack only once since the night he and Tim had the drag-down fight over Lenora. In late May, he and Mack went to Angie's. Joey sat nursing beers while Mack hit on the college girls. Mack ended up ditching Joey when he scored with one of the older waitresses.

Most of the summer, Joey stayed holed up in Inez's house, writing or reading poetry and going over pamphlets for grad schools. He had a job at the college library, thanks to Professor Itch, which meant he ate regular meals, bought his own beer and pot, and had more than five bucks to his name. It also meant he no longer had to work at Angie's washing dishes covered with spaghetti sauce and cigarette butts.

He knew fewer people going to Westbridge State College than he ever did. Once at Jimmy's, he overheard two professors from the history department complain that the new kids were bright but terribly boring. They mourned the days when hairy kids begged for extensions because their best friend took some bad acid, man, and they stayed up all night helping him come down, so naturally they couldn't finish their paper on the Industrial Revolution. Or they had a protest to plan or were sweating out an induction physical or a pregnancy test. The kids came up with all kinds of excuses, driving the professors crazy. But they didn't deny their energy and convictions fired up their classes.

The only old friend Joey saw steadily was Tim, when he wasn't working or driving to New Hampshire to see Lenora and Isabel. Once he hitched a ride with Tim to Great Meadow. It blew him away watching Tim, Lenora, and the baby together. Tim finally got it right, and Joey was happy for them.

Tim didn't make it to Ray's place last night or to pick up his rental. He told Ray he'd take his chances whether the suit fit. The newsroom at the *Brockville Enterprise* was on the Watergate watch and Tim was moved temporarily to the news crew. His son-of-a-bitch editor told him he had to stay until midnight in case Nixon resigned, so Tim called Ray to explain he wouldn't be there until the morning. Of course, Ray forgave him because it was for a noble cause although he said, "that crook Nixon" instead of "that goddamn Nixon" now that he was a man of the cloth.

After the three of them picked up the orange monkey suits at the rental shop, they took Big Ray out to dinner and a bar for his last night as a free man. Mack billed it that way, as if Ray had been a stud at Westbridge and now he was going to be out of action. Mack wanted to go to a strip joint, but the Rev. Ray rejected that idea. He was afraid he might run into somebody from his congregation, so they ended up buying a bottle of top-shelf scotch and taking it to his place. They smoked pot, getting Ray to take a few hits, but he warned them not to tell Janice. "She thinks I put all that behind me," he said.

Joey stood in Ray's small office. His legs wouldn't let him sit any longer. He forced himself not to touch the white rose pinned to the lapel of his orange jacket. He stood in the open doorway facing the empty church. Janice's family went all out with flowers and bows at the end of each pew. Large bouquets were arranged around the altar. All Big Ray had to do was dress himself, put the box of rings in his pocket, and get to the church in time. He made Mack drive him extra, extra early to be sure.

Joey glanced back at Ray, who mumbled with his eyes shut as if he were in deep prayer.

"Can you tell me again what we're supposed to do?" Joey asked him.

Big Ray's eyes popped open. He cleared his throat.

"We went over it last night. It's simple. When people come to the door, you ask them if they're here for the bride or the groom, and then you walk with them to a pew so they can sit down. When everybody is there, you come up to the front of the church and stand next to me. At the end of the ceremony, you walk with one of the bridesmaids out of the church. We'll all pose for photos on the steps before we drive to the reception."

"Then what?"

Ray filled his cheeks with air and let them deflate with one big blow.

"At the reception, you sit at the head table. After Tim makes a toast, we get to eat. Janice and I will have the first dance and the rest of you will join in with the bridesmaids when I give you the signal." He shook one of his fat fingers. "After that, you just have a good time, but not too good a time, if you catch my drift. Any other questions?"

Joey's head bobbed.

"Yeah. Which side is which?"

Ray arched one brow.

"Janice's side is on the left. Mine's on the right. That's facing the altar. Got it?"

"Bride left. Groom right. Got it. When do we start?"

Ray checked the clock above the door and snorted.

"Soon. Maybe you should wake Mack up and tell him to zip his fly."

Manny nudged Mack when the outside door to the office opened. Tim stepped inside and choked out a laugh.

"What kind of a get-up is that?"

Joey raised a finger to his lips as he tipped his head toward Ray.

"Janice picked it out," he said.

Manny pointed toward the bag hanging off the door.

"Don't worry, Tim, you get to wear one, too. See?"

Tim made a you-got-to-be-shitting-me face as he rubbed his clean jaw. But he recovered quickly and walked with his hand out toward Big Ray.

"Congratulations, Ray. Manny and Joey say you found someone special to love."

Big Ray pulled himself upright. His belly was bound in his white, satin vest.

"I did. What's the latest on Nixon?"

"Nothing so far, but the rumors are he'll be quitting next week. The noose gets tighter and tighter."

Ray started to get red in the face as he sputtered about Watergate and the war. He pounded his fist on his desk like he used to at *The Hard Truth* office.

"Serves the crook right," he bellowed.

"What the fuck," Mack said, startled awake.

Mack grunted when he saw Tim. They hadn't spoken since their fight, but Mack promised Joey on the ride here from Westbridge that he'd be on his best behavior at Big Ray's wedding. Of course, Mack wanted to hear where Joey stood. Joey, who was on Tim's side but needed the ride, deflected the subject fast with a bit of poetry. Then he brought up Watergate, everybody's favorite topic these days.

Tim stood bare-chested in the church office. He reached for the ruffled shirt on the arm of the couch.

"Mack, how's it going?" And then he said to Joey, "How about shutting the door so I can get dressed?"

Joey went to the door.

"Did you have to write a story last night?" he asked.

Tim fished the buttons through the ruffles.

"Oh, yeah. I went down to this bar to interview a bunch of Vietnam vets about what they thought of their commander in chief. It was my idea."

"What'd they say?" Joey asked.

"Mixed views from the vets. At one point, I thought two guys were going to pound each other over whether Nixon should resign. That was cool. My favorite was the vet with one leg. He lost the other in Vietnam. He said he wanted Nixon to give it back." Tim finished the last button. "I've got the morning paper in my van. I can show you later."

Mack was fully awake. His cheek twitched as if he had something super smart to say but he didn't speak. The small room had gotten smaller fast.

Tim dropped his pants.

"You guys have a good time last night? Sorry I couldn't make it. You should've heard my editor. He had a fit when I reminded him I had to go to a wedding today. You know what he said? 'Well, kid, it's not like you're the one getting married.' The guy thinks I'm his personal slave."

"We had an okay time," Joey said. "When are Lenora and Isabel getting here?"

Tim checked the wall clock as he pushed his foot through an orange pants leg.

"They should be here any time now. When I talked with Lenora this morning, she and Inez were about to leave with Itch." His head was down. "There's no belt with these pants?"

Manny grinned.

"Wait 'til Lenora sees you dressed like that."

"God, I hope she still loves me."

"If she does, that's what I'd call true love," Manny said. "Right, Joey?"

"*I wish I could remember that first day,/ First hour, first moment of your meeting me.*"

"Wait. I think I know that one. Shakespeare?" Manny said.

Joey shrugged.

"Close. Christina Rossetti."

Tim slipped his feet into his shoes. He lifted the bowtie from the desk.

"Thank, God, it's fake. I couldn't tie a real one to save my life."

MIDDLE OF SOMEWHERE

tch took a right at the traffic lights. Inez pointed toward a gas station on the corner.

"Mitchell, swallow your manly pride. You got off at the wrong exit and now we're stuck in the middle of somewhere. Please pull into that gas station and ask the attendant where in God's name we are."

"I'm positive I know."

"That's what you said a half hour ago and we aren't any closer to the wedding."

Itch flicked his head toward the back seat, looking for a little help from Lenora. She kissed the top of Isabel's head.

"Want me to go inside and ask?" she said.

Itch steered the car toward the station.

"No, no, I'll do it."

Inez's charm bracelet spun when she raised her hand.

"That's what I like about you, Mitchell. You'll listen to reason. Now, if Ned were here, we'd be driving all the way to the West Coast."

Itch killed the engine.

"Don't go anywhere," he told Inez.

"Hey, that's my idea," she said.

Itch shut the car door. He strolled toward the garage where a kid with a greasy rag in his back pocket fed coins into a soda machine. Itch's gray ponytail bounced over the back of his navy blue jacket. He talked with the kid, who shook his head and jabbed a finger toward the office, which is where Itch went next.

Inez smiled at Isabel.

"What do you think, honey? I bet that nice man couldn't find his way along a straight line."

Isabel thrust a stuffed dog toward Inez.

"My dog."

Inez made a husky chuckle. She bought the toy for Isabel at FAO Schwartz.

"That's right. Only the best for you, kid." The light glanced off Inez's glasses. "I enjoyed having you both around the past couple of days. You filled my home nicely. Come again and next time bring what's his name."

"Tim. His name is Tim."

Inez smiled as she nodded toward the newspaper on the seat beside Lenora. Itch picked it up for her. Tim's story was on the front page.

"I know he's Tim. I'm only playing with you. I heard you on the phone this morning. You should have seen the expression on your face when you talked with him." She sighed. "I remember feeling like that once."

Lenora folded the paper so Isabel could walk on the seat. Inez raised her eyebrows and nodded at the girl in encouragement. She spoiled Isabel, letting her touch or do whatever she wanted in that house of antiques she owned in Boston's Back Bay.

After the wedding, Lenora and Isabel were going to spend a few days with Tim, and then see her folks. Her parents complained too many months had gone by since they last visited. She got George to let one of the other women at Great Meadow do her job at the farm while she was away. He wasn't happy about it. He grumbled, "I don't think I'm gonna like her as much as you. You're not thinking of leaving to be with that fellow, are you?" And then, "I wish you'd change your mind about living at my house. It's because of him, isn't it?" George never called Tim by his name.

Isabel shook her dog and said, "Go. Go. Go." She was tired of being in the car.

"We'll be there soon, Isabel, and we're going to see Tim." Her daughter's face brightened as she repeated his name. "That's right, Tim."

Inez lit a cigarette and blew the smoke through the open window. Itch stood in front of the gas station, nodding and talking with the attendant, who gestured toward the intersection.

"It's been over a year now and I still miss Ned." Inez held the cigarette outside the car. Her head swung toward Lenora. "That man caused me a great deal of pain, and, hell, I probably only knew half of it. Maybe a third." She took another drag. "People must wonder why I put up with all his shit. The truth? I couldn't imagine being with another man. I don't think your Tim's the kind of guy to run around like Ned, but I hope you feel that same way about him."

Lenora smiled. Beside her, Isabel jumped and tossed her dog so it hit the car's ceiling.

"Oh, I do," she said.

WE'VE ONLY JUST BEGUN

Tim poked his head outside the church. Manny did the same.

"Where in the hell are they?" Tim said, and then, "I should've picked them up in Boston."

Manny patted the padded shoulder of Tim's tangerine jacket.

"They'll get here. So what if they're a little late?" Manny slapped his forehead. "Never mind. What am I talking about?"

"It's been three weeks since I saw her and Isabel. I couldn't get away. They kept thinking Watergate was going to break and we had to be ready."

"Why don't you ask her to move in with you?"

"At the Roach Motel? That's not good enough." He shook his head. "I'm waiting for Itch to finish fixing up Winter Street. I've got dibs on the first-floor apartment."

"You ask her yet?"

"Not yet. You know me. I'm a slow worker."

Manny glanced back. Joey stood behind them.

"Slow worker? What're you guys talking about?" Joey asked.

"Tim wants to ask Lenora to live with him. My advice is to ask her fast. Don't let her figure it out first. She likes it that way."

"Manny's right, and I was right the last time," Joey said. "Remember?"

"Yeah, yeah, geniuses, I'll keep that in mind."

Tim watched the wedding guests file into the church until the vestibule was jammed with people. Joey's hands shook as if he were playing a drum solo when he asked, "Friends of the bride or groom?" as if he couldn't tell. Ray didn't have any family, except for two stepsisters who were already in the front pew. So, a friend of the groom was anyone who had long hair, a beard or mustache, or both, and freaky clothes although not as freaky as the clothes Ray's best men had to wear to the wedding. Or they knew them from Westbridge like one of the Dirty Old Bastards. Everyone else was a friend of the bride, including the folks standing in front of Joey. Even so, Joey kept messing up. For such an egghead, he couldn't seem to tell his right from his left, and the sides were getting mixed. Then Tim or Manny had to go down the aisle to shuffle people around.

Tim didn't care about the mix-up. Manny didn't either. It was kind of neat seeing the kid who used to play air guitar sitting next to one of Janice's uncles, who handed out cards for his insurance business. Likewise, Janice's next-door neighbors, the ones who owned the Buick dealership, got an earful from the loser who became a Jesus freak for three months after he ran away with the Christian acting troupe. Of course, the drama club freaks made a splash when they showed up in white capes and top hats. They were the only ones who were genuine when they said they liked the tangerine suits.

But the best men were on strict orders from Big Ray to get it right. Tim and Manny got the idea Ray was nervous someone on his side might spill something juicy to someone on his bride's side, like maybe the time he drew up a plan to take over the campus. Or how he used to give his well-known monologue on the three types of assholes—flaming, flying and fucking—and how he could tell who was what and how. Or how much beer he drank or pot he smoked. Or some of the editorials he wrote about the war, because, now, whether the Rev. Big Ray wanted to admit it, he was part of the establishment.

Mack left the ushering job to Joey, Manny, and Tim. He leaned against the wall of the vestibule, except whenever a pretty woman arrived, and then he was all over her. He did something corny like kiss her hand as if it were part of the routine, making the poor girl giggle and blush when he escorted her to a pew. Afterward he called Manny over to share his raunchy observations.

266

After the third time, Manny waved him off and took Tim aside, "You're right. Mack's a flaming a-hole."

Geneva made her entrance wearing something sparkly and just long enough to cover her butt. She walked arm in arm with her rhinestone cowboy singer, who whipped off his black hat respectfully when he entered the church. She had a large, lipstick smile and big hair, and as she shimmied in her dress the old man behind her, definitely a friend of the bride, took a peek to see how high the fabric rose.

Geneva saw Mack and Mack saw her. They had a loud, mushy reunion. The rhinestone cowboy singer rolled his eyes, because he was probably wondering how he got roped into this lame trip. Geneva squealed when she noticed Tim, Joey, and Manny, and there were kisses all around. They all got to meet the cowboy, who puffed up when some of the bride's side recognized him. Tim wiped Geneva's lipstick off his face as Joey led the happy couple up the aisle. Manny shouted in a stage whisper, "Right, right. No, damn it, your other right." And then he ran up there, because Joey was putting Geneva and her cowboy where the bride's parents were supposed to sit.

Tim led a cluster of Janice's family to a seat in front. He walked back toward the entrance, checking outside for Lenora, but still there was no sign of her. It had been much too long since he saw her even though they talked on the phone every few days. His editor caught him once at work and told him to cut it out. He said it made him too miserable to see someone so goddamned happy.

The doorway filled with the Roach Motel tribe, and as Tim got closer, he smelled pot smoke. Knowing the group, they wanted something to put a crooked edge on this square event. Tim gave backslapping hugs to the Roach Brothers. He and Roach Brother Bob were back on decent terms after Bob showed up one night with a bag of pot and an apology. His stoned eyes blinked that night as Tim congratulated him about Nina. He had wanted to thank the guy for doing him a huge favor, but it wouldn't have been a cool move. Nina squeezed through the group to catch up with Bob. Tim said hello and felt absolutely nothing at all.

Joey blocked the way to the main aisle. The Roach Motel tribe laughed when Joey asked, "Friends of the bride or groom?"

Tim went outside again. A limo stopped at the curb. Big Ray's little bride was here. A couple of stragglers rushed up the steps. Manny came beside him.

"Ray wants us up front with him. We'll seat these folks. The rest of the guests are on their own. Take it easy. They'll make it."

Manny led the friends of the bride to their places while Tim brought up the rear. The church was nearly full. The straights were on the left and the freaks were on the right although when he thought about it, it should be the other way around. Grinning, Tim gave a thumbs-up to the people he knew, like the guy who used to bring his little kids to the Winter Street parties, the libbers Nancy and Lorraine who lived next door, and the math majors from downstairs. Their uncles, the Dirty Old Bastards sat among them. The last time they were all together for a happy time was that last weekend in Westbridge. The only one missing was Ned Burke. They were good people, as Manny would say. Tim hoped they were doing as well as he was.

Tim checked the altar. Mack was there, and so was Joey. Big Ray stood in a trance. Behind Tim, fabric rustled as the bride came into the church. Her bridesmaids fluttered in bouncy gowns of some unnatural blue before the doors to the vestibule swung close. Tim took his place between Manny and Joey. White rose petals were crushed on the red carpet near Joey's shoes. All that was left of his boutonniere was the stem pinned to his jacket.

Tim whispered to Ray, "You ready?"

"Yeah," he gasped.

From the choir loft, a woman began to sing, "We've Only Just Begun," in a soprano that wobbled and broke in all the wrong places. She was one of Janice's aunts, her favorite they were told, but the woman had no business singing in public. She tortured the song and any normal person who listened to it. Those on the groom's side goofed on the woman's voice while those on the bride's side wiped their eyes. Geneva's rhinestone cowboy grimaced as if he got punched hard in the gut.

Tim studied the red carpeting so no one saw him laugh.

"I can't believe this," he whispered to himself.

He raised his head when he felt an elbow poke his side.

Manny hissed, "She's here."

A side door was open. Itch held it for Inez, and finally Lenora, who carried Isabel on her hip. Tim exhaled. Lenora wore a pale pink sundress and a straw hat that belonged to the bachelor farmer's mother. Her hair hung loosely.

In the loft above, Janice's favorite aunt labored through the song.

Tim whispered to Joey and Manny.

"I've gotta see her. Be back."

"You don't have much time," Manny whispered.

Ray stared straight ahead as Mack bent forward to see what was happening.

"Go ahead, Tim. We'll cover for you," Joey whispered.

"Don't start the ceremony without me."

Tim stepped from the altar, almost losing his balance on the Cuban heels. But he recovered as he headed left, past the wedding guests who now swiveled in their pews to check out the scene.

From the choir loft, the woman sang.

Tim reached Lenora in the back corner of the church. Her hand was over her mouth. She was getting a charge out of his stupid suit.

So was Inez, who shook her head as she remarked, "Jesus, what'd they do to you, Tim? If I were you, I'd sue whoever it was."

Lenora giggled as she fingered his lapel.

"Shouldn't you be up there with the rest of the band?"

Tim made a half-laugh. He didn't have much time. If he didn't talk with her now, he wouldn't get another chance until later at the reception, and what he wanted to say had been on his mind for the past few weeks.

"I was worried, cause you were late. I had to see you and Isabel."

"Professor Mitchell got a little lost."

Inez's charm bracelet clinked.

"What can I say? The man has no sense of direction. Now, let's see if he can find me a seat," she said.

Isabel's hands reached toward him as she said "Tim" in that sweet, wee voice of hers. He took her in his arms and kissed her cheek.

"Have you been good?"

She nodded.

"That's my girl."

The singer strangled another line.

Tim glanced at the choir loft, then the altar. Manny waved for him to come back, but Tim shook his head.

"I missed you both too much."

"We missed you, too."

The organist hit the last chords of the song with a flourish.

"Shoot. Not yet," he whispered.

Lenora pointed toward the altar where Joey and Manny had their heads together. They talked with Mack, who nodded.

"Tim, I think they might need you up there," Lenora told him.

"Here, you'd better take her."

Lenora reached for Isabel as a loud whistle shot through the church. She and Tim turned toward the altar, where Joey pulled two fingers from his mouth. One of the goofiest grins Joey ever made was plastered all over his hairy face.

Manny was next to him, addressing the guests, "I dunno about you, folks, but I've never heard 'We've Only Just Begun' sung quite that way before. I sure would love to hear it again, and I bet you would, too." He raised his hand in a salute toward the choir loft. "Ma'am, how about singing it for us again?"

Janice's aunt gave a little bow as the wedding guests made a loud and steady hum. The groom's side was thinking this was some groovy show. The bride's side didn't understand why these longhaired hippies were asking for an encore. This wasn't some rock concert. Just then, Janice's father stuck his head between the vestibule's doors and said "huh?" for the rest of them. Ray's head swung from one side to the other and to the choir loft, where Janice's aunt tapped the organist on the shoulder, and moments later "We've Only Just Begun" began again.

At the altar, Joey and Manny pointed at Tim and Lenora. Mack and Big Ray did the same. People twisted in their pews toward the back of the church to see who they were signaling while above them Janice's favorite aunt sang off-key.

Lenora shifted Isabel so she straddled her hip. She mouthed, "Tim, what's going on?"

Tim touched her shoulder.

"I have to ask you something, Lenora. Please. It's important, and I really, really want you to say yes."

Lenora tipped her head to one side. Her lips curled into smile.

"Go ahead, Tim," she said. "Why don't you ask me? We're all waiting."

THE END

ACKNOVLEDGEMENTS

An author doesn't do it alone, at least not in my case. I've been fortunate to know people who have encouraged me with my writing. At the top of the list are my children, Sarah, Ezra, Emily, Nate, Zack, and Julia, along with John and Chris. Of course, there are my parents, Antone and Algerina Medeiros, who gave me opportunities they never had.

I offer thanks to those who helped me birth this novel, especially Michelle M. Gutierrez, who created the book's cover and design.

I've been blessed to have the encouragement of dear friends: Fred Fullerton, Teresa Dovalpage, and Amy Peck Murphy. And then there is Craig Dirgo, who urged me over coffee one day to publish this novel myself.

Finally, while this is a work of fiction inspired by a place and time I once lived, I smile when I think of the people I knew then.

A NOTE ABOUT THE AUTHOR

Joan Livingston is the author of books for adults and young readers, including los Primos bilingual series.

She was an award-winning journalist who started as a reporter covering the hill towns of Western Massachusetts. Her most recent gig was the managing editor for *The Taos News*.

She and her husband Hank live in Northern New Mexico. For more, visit *www.joanlivingston.net.*